STORM SURGE
A JONIE WATERS
MYSTERY

Tamara Ward

Printed in the United States of America
ISBN 13: 9781935711063
ISBN 10: 1935711067
LCCN: 2011921876
Fiction/Mystery
First Edition
1 2 3 4 5 6 7 8 9 10

PROLOGUE

I didn't set out to kill her. But if I'd been planning ahead, I couldn't have arranged it better.

"I'm not changing my mind," she said. The steamy, still air, stinking of salt marsh, where even the summer insects knew better than to break the silence, amplified her shaking, childlike voice.

Not that anyone was around to hear us. Not at this time of night. Not on this boardwalk ten feet above some no-name tidal creek dotted with dried-up oyster beds and hurricane-splintered trees.

"You can't make me change my mind," she said.

The moonlight was hidden behind mile-thick storm clouds that flashed lightning like a snake flicking its tongue. In the white-hot bursts, I could see the wetness of her eyes.

I took another step toward her, and she took a step backward, like we were dance partners.

"I'm not changing my mind," she repeated.

Before I knew it, I punched her face so hard her nose crunched. I heard blood spatter on the boardwalk. In the next flash, I saw she had landed against the railing, cracking the wood beam. She was wobbling away from the drop to the creek. I lunged at her back. Grabbing her, I forced her to the railing. She tried to push away from the edge, but I slammed my fist into her spine and shoved her off. I heard a snap and a splash.

I paused and listened. Nothing. I peered over the edge. Her body lay face-up under the brackish water, not moving. I waited. Nothing. She hadn't even screamed.

I shook my head at her limp body; her hair trailing in the current. As I waited, I replayed the last half hour in my mind. I hadn't wanted this, but no other outcome had been possible. I was sorry she had to die. Yet, I was certain she had to die; so certain now, that I knew if she moved, I'd have to climb down there somehow and finish it.

A raindrop splattered on the broken railing, its ricochet wetting my arm. I smiled. Torrential rains always were good for washing away refuse—her body, perhaps—and evidence of my presence. I turned back toward my car. I wasn't surprised that I felt sure-footed. Because some things—some things are worth killing for—despite any possible consequences.

CHAPTER 1

I had that feeling, the telltale sinking beneath my breastbone coupled with a queasy, metallic fluttering at the back of my throat. It was the feeling I always ignored just before my life was yanked from under me the same way a riptide sucks a swimmer from the shore.

You'd think I'd learn.

But no—like that flailing swimmer, resisting the current was impossible for me.

The part of me that listened to feminine intuition wanted to scurry back to my truck, throw it in reverse, and lie about investigating the news tip I just received. The forested garden beside the university's marine biology research center simply felt evil. My fingers tingled as I hesitated at the entrance, at the fringe where light met darkness and pavement met mulch, under an arching trellis entwined with purple-blossomed wisteria vines. Despite the heat and humidity, goose bumps dotted my arms. I felt as if someone was watching me. My feet edged backward reflexively.

Fighting the impulse to run, I took a deep breath and thought about my circumstances. I was nearing 35, alone in life and returning to the hometown I once fled—because I'd been driven out of the town I just left. Nearly broke, I was hoping my only job prospect would evolve into steady employment. That job was why I was standing here, contemplating my future. I refused to return to the *Tribune* with a lame excuse for failing to investigate my first—albeit peculiar—news tip.

I stepped forward into an oppressive gloom cast by the web of Spanish-moss-laced branches above me. Dead leaves trapped in the undergrowth crackled a couple of steps ahead of me. I froze but then saw a squirrel dart away. I huffed out a breath and continued on, past a gazebo, through thick, waist-high marsh grass. Wet mulch sucked at my feet, and the sharp edges of the grass snagged on my slacks. The rich sulfur smell of saltwater marsh-mud intensified.

I finally reached a long, curving boardwalk, wide enough to drive across and more than high enough to accommodate storm surges from the tidal creek below. The caller with the news tip had said to come here. At the crest of the boardwalk, a broken railing bent outward as if the wood had been kicked. Walking to the breach, nothing seemed worthy enough to warrant a newspaper article. Nevertheless, as I walked, I squeezed my leather saddlebag purse to check for my notepad, pen, and secondhand digital camera while my eyes continually scanned the scene around me. My steps sounded loud and hollow against the wood. I reached the boardwalk's edge and peered over it into the dark, brackish water. And then I saw her.

Her nose was smashed, crooked and bloody. The portions of pale blonde hair not submerged in slick, black mud shone dimly, feathering to merge with the marsh grass. Her eyes were barely open, as if she daydreamed. A blood and mud-smeared silk scarf boiled with movement from fingernail-sized crabs; dozens and dozens of crabs; hungry pinchers snipping and tugging and then gobbling.

The trees seemed to spin. Spots exploded before my eyes. I retched. Retched until nothing was left and then dry heaved some more. My eyes blurred with tears; my knees trembled. I crouched down and forced myself to stare back at her. I choked on my breath. In spite of her bloated, ashen appearance, I recognized her—even though years had passed since we'd last seen each other.

"Abby." My voice came out a croak.

This wasn't a news tip. This was murder.

CHAPTER 2

Fingers fumbling, I pulled my cell phone from my bag.

"Are you alright?"

I jerked at the voice and lost hold of my phone. It clattered onto the boardwalk and fell off the edge, down into the muck next to Abby. A few crabs scuttled away, but the majority remained.

A student carrying a notebook with a glittery, silver cover stood beside me.

"Are you here for the class?" she asked. "It's back at the gazebo." Then her eyes found Abby. Her mouth fell open. Then she began stuttering.

"We need to call someone," I said. "Do you have a phone?" Only the upper edge of mine was visible above the wet mud.

Her eyes darted back and forth. She stopped stuttering.

"Find a phone, and call for help," I said.

She went running back toward the university. My leaden feet wouldn't move. My mind kept shrieking—Abby! Sweat dripped down my face. I swiped at it, smearing the small amount of makeup I'd applied before keeping my appointment at the *Tribune*. I no longer cared if the black circles under my eyes and the pallor from my through-the-night drive were revealed. Forget it, I thought, Abby's dead.

I was still anchored on the boardwalk when I heard sirens.

I slapped the side of the drink machine harder this time, figuring the police taping off the nature garden were too busy to care about my abuse of malfunctioning campus equipment.

"Come on," I whined. Another bead of sweat trickled to my jaw. I ran my hand under my shoulder-length hair, trying to un-stick it from my neck.

I poked the buttons for each drink option. At this point, I didn't care what kind of soda I got. I'd welcome any variety of relief from the summer heat while waiting for the police to question me. The machine made no response. I was being mocked. I glanced at the officer on the shady side of the picnic area. He'd escorted me from the boardwalk to the picnic tables and was trying to appear nonchalant while babysitting me. Ensuring I don't run away, I thought, at least not until the police interview me. I couldn't even tell if the officer was watching me from behind his dark sunglasses.

I balled up a fist and hit the side of the machine. Repeatedly. I punched the buttons again; still nothing. I grabbed the sides of the machine, growled at it, tried to shake it, banged my fist against the Coke button one last time, and pushed away, right into a solid, masculine body. Large, warm hands caught my sides, pushed me upright, and released me when I was steady. I whirled around. I hadn't heard anyone approach me.

"I'm so sorry," I stammered, feeling my face, already flushed from the heat, blush in embarrassment. Then I noticed the man who had caught me. I glanced up into blue-gray eyes the color of the ocean before a storm. They were topped by short, dirty blonde hair—slightly spiked on the top as if, when wet, fingers ran through it and left it to dry uncombed. I found myself drawn to his eyes, almost unable to blink, flustered. I considered re-enrolling in college to get a degree in whatever it was the marine center offered if he was my professor.

"Can I help?" he asked. His voice, a deep, seductive tenor, held hints of playfulness. Stubble grizzled his chin. He grinned at me, not revealing any teeth. Casual and yet professionally dressed, a crisp black polo shirt hinted at a toned chest.

"The drink machine stole my money. I was trying for a Coke, but I think the machine's fried."

He walked around me and pushed the Coke button, the one I'd pushed and jabbed and pounded about a hundred times in the last couple of minutes. Obediently, the machine answered with a metallic whir and the resounding clang of a soda can hitting the floor and rolling to the flap. He passed the can to me, our fingers brushing. His grin widened, perhaps at my expression.

"Thanks," I said through my teeth. I forced out a breath and consciously relaxed my shoulders. "Can I buy you one?"

He shook his head. "I'm on duty." The grin disappeared.

It was then I noticed the assortment of police equipment—a badge, gun, cell phone and who knew what else—that hung from his belt.

"Right," I said, instantly brought back to reality.

"You're the one who found the body," he said.

I nodded.

"I'm Daniel Wyeth, detective with the Wilmington police force," he said to me.

"I'm Jonie."

After a moment of continued assessment, Daniel spoke again. "I need to take care of some things." He gestured toward the garden. "Sit tight. I'll get to you as soon as I can."

With his comment, he walked off, leaving me to return to the picnic tables. While drinking my Coke, I watched Daniel direct other officers in the garden's distant depths. His arm movements looked relaxed, but something about the way he held himself also suggested unwavering authority and safety. I wanted to feel his arms around me, shielding me from my memories of Abby's body. He wasn't wearing a wedding band. I'd already noticed—though noticing made me nauseous. Abby was dead, I reminded myself, and neither Daniel nor I was here to flirt.

"So, you discovered the body," Daniel said, after he exited the garden and approached me at my picnic table.

5

It wasn't a question, but he stopped talking to observe my response. He stood so close our knees almost touched. The sun behind his shoulder brought tears to my eyes. He was waiting for me to speak, waiting like a hunter with a deer in his crosshairs, pausing to allow the deer to turn on its own and provide the proper angle for a shot.

I stood up, forcing him back.

"So that's Abby down there?" I asked, hoping I'd been wrong.

"You knew her?" His louder tone betrayed surprise.

"We were girlhood friends," I said.

A few years older than me, my next-door neighbor when I lived at home, Abby Pridgen taught me how to surf, how to survive adolescence. We hadn't contacted each other since I'd stormed out of town years ago. She wouldn't have known how to reach me, and even if she had, I'd have been too embarrassed to relay the bumps along the plummet my life took as I crashed.

"I can't believe she's—" I sucked in a breath. "I just got into town this morning."

Daniel frowned and waited for me to continue.

"I'm a new reporter for the *Tribune*."

His eyes narrowed a fraction. He crossed his arms. I sidestepped around him so I no longer looked into the sun.

"I was called out here on a news tip. Someone called me and said for me to come here, to the boardwalk, for me to hurry."

Flouncing, clown-orange hair, twice as wide with natural curls and humidity-induced volume as the face the hair sandwiched, appeared behind Daniel's shoulder. I knew the hair, and I knew the face, flat and bland as an ivory serving platter, with the exception of its oddly deep chin cleft. My stomach clenched, along with my fists. I'd heard she'd joined the police, but I didn't expect to see her. Not so soon after returning to town. Not at a crime scene. I felt the muscles of my jaws involuntarily tighten.

"Jonie?" She fingered the collar of her long-sleeved, button-down cotton shirt as she looked me over. She'd recognized me instantly too.

"Kimmie."

We glared at each other, taking in how the years altered our appearances. My hair had darkened slightly over the years but retained its light blonde hue, which graciously masked a few gray hairs I hadn't gotten around to plucking yet. The beginnings of wrinkles caused by exposure to both time and sun could be found at the corners of my eyes and mouth. I wondered if Kimmie noticed the thin scar that cut about half an inch up from my lip near my right eye tooth, a souvenir from my early years on my own. Kimmie remained as solid and straight as a pillar. A head taller than my petite 5'5" frame, she was half a body wider and not afraid to show it. I listened to the rhythmic ringing in my ears and reminded myself that part of returning to town involved trying for a fresh start with my family. Unclenching my fists took effort.

Daniel glanced at Kimmie.

"We're stepsisters," Kimmie explained, "but we haven't spoken in—how many years? A dozen?" She frowned at me. "You found the body—Abby's body?" As she spoke, her hair jiggled, making it seem as if the words were coming from her frizzy hair instead of her mouth. "How did you happen to do that?"

Daniel held his mouth tense, restraining from intervening. Maybe he assumed Kimmie knew how to handle me.

"Why are you being so—" I tried to think of a word. 'Callous' didn't quite cut it. "Abby's dead!"

"And I'm asking a question. You get to answer it. I'm a police detective now, partner to Detective Wyeth."

Kimmie rested a hand on Daniel's shoulder and cocked her hip toward him, taunting me with a smirk and a raised eyebrow. I took a breath, a futile effort to slow my pounding heart, and again reminded myself why I was being questioned.

"So, again," Kimmie asked, "how is it that you came to be here?"

I started at the beginning—when I had arrived back in town. I was still stinging from the memory of tense determination I'd felt not an hour ago when I was forcing a smile in an effort to appear confident and friendly instead of betraying my desperation for employment and my obvious inexperience. My discomfort was augmented by my expectation that compared to Lee Sanford, the editor-in-chief at the *Tribune*, I must resemble a frog that has yet to lose its tadpole tail. My memory of our encounter was still all too fresh in my mind.

CHAPTER 3

Lee's dark office air had hinted at an accumulation of years of smoke sneaked in from under collars and concealed in jacket folds. I'd imagined the hidden, invisible smoke unfurling and settling into his office like the sweet scent of a secret lover.

"So, you're Jonie Waters," he'd said. The only light in his office, aside from the window that overlooked the retired battleship docked across the Cape Fear River eight stories below, had come from a small desk lamp with a green glass shade. Its jade glow had glinted off thick bifocals and had added dimension to Lee's wrinkled, tissue-paper skin. "You're the reporter who broke the Cheatham scandal and is now being chased from that Podunk Tennessee County by the sheriff and two deputies?" He'd given me a scrutinizing stare. "You ran from Cheatham back home to Wilmington, right?"

My smile had faded. I'd wanted to disagree with him. First off, I wouldn't have called Cheatham County Podunk; farmlands were vanishing beneath bedrooms for Nashville commuters faster than kudzu overtook a field. But I could agree that my former county of residence appeared sedentary compared with Wilmington, one of North Carolina's busiest port cities. Interstate 40 ends in Wilmington at an overdeveloped street that travels past car dealerships and strip malls, back-in-time past sprawling live oaks, crumbling cemeteries, and historic homes. It travels to the Cape Fear River, the heart of this, my favorite city in the whole world.

Although I loved Wilmington, I had to wonder if it was still my home. I'd grown up here, and my family still lived here; but I'd chosen to abandon it. Didn't that divorce me from my ability to call the city my home? And I'd never admit I was running, even though that's exactly what I was doing.

Lee had leaned back in his chair. Magnified behind his glasses, his eyes had revealed un-aged sharpness, measuring me like a jeweler examining a gem of dubious quality. I was used to people underestimating me based on my appearance. I still got carded occasionally, despite being more than a decade over the legal age limit, but mostly by single men, which made asking to see my license somewhat questionable.

I'd thought to fill in the silence, had thought to explain why I couldn't stay in the Tennessee county with that sheriff and his two deputies, but it wasn't just them. Before leaving, I'd come home to find items in my apartment rearranged; one day dresser drawers had been switched around, another day cabinet doors had been left open, and once the covers and sheets had been ripped off my bed. Five times in the last three weeks I'd lived there, I'd been pulled over for "routine" traffic checks. Twice at different grocery stores, after unloading the entire contents of my grocery carts on the conveyor belts, the cashiers had turned off their lights and walked away. Finally, I asked my former editor if he had any contacts with newspapers in Wilmington, my old hometown, expecting his apologies. To my shock, he'd somehow managed to connect me with the *Tribune*. A couple of steps up for me as a journalist, the *Tribune* was a daily paper and circulated throughout southeastern North Carolina.

Although returning to Wilmington after fleeing years ago meant facing my family, I'd believed I was ready for the confrontation and for resolution. My life in Cheatham had ended when I broke the story about how the sheriff used taxpayer money to court his unwed, pregnant secretary and to stockpile self-indulgent luxuries.

"That was a big story for Cheatham," Lee had said. "A big story for the state. And it was pretty impressive that a weekly paper reporter broke it—a reporter without a college degree—a reporter with maybe a handful of years of experience."

At least he hadn't added blonde and female to his assessment, I'd noted, wondering if he had refrained out of politeness or political correctness.

"I'll be interested to read what you can dredge up here," he'd said.

"Thank you for agreeing to give me a chance."

Lee sat upright. "Why did you...?"

His phone had beeped, and the receptionist's voice had sounded from his speaker. "Sorry to interrupt, Mr. Sanford, but I've got an urgent call for Ms. Waters."

Lee's eyes had bored into mine.

An urgent call? Not even family had known I was beginning work at the *Tribune*. I'd wanted to break the news face-to-face under favorable conditions.

"Patch it through." Lee had said before handing the receiver to me.

"Jonie Waters?" A man had asked in a gravelly voice.

"Who is this?"

You need to come. Come across the boardwalk in the garden beside the Cooperative Center for Marine Biology."

"Why?"

He hadn't answered.

"Who are you?" I'd asked. "How do you know me?"

Silence.

"How did you know I'm even in town, working here?"

"Are you coming?"

"Is this a joke?"

"Come now. It's important."

I'd heard a click and the line had gone dead.

"I suppose it was a news tip," I'd said, though the twanging in my bones had told me categorizing the call as a news tip was an error. "The caller didn't say what was happening. I don't know how he knew my name or found out I was working here."

Surely the caller hadn't been one of my former colleagues from Cheatham playing a joke. I would have recognized the voice. Or were the Cheatham sheriff and his goonies taunting me still? How would they have known where I was? Why would they have sent me to a local university's satellite campus, a multi-million dollar research facility on the Intracoastal Waterway?

"Why don't you go check it out?" Lee had asked. "You've filled out our paperwork?"

I'd nodded.

"You've signed the contract?"

I'd nodded again. I'd be paid by the column inch with a bit of extra money if I happened to take a publishable photo, too. The paper had hired me as a freelancer, with no benefits, during an unspecified trial period. If the paper liked my work, I could be brought on staff later, two days from now or two years from now. If the paper didn't like my work, I could be fired on the spot. It was dog food, but I would take it and push to prove myself and be hired permanently as soon as possible.

CHAPTER 4

I finished my recap to Daniel and Kimmie by recalling how I'd followed the news tip to the marine center and found Abby's body. As Kimmie finished taking notes, a black bird cawed from a scrubby pine tree.

"The caller didn't give a name?" Kimmie asked.

"No."

"And the paper just let you—you—run out here?"

I gritted my teeth.

"We'll be checking into your phone records."

"What? Why?" My voice was raised. "Do that. It's the paper's phone records. The tip came in on the main line."

"How did you end up with the call?" Daniel resumed asking the questions.

"The caller asked for me specifically."

"But didn't you say you just got into town?"

"Earlier this morning. I drove through the night from Tennessee." I'd broken free of Cheatham as quickly as possible and couldn't afford a break in pay between jobs.

Did you stop for gas?"

I nodded.

"Then you have a receipt?"

I'd paid in cash because passing paper money made keeping track of my ever-diminutive, dwindling bank account balance easier than attempting to tally credit card purchases.

"I told the gas station attendant I didn't need one."

Kimmie rolled her eyes. "You at least remember where the gas station was located, right?"

"It was just some mountain town off the interstate. I think it started with an 'M.' Marion, maybe, or Morganton." I vaguely remembered a reddish orange sign beckoning within view of the highway. "I admit getting the call at the newspaper this morning was curious. I don't know how anyone, other than former colleagues in Tennessee and the few *Tribune* employees I met today, would have known I was here."

"Maybe," Kimmie said, "the caller, if there really was a caller—"

"You think I want this to be my first story—Abby murdered?" I balled my fist around my pen.

"It wouldn't be the first time you've manipulated yourself into a self-serving spotlight."

I stepped closer to her, my fingers burning from clutching my pen so tightly.

Daniel pushed between us. He gave Kimmie a stern look. "And you," he growled at me. "Sit." He pointed at the picnic table.

I backed away and tried to calm my breathing while he led Kimmie away by the arm.

Did old wounds ever heal, I wondered, taking solace in remembering our senior year in high school when I spread four packages of raw ground beef on Kimmie's Mercedes and wrote "cheap meat" in bright red paint on her tinted windows. While the effort marked a crowning achievement in our all-out war that stemmed from our first meeting, I also couldn't forget the day our family cracked between the Jonie/Kimmie fissure—how I left, how I wished I could take back what I did that day—some of it, anyway.

But I didn't need to dredge up the past. Not now. Now I needed to focus, I thought, to separate myself between being a person and being a reporter. I had done it a couple of times before now, torn my emotions from my mind—when I was writing a story about a girl horribly mauled by a bear caged in her neighbor's back yard—when interviewing the parents of a teenaged soccer player who was killed in the passenger seat of his best friend's crashed Miata speeding upwards of 110 mph on I-40's loop around Nashville. But I'd never splintered myself to write a story about someone I knew well. Could I separate from my feelings and be just a reporter for Abby? I pulled out my pad of paper. Right this moment, I told myself, I would be a reporter.

I began to write what I knew. The approximate time the call to the *Tribune* came in, that the caller was a man, his voice gruff and disguised. That about a half hour passed between the time the call came in and the time I arrived at the marine center. I checked my watch and wrote down the current time. How much time passed while I stood on the boardwalk?

I looked around and wrote what I observed. Students gathered in bunches outside the marine center. Built to look modern and incongruous, the center's entryway consisted of a single black column propping up a sweeping, white concrete canopy that curved over the front door. A fountain squirted graceful arcs that distorted the reflection of the center's towering wall of mirrored windows. I retrieved my camera from my pocket and took a photo.

I wrote down what the body had looked like: bloody, soggy, grimy with marsh mud, and bubbling with crabs. The body— Abby's body—the body, I redirected my mind, again veering away from the intersection of friend and reporter.

I wrote down what I didn't know. Who was the caller? Why didn't he call the police himself? Why did he call me? How did he know I was at the *Tribune*? Did he realize I knew Abby? How did her body end up down there?

I glanced beyond the yellow police tape and into the garden. Officers still were examining the gazebo area. I took a photo and then used the zoom button to study Daniel. He'd released Kimmie, who now was frowning at him. A silver cross on a thin chain around his neck had worked its way out from under his shirt. I took a picture of him, Kimmie, and the swarm of officers beyond them. Then, over the distance,

Daniel's eyes connected with mine. I looked away. When I looked back, Daniel was headed in my direction with Kimmie remaining a step behind him. I shoved the camera into my bag.

Before they could speak, I said, "I was in the editor's office when the call came in. You can verify that with the editor-in-chief, Lee Sanford."

"Was the conversation on speaker phone?" Kimmie asked.

Daniel glanced at her.

"No," I said.

"Can you tell us anything about the caller?" he asked.

I thought I already told them everything I knew. I shook my head. "It sounded like the caller was trying to disguise his voice, but he didn't sound like anyone I know, anyway."

"Did he sound agitated? Nervous?"

"Nervous. Winded."

I looked into the garden. Abby's body was enveloped in a bag at the base of the marsh grasses. Part of me itched to take another photo. Another part of me wanted to throw up.

"You're interrogating me, acting like you think I'm involved in this. You're categorizing Abby's death as a murder, right?" I asked.

"It's too early to call right now."

I jotted down what he said.

"There's no way she tripped, smashed the railing, and then fell," I said. "For one, the railing seems too sturdy to be broken without significant force."

Daniel stared at me, eyebrows furled, eyes unfathomable. I stared back at him.

"How can it not be murder?" I asked.

"We'll be taking the body to autopsy," Daniel said, avoiding my question. "We'll investigate the death and determine whether her death was an accident or something more insidious."

"How soon do you think you'll know?"

"Within a day or two."

"How… ?"

"That's all I'm going to say. Our department will issue a media release. We'll need a number where you can be reached in case we have more questions for you."

I gave Daniel the number at the *Tribune* and the address to my apartment. When my father's childless sister died, my aunt bequeathed her downtown, crumbling two-story building with downstairs and upstairs apartments, complete with antiquated furnishings, to me. I offered my stepbrother cheap rent to live in the downstairs apartment and keep up the building. My stepbrother was Kimmie's twin and the only family member with whom I maintained regular contact. I often wondered how twins could be so different.

"I gave you the *Tribune's* number because my cell phone is down there with Abby," I said.

"This should be another good tale," Kimmie said.

"Kimmie," Daniel said as though admonishing her, but he hadn't looked away from me.

"I dropped it when I was going to call 911. A student came up, startled me, and the phone fell out of my hands."

"Can you point out this alleged student?" Kimmie asked.

I looked into the crowds of students, searching to find the girl. I didn't even remember what she looked like. All I remembered was her silver notebook cover.

"When my phone fell, I told her to go to a phone and call you, call the police," I said. "She went running away."

"It was a male professor who called us," Kimmie said.

"Then the student must have told the professor. Why don't you check with him and see who told him to make the call?"

"You're leaving us with a lot of unanswered questions to research."

I stood up. Again Daniel stepped between me and Kimmie.

"I'll escort you back to your car. Kimmie, check on the progress back there."

After Kimmie stormed off, we stood in silence for a few beats; Daniel not taking his eyes off mine; me refusing to demurely look away. His eyes were unreadable. I felt a small tremor as we kept eye contact. He shook his head and finally broke the standoff by asking if I minded him examining my hands. I held them out and allowed him to turn them over. His touch was still warm, and his hands were calloused. I wondered if he noticed how my breath sped up. He nodded and released my hands, then steered me past the students, through the parking lot, and to my truck. I thought of him not as Detective Wyeth but as Daniel. I needed to watch myself.

"Is there anything you want to say, anything else you want to add?" Daniel asked.

I shook my head. Again, he seemed to be waiting for something. What did he want me to say?

"I'm telling the truth," I said, looking directly into those deep blue eyes again. "Check the newspaper phone records, check with the professor who called to verify the student's identity. Abby was a good person. She was beautiful, nice, and full of grace." I felt my eyes tear. "In a lot of ways, she was the opposite of me. For her to be killed, to find her dead—it just doesn't make sense."

"I'm sorry." Daniel's words reached his eyes, softening them, and his hand rested briefly on my back. "I'm sorry you had to see your friend that way. Let us know if you think of anything you forgot to mention."

We reached my beat-up truck. I'd rolled down its windows as usual in an attempt to keep the interior slightly cooler than a kiln. My air conditioning had broken just after passing 210,000 on the odometer. Daniel handed me his business card and tugged open my door, glancing around my truck's cab.

"You can tear my truck apart," I said.

He backed away, and I climbed in, tugging the rusty door shut behind me. I turned the key in my ignition, and my truck coughed to life. I drove away, periodically checking the side mirror, watching Daniel observe me until I rounded the corner. I didn't like how our conversation had gone, how Kimmie and Daniel seemed to be suspicious of me, and what their attitude suggested about how Abby died, but I couldn't dwell on that. I had an article to write.

CHAPTER 5

I wrote the story at Port Java House. A block from *Tribune* headquarters, fronting the Cape Fear River, the café was jammed into one of the old brick storefronts that served customers before automobiles replaced horses; before steamboats were used only for ferrying tourists on sightseeing cruises. The Cape Fear River had been the lifeblood of Wilmington, attracting early settlers with a port that served industries evolving from lumber and rice to tar and turpentine. Today a person sitting in front of one of the trendy, river-front restaurants or shops could drink imported coffee just upriver from lines of metal cranes unloading cargo ships stacked with multicolored containers. Perhaps because of the river, Wilmington continued to flourish and thrive despite hurricanes, despite wars, despite fires and epidemics, and economic free-falls.

Port Java House granted customers both a view of the river and the novelty of enjoying an old building's nuances. Its wooden floors sloped, and its scratched front windows curved out like rounded bays, the semicircular spaces hosting elevated platforms with a couple of chairs stationed around tables designed to encourage intimacy.

I ordered a tall mocha, found a seat by a wall, shoved away the emotions that had been swirling in my chest and threatening to spill out during the drive over, and set down to business. With so few facts, writing the article didn't take long.

I e-mailed the article and photos to the *Tribune*. The piece would make tomorrow morning's paper. Walking back to my truck, the air so humid a fish could breathe it, exhaustion slammed into me. By the time I drove to my apartment and unloaded my meager belongings from the bed of my truck, I felt too tired to eat or even investigate the abandoned possessions I'd inherited with the house. I tugged the plastic trash bags I'd crammed with my clothes to the bedroom, along with my secret stash of romance novels, their bindings cracked and pages worn from handling. I leaned a few framed prints—a Monet, a still life of some daisies, and one of the ocean at sunrise—as well as my acoustic guitar against the living room walls. I stacked several boxes of miscellaneous possessions in the hallway and kitchen. Then I fell onto the dusty couch, one of the many fusty furniture pieces my aunt had left. I turned the ancient television on for some company, closed my eyes, and slept dreamlessly until I jolted awake, my heart pounding.

I thought I'd heard someone scream.

CHAPTER 6

I threw off the scratchy afghan and sat up on the couch. The only noise in the room sounded from my aunt's television. Grandparent-aged actors wearing farm attire belted out a hokey children's song. The mechanical clock on the mantel read 3:47 a.m. I glanced through the den and vacant kitchen. Beyond, stairs led down to a claustrophobic foyer and the front door, the only door out, unless I counted the door off the bedroom to the porch, which didn't have stairs to the alleyway below. The only rooms I couldn't see from the couch were the bedroom and bathroom. Maybe, I thought, what had startled me awake was a squeal from a mouse scrounging for food. Maybe it was one of the actors on television trying to sound like a barnyard animal. Maybe I was jumpy from finding Abby, and from being surrounded by my aunt's musty belongings.

Then I heard the noise again. Something screeched in the bedroom. The noise sounded like a parrot shrieking, or like a stubborn window being forced open.

Adrenaline sparked through my veins. The kitchen and stairwell were on the opposite side of the bedroom door from where I sat, and I didn't remember where I'd left my keys. I couldn't unlock the deadbolt without them. Since I couldn't run, and I was fairly certain an intruder was entering my apartment, I'd be forced to fight. I jumped from the couch and scanned the room for a weapon, something hard and straight that I could wield, like a bat. A golden lamp stand rested on a corner table, but it was plugged in and had a shade the size of a small umbrella. A coat rack missing an arm listed toward one wall, but the rack was too long to manage. I spotted a metal cane behind the television. I grabbed it and flattened myself against the wall beside the bedroom door. Inching closer to the door, I raised the cane above my head, gripping the cold metal.

I heard something that sounded like fabric scraping against wood and crinkling—weight bearing down on the plastic bags containing my clothes. Someone was coming in through the window. My best chance at defending myself was to clobber the intruder just outside the bedroom doorway, so I waited. I heard the creaking of the wood floor beams. The actors on the television were merrily singing "The Farmer in the Dell," oblivious to my hammering heart. A bulking, masculine body crossed the threshold.

I brought the cane down. He blocked the blow with his arm and twisted the cane out of my hands. I aimed a kick at his groin, but he turned and shielded my foot with his thigh. I followed with a punch toward his nose. He jerked his head back so my punch landed on his jaw. He brandished the cane, but as it swung toward me, it thumped inside the door frame and instead a fist came through and caught my chin. I fell; my cheek scraped the wooden box my aunt used as a coffee table. I landed hard enough to raise a cloud of dust from the floor and immediately pushed up. The man caught me from behind, pinning my arms to my body. I reared both knees to my chest, and then yanked my heels down on what I hoped were his knees, flailing my arms. He let go, propelling me across the room. I spun around and aimed a roundhouse kick at his face. As my foot connected near his ear, I recognized those large, pale gray eyes.

My stepbrother, Phaser, landed on the couch. A line of blood trickled from a cut.

We stared at each other. Then we laughed. On the cuddly side of the scale, Phaser was handsome with a freckled, square face. I had to give my stepmother, who owned a chain of spas that specialized in transforming women with deep pockets into women with deeply layered haircuts, credit for the way she cut his light brown hair. She allowed it just enough length for its natural waves to take shape. The years hadn't changed Phaser's appearance much. I touched my cheek and found it wet with blood.

"You—" I sucked in a breath. "You scared me. I—"

He sat up and fingered his face. "Great gobs of goat shit, Jonie."

I grinned at the way his southern accent crooned the phrase.

"Damn, you weren't kidding when you said you won yourself a black belt. Gave me a run for my money, girl. I thought you were another drifter using the place to crash."

"There have been bums in here?"

"Just one, once. I'll put locks on the windows. That should fix it."

"Use the doorbell or your key next time. That would fix it."

"You hurt badly?" he asked.

"I don't think so. My chin's tender. But I'm not sure about this cut."

"Don't look too deep."

"Are you okay?"

"'S all good." Phaser's familiar euphemism remained unchanged in my absence. "But my ego's crushed. I been beat up by my little sister."

I pulled him off the couch and into an embrace. That was one of our old jokes—little sister, big brother—I was younger only by a few months.

"Got ice?" he asked.

I walked to the kitchen and scrounged through a couple of drawers until I found some dish towels, which were patterned with ugly glaring roosters. I wrapped ice in two towels and tossed one to Phaser. I tore off a paper towel and pressed it against my cheek. The blood flow seemed to have stopped, but I could feel a bruise rising.

"So what're you doing here?" Phaser asked, reclining on the couch and propping his feet on the upturned wooden box.

"I'm moving back. I've got a job with the Wilmington *Tribune*."

"How come you didn't tell me? You called me last week."

"I thought I'd surprise you."

"Some surprise."

I rolled my eyes. "Anyway, I thought Kimmie might have called you."

"You told Kimmie you were back? You and Kimmie suddenly are speaking to each other?"

Phaser didn't know. Kimmie hadn't told him—not about me and not about Abby.

"Phaser," I said, my voice suddenly sounding foreign. "Abby Pridgen is dead."

"No! What?" Phaser looked blank, as if he hadn't comprehended.

"Abby. She's dead."

Phaser's eyes found mine. They looked pleading and then heavy. His scabbed hand clutched the dish towel tighter. I heard the ice cubes crunch and fracture.

I shouldn't have said it so abruptly. I should have told him to prepare himself first. Ever since I knew him, Phaser had pined for Abby. I'd never sat down with him for a heart-to-heart explanation about how and why she, and other smart and goddess-gorgeous women, were more than a little out of his league—not that Phaser was a toad. He was just alternative and a tad goofy—not desperately so, but enough to put corners in wheels cool chicks like Abby expected to roll.

Phaser moved the dish towel to his forehead and shielded his eyes.

I backtracked, filling Phaser in on everything that happened earlier, from driving overnight into town and meeting Lee, to the phone call, to finding Abby, to Kimmie questioning me as if I were a suspect. When I finished, I wiped tears from my eyes. Phaser's cheeks were wet too. His pinkish face appeared as a bright smudge in the dark, cool room.

"Do you think the person who called you had something to do with Abby's death?" he asked. "Or, do you think maybe he just found her? But if that's the case, why wouldn't he have gone straight to the cops? You think he got spooked? Why did he call you at all?"

"I don't know," I said. "No way could she have tripped. I suppose it's possible, but not at an angle perpendicular to the boardwalk and with enough force to crack the railing, and besides, she was so—"

"Elegant," Phaser finished. "She and I—" Phaser glanced at me, his eyes bloodshot. "We kept in touch. It wasn't like we were close or anything, but at least a couple of times a year one of us would phone. We were friends too. I spoke to her last weekend. At the roadhouse."

I stood in silence, in the middle of the unfamiliar room full of inherited belongings, feeling disconnected. This apartment with all its wacky old furnishings wasn't home, at least not yet. And Abby—Abby was dead, and the way she looked with those crabs—how could her death be real? This wasn't my world. Maybe this wasn't me.

"When I spoke with her," Phaser said, "she was upbeat, consumed with her research, chasing after some theory, just the way she liked to be."

One corner of his mouth widened in a grimace, and his fist tightened again around the dish towel.

"Her life wasn't as carefree as she let on," he said. "I knew her, enough to know she was an expert at hiding the cracks inside."

He stood abruptly and walked through my bedroom. I heard him climb out my window. I gave him a few minutes and then followed him outside. Phaser leaned against the porch railing. I looked down into the shallow backyard at the azaleas he planted years ago. They were a riot of color when blooming—sweet pinks, pure whites, and an almost vulgar magenta exploded off photos he mailed me with the names he'd christened the plants penned on the back. Phaser was full of ironies, working as a technological geek by day, a bouncer at the Riverside Roadhouse by night, and an expert gardener in between. I never was successful with caring for plants; houseplants esteemed for their self-sufficiency, even bamboo, died within a month, tops, of my guardianship.

"So you and Kimmie reunited," Phaser said quietly. "How'd it go?"

I shrugged. I supposed Kimmie had been as surprised as I'd been at our run-in at the university. But Wilmington was like that, despite the metamorphic changes I'd witnessed in my adolescence, and apparently even despite the city's boggling growth since I'd left. I still couldn't disappear in Wilmington. Between large families and old money and friends of friends, run-ins and mutual acquaintances were unavoidable. This was the South, after all. We kept tabs. Also, with the river and nearby beach, the history and distinct charm, not many people wanted to leave Wilmington. The city bred closeness.

"Come on," Phaser said. "You haven't seen us in more than a decade, and I missed the big reunion."

"I think she was more shocked than happy to see me."

"I'm more shocked than happy to see you. Besides, what did you expect from her?"

What had I expected? I didn't expect to meet her at a crime scene. I'd hoped to talk with her eventually, just the two of us. And then I'd hoped for forgiveness. Maybe me giving a tearful apology and Kimmie saying she was sorry too, hugging me, laughing at how crazy we all were. And a new beginning from there. I usually was optimistic, a believer in redemption and goodness. But then again, deep down, I knew a joyful reunion was beyond reasonable hopes. Even a civil reunion would have been pushing luck, as never in our history had we been civil except at surface levels when our parents were watching.

"Girl, don't take this wrong, but the way you left—"

I envisioned that evening, when I left Wilmington. My family's faces lit up, ghostlike, in the darkened living room. And then the cloudburst, my father's and stepmother's shouts and punishment threats crashing down on me, my failsafe plan to serve Kimmie with justice horribly backfired. My hands moved like nervous birds, cramming my clothes and belongings into my backpack, not bothering to organize anything, grabbing my guitar and running out to my truck, thinking I was leaving nothing behind but burned rubber, feeling not the empathy or trepidation or hideous shame that I should have felt, but instead invincible glee and salty, crisp spring wind ripping through my hair. I opened my eyes.

"It was a mistake," I said.

"It weren't a mistake. What you did to Kimmie took planning."

"I meant doing it was a mistake. I went too far."

"Way too far."

"It was a dozen years ago." I punched the railing. "Kimmie pulled off just as many planned-out schemes—"

"All I'm saying—" Phaser held up his hands, "is, it was such a shock. That whole night. And we all were left spinning, not knowing what to think. And there's Kimmie, wounded. Yes, she really was wounded," he said, shaking his head, "and mom and dad are getting her side of the story for all these years."

"Kimmie can do no wrong. They never listened to me."

"Look," Phaser pushed off the railing and wrapped his bear arms around me. "It's going to take a while for everyone to accept you back with open arms. Especially Kimmie. You just can't snap your fingers and wish it back to what it was."

"And do I even want what it was?"

"You want a family," Phaser said, softly rubbing my shoulders.

We had talked about this on the phone. Even hundreds of miles away, Phaser was my closest friend. He was there when I thought I was completely alone. Knowing him was what kept me going some days—knowing him and punishing the punching bag during tae kwon do classes.

Our conversation lapsed into silence. Seconds turned into minutes. Neither of us wanted to talk about Abby, and nothing else seemed relevant any longer. Finally, we said goodnight, and I climbed inside and forced the window shut. Lightheaded, I wandered into the mustard yellow bathroom. A purplish tinge surrounded my cut and contrasted deliciously with my vivid green eyes. I frowned at my straight, static-frizzed hair and my nose, which bent slightly at the bridge before realigning itself, a permanent memory of a childhood tree-climbing accident. I looked like a freak. Foundation might hide the cut, at least, and a shower and conditioner might tame my hair. I left the bathroom light on and plopped onto the unmade bed, hugging my oversized pink quilted pillow—another childhood souvenir—snugly against my chest. The mattress smelled like a rain puddle.

CHAPTER 7

I slept in fits, my stomach churning, and climbed out of bed before the sun, entirely awake—jittery, even, but simultaneously exhausted. I decided to go for a run in an effort to burn off energy, or to at least purge some of what felt like guilt caught in my throat. After slipping my lean legs into a pair of silky black running shorts, I took a challenging course that weaved through the nearby neighborhood blocks, pushing myself so hard I felt like I was sucking air through a straw. I couldn't help but notice copies of this morning's *Tribune* rolled tight and secured with rubber bands, waiting on driveways to announce Abby's death to subscribers.

Writing about her death, taking those photos—I was doing my job, I told myself. I had no other options but to report what I witnessed. My thoughts wandered to Daniel, Detective Wyeth. Was he really thinking I was involved in Abby's death, or was he just doing his job, covering all his bases? My stomach quivered at the memory of his warm, strong hands holding mine. He had to feel our connection too. By the time I rounded the corner to return to my apartment, the sun rebounded in golden flashes off windows. If the light hadn't temporarily blinded me, if I hadn't failed to see who was waiting at my doorstep, I would have been tempted to turn around and jog another couple of miles. Kimmie and Daniel both turned their heads to face me as my footsteps slowed to a walk and carried me across the crunchy brick walkway to my door.

My heart rate accelerated as I approached them, despite the end of my aerobic activity. So much for a cool down, I thought. Daniel, stoic-faced and weary-eyed, nodded at me, taking in my flushed cheeks and loose, sweat-drenched tank top that barely concealed my sports bra, before his eyes found mine again. A thin, straight scar ran from his lower cheek and disappeared beneath his chin—something I hadn't noticed yesterday. With a manila folder wedged beneath her arm, Kimmie merely wrinkled her nose as if my deodorant had failed. A tightly stretched knit band strapped her unruly orange curls back from her face; beyond, the frizz exploded on the sides and back of her head like a bouquet of snarled fireworks.

"We wanted to catch you before you left for work," Daniel explained.

"Why's that?"

Kimmie shook her head at me behind Daniel's back.

"We wanted to follow up with you," Daniel said. "We had some additional questions. I'm glad we didn't wake you." A small smile tugged his lips, probably because of my sweaty appearance. So he wasn't all business, I thought.

I continued to wonder what was causing his smile as I unlocked the door. If he was imagining catching me in a silky nightgown, he'd have been sorely disappointed. My pajama wardrobe primarily consisted of old shirts.

"Come up," I said.

At the top of my stairs, I turned into the kitchen and rummaged through boxes until I found my coffee maker. I plugged it in and shook out a portion of the half-used bag of ground coffee I transported from my Cheatham home. Daniel and Kimmie slid into mismatched chairs at the kitchen table and watched in silence as I worked.

"I don't have any donuts," I said, inwardly groaning at my ridiculous attempt at lifting the mood, "or any other breakfast food, but can I get you anything other than coffee? I've got water."

"No, thanks," Daniel answered.

Kimmie made a noise halfway between clearing her throat and gagging. A picky eater, donuts were never Kimmie's style, and her hotdog figure—not lean but not bumpy, either— proved her food preferences remained selective. I, on the other hand, had curves and softness where most men wanted them.

With the coffee maker eagerly dripping in the background and a disposable plastic cup of ice water chilling my hand, I joined them at the table.

I took a sip of the water. "Ask away."

"When was the last time you had contact with Abby?" Daniel asked.

"About a dozen years ago. I haven't spoken with her since I last lived here."

Daniel frowned, and I mentally double checked my math. It was correct, so I didn't elaborate. I shimmied out a cocktail napkin from the dusty stack centered on the table and dabbed sweat from my forehead and cheeks.

"Did she ever try to contact you after you left town twelve years ago?"

I shook my head.

"Did you speak on the telephone? Email? Write?"

I kept shaking my head.

"But you let her know you were coming back to town."

"No."

"You haven't contacted her in any way in the last month?"

"No."

"Not even passing on a message through a mutual acquaintance?"

I shook my head again.

"Then do you know how she would have a printout of your article on the Cheatham sheriff in her car?"

My jaw locked as my mind bypassed the shock and kicked into overdrive. How would Abby have known about the article I wrote? Would Phaser have told Abby about the trouble writing about the scandal had caused me? Even if he had, why would Abby have gone to the Cheatham paper's website and printed my story?

"Do you need me to repeat my question?" Daniel asked.

"No," I said, my voice sounding like a stubborn teenager. "I don't know. Maybe Abby was looking up old friends on the internet. Maybe someone we both knew told her about it." I tried to envision Abby reading my article. What would cause her to be so interested in it that she printed it out? "I haven't spoken to Abby in years, so of course I didn't tell her about the article, or where I worked, and I didn't ask anyone to pass along the information." I forced another sip of ice water.

"You said yesterday that hardly anyone knew you were coming to Wilmington and writing with the *Tribune*."

"That's right."

"Who, exactly, knew?"

"My colleagues in Cheatham—my former editor and his staff—and Lee Sanford, the *Tribune* editor, and anyone he decided to tell." I patted my forehead and cheeks with the napkin again, racking my brain. "That's all. Why?"

"I was wondering why Abby wrote the *Tribune's* phone number on the printout of your story."

"What?"

Daniel merely studied me.

How would Abby have known to write the *Tribune's* number on the article from my former paper? "No one other than coworkers knew I was coming to Wilmington." My dry voice sounded phony.

The sound of the last of the water coughing violently through the coffee maker caused me to glance over my shoulder.

"What happened to your face?"

A couple of seconds passed before I realized Daniel was referring to the cut that must have been concealed by my flushed cheeks when I first returned home. I jumped when his fingers touched my chin. He gently turned my head so my injured cheek faced him. In the action, I noticed that his arms were evenly built with the type of lean muscle that comes from use and not from a weight room. No, I thought. I couldn't allow myself to be distracted. I closed my eyes. When I opened them, Daniel stared into mine as if he thought, through his close, steady gaze, he could penetrate my soul. His face was so near, I felt his breath on my jaw. He cleared his throat and released me.

"I didn't notice this abrasion yesterday," he said.

I winced. "That's because it happened last night. Phaser broke into my apartment while I was sleeping. He saw some lights on and thought I was a bum crashing here. I thought an intruder was breaking in, so I tried to knock him out. I fell on the coffee table and kicked him back before either of us knew who we were fighting."

Kimmie blew air out her nose in a suppressed chuckle.

"You can verify that with Phaser," I said.

"Phaser?" Daniel asked.

"My twin brother, Phillip," Kimmie said. "Phaser's his nickname, because he's so laid back nothing ever phases him. This is his upstairs apartment."

"My upstairs apartment. My building. He rents his apartment from me."

Kimmie wrinkled her nose again.

"What is it between you two?" Daniel asked. His question was purely rhetorical, because before I could think of a suitable explanation, he continued. "Why didn't you call the police if you thought your apartment was being broken into?"

"I thought I could take care of it myself, and I did," I said, as Kimmie mouthed 'yahoo.' "Besides, going for the phone would have revealed my location to the intruder while wasting time I needed to find a makeshift weapon and get into position, and I didn't want to give him that advantage."

Daniel raised his eyebrows, and Kimmie snickered.

"Phaser told me you bought yourself a black belt," she said. "I didn't realize you actually took yourself seriously." Kimmie giggled.

"Ladies," Daniel said, addressing me. "Back on topic: for Abby to have a printout of an article you wrote at some Tennessee paper and to have written on it a number for the *Tribune* where she could reach you seems to be too much for coincidence."

I met his statement with silence. What could I say—that I agreed? Was he insinuating that I was lying?

"In addition to those alleged coincidences is the huge fact that you were found with her body," Daniel continued. "One plus one, plus one, equals—" he let his voice fade.

"Equals what?" I asked, hazarding a glance at Kimmie. She was enjoying the show, her lips stretched in a contented grin that took me back to high school, passing her in the hallway—the look told me something nasty was brewing. "I was as surprised—as horrified—as anyone at her death." My voice cracked.

"But you sure did a good job taking advantage of the situation," Kimmie said, smugly pulling the front section of today's *Tribune* from her folder and slapping it down on the kitchen table directly in front of me. The photo of the students huddling together as if for warmth at the marine center, yellow police tape cordoning off the garden in the background, stared back at me from the paper's front page. "Your first story was a killer."

I snapped. My hands clenched, and the plastic cup I held cracked and split, slopping ice and water across the newspaper and table. Daniel, Kimmie, and I simultaneously jumped up. I had lunged back to escape being drenched in ice water, but it appeared as if Kimmie arose in preparation to defend herself, and Daniel froze mid-stride halfway around the kitchen table like he was ready to restrain me from attacking Kimmie. I was shaking.

"Not necessary." I was surprised I managed to choke out the words. As I mopped up the mess, Daniel and Kimmie straightened up and tried to appear nonchalant. "Do you mind leaving now, if you're through questioning me? I need to get ready for work."

I locked the door behind Daniel and Kimmie and took a long shower, allowing burning hot water to trickle down my body until all that was left was cold water, and then I remained in the shower a few minutes longer, just to feel my skin throb. I had no options, I told myself again. I did my job in reporting Abby's death. Daniel and Kimmie had nothing on me but a teetering stack of coincidence. I didn't have anything to fear because I hadn't done anything wrong.

If that was true, a quiet voice inside me said, then why was I trembling?

CHAPTER 8

I take full fault. The shame is on me. I should have checked the identity of the writers the *Tribune* employed when I decided to move back. Even when Lee told me that for my first month with the paper, he was pairing me with a writer named Jason, the internal bells that should have clanged remained still and cobwebbed.

At the newspaper office for my second day on the job, Lee showed me to my cubicle. It sat at the back of a row against an internal wall, furthest from a window. My area, which encompassed a square of carpet about the size of a bathroom stall, was outfitted with an ancient computer and a telephone with its "3" button missing. I supposed the nicer office furnishings I passed in the cubicles closer to the window and main walkway belonged to salaried reporters. But I liked my cubicle bordering a wall. I'd rather neighbor a wall than the walkway with fellow employees and supervisors looking over my shoulder or voicing obligatory greetings all day long. And if the cubicle became too depressing, I could always pack up and work somewhere else on my outdated laptop. Other reporters were beginning to filter into cubicles nearby. Lee glanced around.

"Jason!" he barked.

Looking to match the name to the face, I then realized the extent of my negligence in failing to look up the writers. Had I completed that research, I would have at least been able to hide my shock at seeing the man striding toward me—Jason Rossini, my high school sweetheart and early college boyfriend. Instead, I was unprepared and ended up sucking in such a deep breath I coughed.

"Jason, meet our new freelancer, Jonie."

This was Jason, my first love. I remembered flowers he picked from the roadside for me and shirts smelling of baseball field clay. I remembered quiet afternoons spent sunbathing on his aluminum boat, watching him drift through the tidal creeks, a minimum of two poles set to catch flounder. Our relationship had been an oddity. We dated for four years, serious longevity for young love, for first love. But as my conflict with Kimmie escalated, the romance became a casualty. Kimmie wanted to take him from me, and not because she wanted him. Even when she succeeded, she continued to date other boys although she and Jason were supposed to be together. Score another battle win for Kimmie. He fell for her and ditched me. Jason didn't recognize Kimmie's tactics, and the night I revealed her true nature to him and to my family was the evening I ran away and dropped out of the local college.

Blinking, I brought myself back to the present time, and found my cheeks burning from recalling history.

"For your first month or so," Lee said, "while you're getting settled here, you're going to be working closely with Jason. Jason will accompany you on interviews, review your articles before they're sent to me, and answer your questions. Jason, take Jonie with you to the staff meeting and show her around the office."

Lee was off before Jason could reply. Jason leaned back in his swivel chair and studied me. The rising sun streaming through the distant window revealed hints of red and a few gray streaks in his short-cropped hair that remained a complimentary deep brown to his hazel eyes.

Jason wore his shirt sleeves rolled up and secured with buttons, revealing a complex silver wristwatch with an intricate winged symbol and three smaller dials inside the main face. Combined with a silk tie loosely knotted around his starched collar, the details showed that Jason had turned yuppie in my absence. But then, looking into his olive complexioned face, he seemed to retain traces of the same boyishness I remembered. His inquisitive, unabashed eyes absorbed me, but then revealed a flicker, as if he still was calculating when to pull a minnow from a hidden bait bucket and throw it at me.

"I never expected—I must say—wow. Hello. How've you been?" I wanted to hide my face. I wanted a do-over.

"When Lee told me you were going to be writing with us, I was as staggered as you appear."

"You knew I was coming?"

"I saw your front page write-up this morning." Jason frowned, and the grim gesture suddenly aged his face.

I sat down, looking around his cubicle for clues about him. Other than framed press association awards hanging from the top of the cubicle wall, Jason's space yielded little. He slurped coffee from a large clay mug with a base of forest green and a lip drizzled gray with blue flecks—the imperfect, obviously handmade kind of craft found at out-of-the-way mom-and-pop pottery stands in the mountains. The mug didn't seem to fit the ever-moving man seated before me nor the Jason I remembered from high school. He set the mug on his desk, using this morning's *Tribune* as a coaster.

"Some scoop," he said, massaging his earlobe, a habit I remembered from before.

I suspected he was jealous, though the Jason I remembered wouldn't have envied a reporter covering a death.

"Someone called the paper and asked for me directly instead of calling the cops himself."

Jason cocked his head.

"I don't understand it, myself," I said, trying to read his reaction. I wanted to ask him if he remembered Abby, or remind him that I knew her, but I restrained myself; a personal connection with news articles never was encouraged in the business. "It was a tough story, not to write especially, but to see."

He abruptly sprung up from his desk, startling me. "Let me show you around before the staff meeting."

Jason collected a couple of notebooks and headed to the walkway, leaving a delicious cologne aroma in his wake. I followed him, grateful he had avoided the subject of our past relationship. I supposed Jason felt awkward, too, considering our past love, his betrayal of me, and how I paid him back the day I left town.

"We have a staff meeting every weekday morning when Lee doles out story assignments. We split up weekends—reporters work one weekend a month—and we all try to write at least one story that can run in a weekend edition during the week. We don't work 9–5 days. Obviously, you don't, since you're getting paid by the story. So long as your stories are completed on time, there's no need to stay here. No need to be present physically at all, except for the staff meeting, unless you want to use our equipment and resources."

I hurried to keep up as he turned a corner.

"Stu!" he yelled, beckoning to a tall, bony man with wavy hair so blonde it was almost white, matching eyelashes, and wire-rimmed glasses, who promptly detached himself from a group and headed our way. Stu looked like an elongated green bean, wearing a dull green shirt with plaid-patterned stitching, a diagonally striped tie the shade of a ripe lime, and pants too brown to be khakis.

"Stu, meet freelancer Jonie."

We shook hands. His was slightly sweaty and painfully firm.

"Stu Bennington," he said in a lazy drawl that drug out the 'u' in Stu. Considering Stu, from his clothes to his demeanor, I decided he couldn't be older than twenty-five.

"Stu is the news staff photographer," Jason explained. "He goes to the important assignments, stays a couple of minutes, shoots a photo or two, and takes home the big bucks."

"I wish."

"Do me a favor and take Jonie to the staff meeting. I've got to settle something in payroll."

Too familiarly, Stu put his arm around my shoulders and steered me back toward the cubicles. While I was surprised by Jason's quick departure, I reminded myself that at least he avoided bringing up our past history both to me and in introducing me to Stu—those were good signs—and Jason seemed to have forgotten I was once Abby's neighbor, though I doubted he was even aware of our girlhood friendship so long ago.

"I started as a freelancer, just like you," Stu said, walking to a desk opposite mine behind the cubicle wall. He leaned a worn leather briefcase against a corner, fitting it beneath a framed photograph of himself surfing. Photos of professional surfers and curling waves were tacked to his cube walls. "I was fresh out of college. Took like a year of busting my butt for them to finally put me on staff. Not having a steady salary or benefits can be a real drag."

"So you surf?" I changed the subject, not wanting to explain how I wasn't just starting out—I'd been writing professionally for half a decade, ever since the day the only full-time reporter at the paper I worked at as a receptionist quit hours before the local high school's homecoming game. Someone had to cover the crowning of the new queen, and the editor had not wanted to cancel dinner plans. I'd clawed my way up to bigger papers and stories, nabbing a couple journalism awards along the way.

"I've been surfing all my life." Stu gestured over the cube to Jason's area. "I taught Jason how to hang ten."

I was taken aback again. Jason never showed any inclination to learn to surf when we dated—an anomaly in a school where the tides and anticipated locations of the best breaks dominated daily conversation. I fiddled with my silver bracelet, straightening the beads.

Stu checked his watch. "We'd better split before we're late to the staff meeting."

As we walked, Stu gave me a tour of the office while greeting everyone we met. It didn't matter which section of the cubicles we were in, Stu seemed to be personal friends with every *Tribune* employee. He didn't merely give a quick, casual hello, either. He commented on something specific to everyone, and he seemed to have his own nicknames for everyone: "How was your date last night, Kelly K?" "Gnarly haircut, Ben-ee!" and "Nice column, Jules."

The cubicles were divided into sections for each department. In addition to news, there were lifestyles, sports, business/finance, and arts and entertainment, each located across the walkway from a window. On the opposite side of the building, beyond the bathrooms, were the design and advertising departments, along with administrative offices. Just down from our news department cubes were the editor's and publisher's offices, as well as the conference room where the staff meeting was to be held. The paper was printed in an out-of-town facility across the river.

Stu and I joined the handful of other reporters already gathered in the conference room. I followed Stu's lead and poured myself a paper cupful of coffee, trying not to gag as I added powdered creamer to offset the muddy taste. We sat opposite a wall of windows, the morning sun already burning the air outside into a thick haze. Jason slid in beside us at the polished but worn wooden table.

The staff meeting passed quickly. As the reporters named their story ideas, Lee asked for more information or discussed story lines, occasionally adding an article for the weekend edition for the reporter to complete or asking if the reporter was willing to turn a faxed-in press release into a story. Since Jason and I were paired together during my probationary period, Lee assigned us complimentary articles. In addition to following up with the police on any developments with Abby's death, Jason's article was to be the reaction to her death at the marine center. My assignment was to be an article on Abby's research at the center. Stu would accompany us then spend his afternoon shooting photos for water conservation and bridge repair articles.

"Don't worry, babe," Stu murmured as he pushed back his chair from the conference table. "You can ride shotgun in the Stumobile." Stu kissed his fingers, then patted my cheek.

I checked my watch. At barely half past nine in the morning, I felt as if I'd already endured a week's worth of harassment. But the trouble in my day was only beginning.

CHAPTER 9

"You want some?" Stu asked, pushing a tube of fruity chapstick too close to my eyes as he sped around corners on the way to the Cooperative Center for Marine Biology.

I tried to ignore the crumpled fast-food bags that kept rolling into my feet. A half melted bar of sandy surfboard wax was stuck to the dashboard of Stu's faded red Civic. Wobbling next to the wax was a scantily clad miniature hula girl statue balancing a Corona on a surfboard. I wondered what had happened to my old surfboard I left at my stepmother's place, wondered if I still could ride it. Once, I had loved surfing.

Stu's chapstick bumped against my nose.

"No, thanks," I said to the chapstick.

Stu rubbed some on his lips. "If you put some on your lips, it'd be like we kissed."

I glanced in the side mirror at Jason. He smirked at me and then shifted out of view. For a moment, I thought I might rather be wiping out on my old surfboard than strapped in a cluttered car with a flirt to my left and an ex in the back seat.

"I haven't washed this car since my parents gave it to me as a Christmas present four years ago," Stu said.

"I don't wash my truck too often, myself."

Jason remained silent.

I dreaded revisiting the center. The image of Abby's lifeless body being tugged to shreds by the crabs flashed through my

43

mind. I tried to shut out the vision as we turned into the center, the white-over-black entryway looming.

We split after parking. Jason and Stu bee-lined toward a group of skinny students in tight jeans and figure-fitting shirts lounging against a shiny cherry red convertible. I continued to the center.

Walking inside the center was like opening a door at the bottom of an alien ocean. A school of metallic fish sculptures glittered along one dark wall while silvery jellyfish statues hung from the two-story ceiling. Live fish in a saltwater tank near the doorway gaped at me. A desk set up at the end of the lobby sat vacant, so I passed it undetected as a guest among students and professors. I turned right and continued down a hallway, searching for room 162, the office the university's website listed as belonging to Abby and Stephen Ballings, her research partner. Abby was paired with Ballings in a type of pilot program that matched beginning professors with those with experience and, in Ballings' case, intellectual celebrity.

According to the website, Ballings was a visiting professor. When I ran his name through a search engine, I found he spent his career skipping from college to college, with stays averaging a year or two at each school. His field-cloistered renown pointed back to a groundbreaking study about saltwater parasites published more than two decades ago.

The ability to research without making verbal or physical contact, without notifying anyone of my interest in advance of an interview, was only one of the many advantages the internet offered reporters. I learned never to underestimate the benefit of the element of surprise, particularly when dealing with subjects who could be inclined to evade an interview—shy people, shifty people, anti-news people already burned by a reporter, people in the midst of tragedy. If office hours were posted online, I knew when I could catch the subject in person, eliminating lengthy bouts of phone tag when the ringing phone with my unfamiliar caller identification could be deferred to voice mail. In addition, completing research before the interview gave me a certain degree of command. Preliminary questions were answered, so more invasive questions could be formulated, the underlying problems or holes in the story seen in advance, so the interview could take a new tack. Days of on-the-fly, blind interviews having diminished even in the few years I'd been reporting taught me to use my hair color and implement a demure demeanor, to sometimes pretend to act uninformed and innocent, giving difficult subjects a false sense of security before posing the questions that struck to the core.

Before leaving the *Tribune*, I had visited the Cooperative Center for Marine Biology's website and found a short description of Abby's research. She was trying to isolate the cause of recent kills of resident fish—namely sunfish varieties that spent their lives in the river. These sunfish were dying, despite a lack of data showing any abnormal or elevated levels of pollutants. Unlike other fish kills that resulted in massive pileups of dead fish rotting on riverbanks after a storm or toxic discharge, the kills Abby researched were more of a steady trickle of dead fish. She was testing water at various points along lower portions the Cape Fear River for chemicals that weren't routinely monitored. Her study was entitled *Pseudopersistent Pollution and its Effects on Marine Life*, whatever that meant. The website also listed Ballings' office hours, so I suspected Abby's research partner would be present when I arrived.

After turning a corner and walking past several more doorways, I found the room. The office hours posted on the door matched the website. I knocked, and the force from my fist jarred the door open. I pushed it open the rest of the way. The room smelled like a high school biology class when frogs were being dissected, only worse. And then I saw why. The room looked as if it had been shaken like a snow globe.

Flasks and jars were toppled over and shattered. Fish with bloody sores—the specimens that I assumed had been contained inside the jars—dripped ooze from countertops onto the floor alongside smashed test tube vials. Drawers had been pulled out, their once sterile metal instruments spilled across the floor. A large, silver microscope lay on its side. Abby's and Ballings' office was an elongated room, like a few walk-in closets stacked together in a row with a window at the end, and the whole unit was in ruins.

CHAPTER 10

Two desks on opposing walls near the window of Abby's and Ballings' office clearly had been rummaged through. Papers were strewn on the floor, drawers were left open, their contents jumbled messes inside. Both computers were smashed. Their casings were dented as if a sledgehammer pounded them, and they were surrounded by tiny metallic fragments. Over one of the desks, a diploma for Stephen Ballings hung cockeyed. I looked at the other desk. A photograph of Abby on the beach with her sister, Martha, and their mother rested on its side. I tore my eyes away from the smiles, all the same crescent shape.

When had this break-in occurred? Who had wrecked this office and why? Had the perpetrator been looking for something? A file, perhaps? Heaps of them were scattered around the desks. But then why break specimen containers and test tube vials? I looked to see if I could find anything obvious that had been removed. Nothing looked blatantly vacant.

I changed my line of thinking. Where would I hide something if I were Abby? I looked under Abby's keyboard and peered into her pencil and pen holder. I looked under her desk. Nothing. I looked around at the files strewn across the floor. Most of the papers contained indecipherable notes and printouts with scientific abbreviations, codes, and numbers. I took another look over Abby's desk, glanced at her bulletin board. Whatever notes and charts that had been pinned there were in shredded ruins or scattered among the papers on the floor.

I wondered if I should alert the campus security or call the police. Just then, Jason walked into the room.

"Don't mean to interrupt, but—" Jason stopped short. I couldn't tell if his face twisted into a grimace because of the smell or the sight.

He was followed closely by Stu and a woman with long, straight black hair parted in the center of her scalp. Her dark eyes looked too sharp for the bifocals hanging from a gold chain, and any soft body curves were confined by a stern plum business suit with a skirt that fell in a straight line to her shins. Her jaw dropped when she saw the mess.

"What is this?" she asked, her English accent emphasizing the vowels.

"I—"

"What happened here?"

"Someone ransacked the lab, it looks like."

"What are you doing in here?" The woman walked toward me, stepping high-heeled feet cautiously over upturned equipment, her eyes scouring the room, taking in the disorder.

"I was here to talk to Professor Ballings."

"He's not here. Obviously."

"I saw his office hours and knocked. Then the door just swung open, and when I saw this mess—" I searched for words to explain why I proceeded into the room and instead decided to change the subject. "Do you work here?"

The woman stared down her nose at me.

"She's Lynne Kipling," Jason explained quietly. "She's the dean of the College of Marine Biology."

"Who are you?" she asked, poking her finger at me.

"Jonie," I said, intentionally leaving off my surname. "Where is Professor Ballings?"

Kipling looked around as if she expected to find him hiding in the rubble.

"Sorry. We'll be going," I said as I stepped around her.

She grabbed my arm. Closer up, the dean seemed spry and wiry beneath her business dress. She held herself so stiffly and compactly I felt as if I could pick her up and carry her under one arm like a cardboard cutout.

"You'll be waiting in my office until the police arrive," she said.

"I didn't do this," I said. "The office looked like this when I entered."

Her grip on me didn't waver. I looked at Jason for help.

"Give me a call when you're done," he said, "and I'll come pick you up."

Before I could lunge at him, Kipling spoke.

"You're both coming, too." She glared at Jason and Stu.

We followed her out of the lab, up a stairwell, past a secretary, and into her office. Although it was significantly larger and wider than Ballings' office, Kipling's quarters were infinitely sparser. A clean black leather mat nearly covered a glass-topped desk. Other than a phone, the only item on her desk was an appointment book precisely positioned in the upper left corner.

Black and white photographs of shells, coral, and other brittle nautical specimens hung, framed in reflective black metal, in neat rows on her walls. While she reported the lab's condition to the police on her desk phone, I admired her view. Kipling's office was at a corner of the marine center with one large window that faced the Intracoastal Waterway and an equally large window that faced the garden. Outside, a pelican perched on a pier piling. The waxy green leaves on the trees of the garden shifted.

"The police will be here shortly." Kipling pulled open a drawer and slid out a green file. She flipped through it, her eyes walking back and forth across the pages too quickly for reading. Her fingers were trembling.

A knock sounded on the door, and I spun around. Surely the police hadn't responded so quickly. Though the visitor wasn't Daniel or even Kimmie, he was someone I had expected to run into, sooner or later. The black jacket tailored for his defensive-end shoulders also accentuated his air of formality, a formality that I knew clung to him, or maybe emanated from within him. He stood, taking up more space than necessary, as if at a podium about to make a speech. That formidable presence had always been there, even when I sang rhymes in princess pajamas, sitting at his feet while he reclined in his black leather armchair reading his journals before bed. Part of me wanted to run to him. Part of me wanted to hide. He was my father, and he had yet to notice me.

"Lynne, I just wanted to thank you and let you know we're out of the conference room if you—" His voice trailed off as his eyes finally met mine.

We stared at each other for a moment. Despite the grayer hair and additional wrinkles, the somber eyes acquaintances forever said mine matched remained the vibrant color of sun-streaked spring grass. I thought I saw his eyes tearing. I wanted to hug him.

"Mr. Waters?" Dean Kipling interrupted.

I looked into my father's eyes again. If I'd seen tears, I had imagined them.

"I see you've met my daughter." My father's voice sounded tight.

Kipling nodded as if she knew all along whom I was. My father was head of the College of Arts and Sciences, Kipling's supervisor, and I wondered if my relationship to him could get me out of trouble.

"Hi, dad," I said. "Sorry I didn't call you and let you know I'm back in town. I just arrived yesterday. I've got a job reporting for the *Tribune*. That's why I'm here. I'm writing an article."

Kipling didn't elaborate.

"Why don't you come over for dinner tonight?" my father asked.

Kipling shifted her weight and turned her head.

I stared up at him, wondering what kind of fit my presence would give my stepmother. She never voiced pleasant words for my father when he invited coworkers or friends to dinner without clearing it with her first.

"Vicki's making her chicken and squash casserole, and we always have enough for eight, let alone three. Be there at six?"

I nodded. I supposed I was ready for my stepmother.

My father turned back to Kipling.

"I have to run before I'm late to my meeting," he said.

He frowned at Jason and waved to Kipling before hurrying away, leaving me wishing he would have hugged me. Or maybe it was me who missed the opportunity to hug him.

Kipling resumed pretending to read through her file. After a few minutes, I decided to break her silence.

"Surely you don't believe I destroyed the lab."

She didn't look up. "It doesn't matter what I believe; you're staying here and speaking with the police."

"But it does matter what you believe," I said. "Who do you think would tear the lab apart like that?"

"No one who works here."

"So you think someone outside the school did it. Or maybe a student vandalized it? But why?"

She finally looked at me and shrugged.

"You don't think Ballings did it?"

"No. Of course not."

Stu flinched at the snap in her voice.

Kipling shook her head, her black mane waving in the motion. "Ballings tear up his own office? Don't be absurd."

"So who? Whoever did it was looking for something."

"Why would you think that?" She tapped her fingers on her desk.

"The papers strewn on the floor, the drawers all opened and rummaged through. Maybe if you contact Ballings he would—"

"I am certain Ballings didn't do it."

"But if you just called him, perhaps he would have an idea of who did."

Kipling clapped the file closed and planted it on her desk. Her phone rang and she poked the speaker button so hard I heard her nail click against the plastic. "Yes?"

"The police are here," a young female voice said.

"I'll greet them in the lobby." She looked up at us. "Wait here. My secretary will be keeping an eye on you."

She stalked out of the room, leaving the door open. Her perfume made me sneeze. I sneezed again.

"I don't suppose she'd mind," Jason said, walking a few strides to a bookshelf, grabbing a couple of tissues from a black glass dispenser, and passing them to me.

"I like a woman who isn't afraid to have a scent," Stu said. "You can smell her after she leaves. I once had a girlfriend who I could smell in my car days after a date. Days." He grinned and leaned back in his chair.

I walked around Kipling's desk to throw away the tissues. As the tissues fell into the compact black metal trashcan, I saw a crumpled page from an appointment book at the bottom. I glanced out the door at the secretary's back. She was nodding and talking loudly on the phone. I retrieved the page and smoothed it. The page contained a week's worth of entries. I looked at yesterday's date, the day Abby died, and scanned down to the evening appointments. Kipling had an 8 p.m. appointment at Southern Skillet, a local home-style eatery, with a heart beside it. A 10 p.m. appointment at "CCMB" was listed, too, but nothing else was written about who Kipling met. I glanced at the secretary again and then at Jason and Stu. I flipped open Kipling's appointment book. Scanning the entries, I spotted another 8 p.m. Southern Skillet entry with another heart beside it in a few days. I flipped another page and found yet another Southern Skillet entry. I didn't notice any other odd or late-night appointments.

Dean Kipling's secretary hung up the phone with a clatter, and I quickly flipped the notebook shut and stepped away from the desk as she turned around.

"Just throwing a tissue away," I called to her.

"What do you have there?" Jason whispered.

I showed him and Stu the appointment book page and pointed out the Southern Skillet and CCMB entries before folding the page and slipping it into my pocket.

"The night Abby was killed has Kipling going to Southern Skillet." I told them about the other Southern Skillet appointments. "Then Kipling was supposed to be at CCMB at 10 p.m. Of course CCMB must be this place, the Cooperative Center for Marine Biology."

"You think the dean trashed the lab?"

"It wasn't me."

Stu bit his lip.

"It wasn't me," I repeated. "I didn't have time to do all that damage, even if I'd wanted to, and why would I do that, anyway? I did look around, but I didn't touch anything. Hardly anything."

CHAPTER 11

Kipling entered the room, accompanied by Daniel and Kimmie, and a policeman I hadn't seen before. He was broader and softer than Daniel but also formidable. His eyes gleamed attentively beneath curly gelled brown hair. His tanned face seemed shiny, like it was scrubbed clean beneath his prematurely high hair line. He looked like a rugby player wearing a police costume.

Daniel turned to Kipling. "We'll take it from here," he said.

She marched out of the room.

Daniel introduced Officer Patrick McGregor. As Patrick copied information from our licenses onto a notepad, Stu's eyes were riveted to Kimmie. Jason was focusing on Kipling's desk and rubbing his ear again. Obviously he and Kimmie remained at odds despite the years since I arranged their cataclysm. Daniel leaned against a wall, surveying the room. Something about him, perhaps his demeanor, suggested military training and experience.

Even if I wasn't being questioned, under a totally different scenario in a completely different location, even if we were strangers and I hadn't known he was a police officer, I would have appreciated his understated authority. Even standing back, even dressed casually, Daniel was in charge. He was not controlling, but in control. Assessing, calculating, prepared. I was surprised to find myself feeling reassured merely by his presence, despite my predicament of being found in the destroyed lab, and, even more, despite insinuations and probing questions about my involvement in Abby's murder. Daniel seemed too wise to erroneously conclude that I was involved.

Daniel grinned quickly when our eyes met. I hoped he didn't notice me catch my breath. Even as observant as he was, I doubted he comprehended how perfectly his deep blue polo shirt set off his eyes, made them seem to sparkle with light like water dancing beneath the summer sun. I looked away and ran fingers through my hair, pushing it away from my face.

"Can I take a picture?" Stu asked, directing his question to Kimmie. "You've probably heard this before, but you have the most amazing hair."

"We're here to talk about a vandalized lab," Kimmie said.

"I didn't have anything to do with it," Stu said. "You can ask Dean Kipling. She was with me and Jason all along, and when we found Jonie alone in the lab."

I glanced at Daniel and found him studying me. Again, he allowed a smile when I made eye contact. I wondered why he was amused.

"Jonie wasn't separated from us but maybe 10 minutes," Jason said.

Patrick, pen paused above his notebook, looked at me. "What do you have to say?"

"Of course I didn't do it," I said, explaining how I went to the office expecting to find Ballings. "The office lab is so completely torn apart, no reasonable person would think I had anything to do with it during the 10 minutes, tops, I was there."

"Did you see anyone in the office or leaving when you got there?"

I shook my head.

Patrick nodded and glanced at Daniel.

"Why didn't you report the vandalism immediately?" Daniel asked. His eyes still focused on me alone. "Why did you go in? Kipling told us she found you at the back of the room."

"Curiosity," I said. It was true. I couldn't stop my feet from venturing forward. "I went in because it was my instinct as a reporter. I didn't even think about it."

Daniel nodded slowly, considering my answer.

"Anything else you want to add?" Patrick asked.

I glanced at Jason and Stu. We shook our heads. Was this it? I wondered. If so, I couldn't believe we were getting off this easy.

As if he read my thoughts, Patrick spoke. "We're going to be investigating this, so we may contact you again, soon." He glanced again at Daniel, who nodded once as if to signify the brief interview was complete.

"Do you have any idea who did destroy the lab?" I asked. "Do you think it has anything to do with Abby's death?"

Patrick chuckled. "Daniel warned me about you." He patted my shoulder playfully. "You all can go now."

"So you do believe the lab's destruction is linked with Abby's death," I said, hoping to force an answer.

Patrick looked to Daniel.

"We checked the room yesterday," Daniel said. "Nothing appeared out of place."

"Do you know anything more about Abby's death?" I asked.

"Any updates will be issued by our spokesperson. Patrick will escort you out."

I recognized the dismissal, and Jason didn't appear to be thinking up additional questions. We stood, Stu's height surpassing even Kimmie's. Stu bowed to Kimmie and passed her his card with a goofy flourish.

As Stu drove us back to downtown Wilmington, I contemplated the culprit behind the ransacked lab, the appointment book entries for the evening of Abby's death, especially the 10 p.m. appointment at the Cooperative Center for Marine Biology, Professor Ballings' absence, and Kipling's quick refusal to entertain his involvement in the destruction of the lab. At least his celebrity seemed to count for something, I thought.

"Anyone could have vandalized that lab, but I bet this has something to do with Abby," I said. "Happening the day after her murder—"

"Some student was probably angry at a low exam score," Jason said from the back seat. "You heard what Daniel said. The lab wasn't damaged yesterday."

"But close enough," I argued. "A student would have to be pretty angry to do that much damage. And all that damage had to be done when no one was around to hear everything getting smashed. Where was campus security when all that destruction was going on? Where was Ballings?"

"No one was at the front desk when Kipling dragged us in," Stu said.

"No one was there when we walked out, either," I said.

"At least you have another front page article to write," Jason said.

I glanced at Jason in the side mirror. His eyes were on the road. Stu, humming beneath his breath, flipped on his turn signal.

"We should work together on the vandalized lab story," I said. I cringed at my charity, but Jason remained too zoned out to notice.

After driving a couple of minutes in silence, Stu cleared his throat. "That Kimmie!" He whistled. "Women in uniform!"

"She wasn't wearing a uniform," Jason said.

Stu's hula girl was rocking as we turned the corner, and Stu hummed on, oblivious.

CHAPTER 12

The front door opened without a squeak. I wasn't expecting one.

"May I help you?" Her sweet southern drawl matched the delicate pink miniature rose topiaries that flanked the door.

"Um, it's me," I said.

No reaction. Unbelievable. I waited. Still the blank stare.

"Jonie?" I said, "your stepdaughter?"

I couldn't tell if the comprehension that turned her frown into a tight smile was real or staged. I didn't think my appearance had changed too much since I'd left. Surely Kimmie had phoned Vicki at her first opportunity to report my return to town. Kimmie and Vicki were as inseparable as cat fur in a hairball. Surely my father hadn't forgotten to call ahead and tell Vicki he invited me for dinner. He'd called ahead to the island gatekeeper.

Vicki and my father lived on an island accessible to vehicular traffic by one bridge tended by a gatekeeper around the clock. The gatekeeper allowed through only residents and their guests. If guests weren't on the schedule, he phoned the resident to verify the visit. Figure Eight Island, the ultimate gated community, housed the very well-to-do and even some celebrities.

"It's been so long, you don't hardly look the same, darlin,'" Vicki said. Vicki always was one of those saccharin women.

Her words tasted sweet at first swallow, but digested and interpreted, a not-so-authentic aftertaste could be detected.

I was silent, thinking that if I told her she'd changed also, she'd be insulted. If I told her she looked the same, I'd be lying, though her tediously shaped layers of gray-dyed-red hair, sprayed securely in an immaculate bob above her bony frame, remained the same. If Kimmie was stone, Vicki was porcelain. Vicki stepped back, and I entered, noting the lack of a verbal invitation.

She led me to the dining room—a short walk but one that afforded me an assessment of Vicki's décor changes since I left. Her home remained in a conservative glitz style with traditional colors and furnishings that were meant for show and not for comfort, more like a museum of a home than a living space. In the gold-and-maroon dining room, I noted that Vicki's flower-patterned dress matched the three place settings on the precisely arranged table, which featured a casserole, four vegetable dishes, rice, and rolls, along with a fresh flower arrangement: southern femininity perfected. We sat opposite each other, leaving the head of the table for my father. Apparently, his routine tardiness had not changed in my absence.

"Your roses smell incredible," I said. Vicki's yard was spotted with rose bushes of different heritages with names I couldn't remember, but I could remember Vicki priding herself on immaculate blooms every summer.

She nodded and didn't bother to conceal her examination of me. I resisted the urge to smooth my hair but hurried to tuck my chewed fingernails beneath the table. She noticed and one corner of her mouth rose. I shouldn't have cared what she thought of me. We lived on different planets. Vicki was the owner of a wildly successful local chain of spas. I didn't care enough to own a hair dryer.

"I was wondering about your sudden return to town," she said.

"My job," I said, even though she hadn't exactly asked. "I write for the *Tribune*."

"But there must be newspapers in—where was it you ran off to? Alabama?"

"Tennessee. Near Nashville."

"Ah."

"And I've got my apartment downtown," I said.

"You must feel so blessed that Phillip has taken such good care of it for you."

"Maybe Phaser feels blessed that I give him such a good deal on rent because he takes care of it," I joked.

"You don't feel blessed."

I shrugged. I remembered enough from my time under Vicki's roof to know I didn't want a religious conversation with her. Vicki had won her ability to continue attending Wilmington's high-society church, North First Baptist, with her chin held high. The house on the locked-down island was part of her divorce settlement from her cheating ex-husband, an orthopedic surgeon who used expensive presents to compensate for his lack of presence in Kimmie's and Phaser's youth.

"I'll pray for you," she said.

"I wish you wouldn't."

What Vicki meant is that she'd put in a prayer request for me at Sunday school, bringing up my name and a detailed description of what she believed to be my spiritual ailment. I was certain that in Vicki's eyes, I was still speeding down the one-way freeway to hell because I didn't bow before her children. I stubbornly remained unrepentant for my past, for misdeeds directed at her daughter, who was ever angelic in Vicki's eyes. That, added to my absence at church every Sunday, proved to Vicki that I was a lost soul, doomed to hell and doomed to be the object of gossip-inspired prayers. I was certain I'd been discussed at Vicki's church group. I could envision wrinkled ladies' hands wearing jewels too heavy for frail fingers clasped in prayer, and could hear wobbling voices cooing over Vicki's plight to save me from some fiery furnace. Seeing how whitewashed Vicki behaved put me off organized religion entirely. Besides, I'd always believed I didn't have to go into a church building to talk to God. I found Him in nature, as did Vicki's son Phaser, much to her chagrin.

"Have you been in contact with your mama lately?" Vicki asked.

"No."

My mother was another subject Vicki liked to moan and pray about—or at least she did when I last lived in Wilmington. Even I could admit that describing my mother as a free spirit would be a kindness. Describing her as a flighty, hippie artist would be more accurate. When I was in elementary school, she left me and my father for another man who was more indulgent of her artistic tendencies, particularly the tendency to get high and paint as the urge struck. For a while I'd received postcards from different towns she camped in, living out of her new man's van. After my father married Vicki, the postcards stopped. I'd searched for her on the internet; she didn't show up. El Paso was where the trail ended with her last postcard.

Through the side window, we saw my father's Mercedes pull to a stop, sparing both Vicki and me the challenge of further conversation.

My father entered, nodded to us both, sat, and blessed the food. While eating, my father talked about a report he was compiling for the university trustees. Vicki completed her obligatory whining about the heat. They briefly expressed mild shock at "the Pridgen tragedy," as if Abby was some untouchable actress caught up in a scandal reported on a trashy magazine cover, as if the Pridgens weren't neighbors, as if my girlhood friendship with Abby had never come to their attention.

And then a quiet friction reigned at the dinner table. No one made eye contact while we ate; barely another word was spoken. Surely volumes could be said about our lives since we last sat together around this table, but the only noise was the clinking of silver against china.

"Thanks for having me over," I said, scooping the last gooey forkful of chicken and squash into my mouth. I was anxious to escape the grating silence.

My father nodded, taking a gulp of sweet tea while cupping his hand beneath the glass to prevent the condensation from dripping onto his tie.

"I'll clean the dishes," I volunteered.

"No, no, darlin'," Vicki said, hurriedly standing up and grabbing my dish with enough force that I was surprised. "You stay seated."

Vicki was setting herself up for martyrdom. I had seen this trick in the past. A guest would come over and offer to help with something, anything, and Vicki would turn the guest down, later complaining to her friends or to my father about how she cooked, and cleaned, and waited so dutifully for this guest who didn't manage to lift the smallest finger to help. The strategy provided the perfect lead into more gossip about the guest and what horrible past or present sins made the guest unworthy of Vicki's sacrifice, but also fascinating to discuss.

I glanced out the window toward the Pridgen house. A light was on in their kitchen window.

"Does Martha still live next door?" I asked. Growing up, I'd never known Abby's older sister well, perhaps because Martha was six years older than Abby. Sometimes Martha would come to the beach and sit on the sand, her nose deep into a book, while Abby and I were in the water.

"Martha never moved away," my father said. "Abby lived there, too, for a few months before—" He took in another mouthful of tea.

"I think I'll go next door and see how Martha's doing," I said.

When no one said anything, I stood and walked out the kitchen door, across my father's manicured lawn, to the light yellow house trimmed in white with a wrap-around porch. I knocked on the front door and saw Mrs. Pridgen's spindly figure approaching through the etched glass window. Wisps of prematurely white hair dangled from her bun and traced her narrow, wrinkled face

"Hello, Mrs. Pridgen. I'm Jonie Waters. I don't know if you remember—"

"Come in," she said softly. She smiled, but her eyes remained somber.

CHAPTER 13

The Pridgen house smelled like dusty cinnamon—more nostalgic than fresh. Family photos lining the entrance way showed Abby and Martha before I knew them; showed their father who I never knew; showed a much younger Mrs. Pridgen when straw-colored hair flowed loose and long.

"I'm so sorry about Abby," I said.

She retained her smile, almost resolutely, but her eyes were tearing.

"Is there anything I can do?"

"No." She tucked a wisp of hair behind an ear. "No, Martha's taking good care of me."

"Is she here?"

She nodded and beckoned toward a staircase that bent perpendicularly halfway up. "Do you remember the way to her room?"

I nodded and headed up the stairs, leaning over slightly to avoid fake wheat fronds sticking out of a wide metal vase at the turn. The Pridgen house was smaller than Vicki's, but it was spacious nonetheless. Abby's and Martha's rooms were upstairs, along with a bathroom. Abby's room was the first on the left. As I passed, I peeked through the open door. A poster-sized nautical map of Wilmington and the nearby coast that looked like it had been annotated by hand covered the majority of an interior wall. Abby's surfboard, a short board with a decorative orange flower stenciled onto its nose, leaned against the walls at a corner. I walked past the bathroom to Martha's room. I could see light in the crack between the door and the carpet. I knocked.

"Come in."

I opened the door slowly. Martha's room was painted cream. A framed reproduction of DaVinci's Vitruvian Man encircled with other sketches by the artist hung near her desk. A four poster bed, topped with a machine-sewn quilt and plush pillows, was perfectly made. Martha sat in her bay window, knees tucked into her chest, facing the marsh. She clasped something small and shiny between her fingers. I saw her looking at my reflection in the window.

While Abby had been lithe with an almost avian air about her, Martha always had seemed more solid, perhaps because of her penetrating stare that, even as a youth, seemed to look right through me to focus on something just behind me. I remembered frequently looking up from breakfast to see Martha jogging past our house at the same time every Saturday morning, dark brown hair pulled back tight in a rubber band. The few times I happened to be outside at that hour, I called to her and waved, but she kept her head straight; and I wondered if she'd heard me at all.

The last I'd been told, Martha was working for pharmaceutical giant Prestol. In North Carolina, a state that bragged of its pharmaceutical research and drug manufacturing facilities and poured millions of taxpayer dollars into incentives to entice even more pharmaceutical companies, Prestol was one of the crown jewels of North Carolina's collection. Prestol's United States headquarters and largest worldwide research facility was located a few miles northwest of Wilmington. Watching a half hour of network television without a Prestol advertisement airing was a rarity. While the company always was developing cutting-edge drugs, its most advertised products were for alleviating allergy symptoms and insomnia.

"How are you, Martha?" I asked.

She didn't answer the question but shifted her eyes off mine. Finally, she turned toward me and shrugged. Her makeup absent and her hair hanging limply over a wrinkled green shirt, Martha looked defeated, almost tattered.

"My father said that Abby had moved back home for a few months."

"After she broke it off with Mark." Martha held her hand toward me, showing me an engagement ring with a sizable hunk of diamond. "Mark was her fiancé."

"I didn't know."

"They'd been living together for a year, dating for two years before that. After he proposed on Valentine's Day, you would've thought Abby won the lottery, the way she was acting. Then something happened. I guess they couldn't handle the pressure, or something. Planning a southern wedding, making sure everyone was happy, I hear it's tough. Abby broke it off and moved back home in May. The last thing I said to her was for her not to wake me up when she came in. She was forever running the shower late at night after getting home from the lab." Martha tried to laugh, but it came out as more of a cough, the corners of her eyes spasming in the motion. "I can't believe she's gone."

I wanted to hug her, but Martha was the type of hard, angular person who seemed untouchable.

"I found her body," I said. It came out sounding like I was bragging—not my intention. I just felt like I needed to tell Martha.

"You? You saw her—found her?"

The doorbell rang. We listened to Mrs. Pridgen's steps tapping across the tiled floor and the squeak of the door. Then I heard a familiar voice.

"Hello, Mrs. Pridgen."

"Kimmie! Detective Wyeth."

"You can call me Daniel, ma'am."

Martha stood abruptly. "They must have news about what happened to Abby," she said. "I'll be back." She rushed out the door and down the hallway, leaving me in her room. I waited until I heard her footsteps beat across the downstairs floor before creeping to the stairwell.

From their greetings to Martha, I could tell that the group had settled in the sitting room near the front door.

"Mrs. Pridgen, Martha," Daniel said. "I wanted to bring you up to speed on where we are so far. I'm just going to jump right into it. I know this may be hard for you to hear, but I firmly believe that Abby's death was not an accident."

"Not an accident?"

"No."

Silence.

My heart was pounding so hard I wondered why no one heard it. I crept down a few steps, breathing heavily, Daniel's words slowly sinking in while I simultaneously pushed them away.

"You're saying she was—" Mrs. Pridgen stopped herself.

"Murdered?" Martha finished.

"Perhaps her death wasn't intentional," Daniel said, "but at the very least, it could be considered manslaughter."

"I don't understand," Mrs. Pridgen said.

"She was shoved off the boardwalk. Because of the distance she fell, she was impaled on a snapped tree trunk."

"I'm sorry," Kimmie said.

"She was shoved?" said Mrs. Pridgen. "Couldn't she have tripped?"

I stepped closer again.

"Her nose was freshly broken," Daniel said.

"But you said she fell—"

"The way she landed...she wouldn't have broken her nose that way in that fall," Kimmie explained.

"The fracture was caused by a head-on hit, perhaps a punch," Daniel said. "Her body was found face up. If her nose had been broken by hitting a stump on her way down, the fracture would have indicated force coming from the side."

"In addition to her broken nose," Kimmie said, "we found bruising on her neck, also not caused by the fall."

No one spoke. I peeked around the corner of the bend of the stairwell, careful not to bump into the vase. Mrs. Pridgen was facing me, crying into her hands, as she sat on the loveseat against the far wall next to Martha. Daniel and Kimmie were sitting in arm chairs, their backs to me.

"It's—" Martha said. "It's just so, so hard to accept. I have trouble believing she's dead at all, at times, and now this?"

"I need to verify where both of you were that night," Daniel said.

"We were at home, of course," Mrs. Pridgen said. "Abby left after dinner to go to the lab, as she often did."

"And neither of you left the house that evening?"

"I did," Martha said. Her voice sounded weak in comparison with Daniel's low, clear tone. "Mother fell asleep early, and I went out and had coffee at the café across the way."

"At what time?"

"About nine thirty, I think." Martha squeezed her hands together. "I might still have the receipt in my purse, if you need to see it."

Daniel nodded and changed the subject. "We'll be doing a press conference tomorrow. It's a high profile case, and we have to release the information on the homicide."

Kimmie walked to Mrs. Pridgen, knelt beside her, and took her hands. "We'll find who did it. Whoever it was, we'll find them."

"There's something else," Daniel said. "I'm not sure if you knew, but Abby was about 10 weeks pregnant."

A sudden stillness swept through the room, like Martha and Mrs. Pridgen had frozen in a photograph. I seemed to see it before anyone else. Mrs. Pridgen's head wobbled back, she blinked as if trying to unscramble a visual puzzle on the ceiling, and then her body slumped forward. I started up, as if I could reach her before she fell, and one of the fronds from the vase caught on my shirt. The vase clanged into the wall. Daniel and Kimmie shot up and fixed their sights on me. Neither looked pleased. Mrs. Pridgen collapsed to the floor.

CHAPTER 14

Martha grabbed her mother's side and rolled her onto her back. Daniel's attention snapped back to Mrs. Pridgen. He stooped down and checked her pulse.

Kimmie met me at the base of the stairs, blocking my passage to the sitting room.

"Is she okay?" I asked.

"She fainted," Daniel said. He instructed Martha to bring a cold washcloth. Mrs. Pridgen's eyelids fluttered.

"What can I do to help?" I asked.

"Leave," Kimmie said. "What are you doing here, anyway? Just leave!"

"But—"

"Has Jonie been bothering you?" Kimmie asked Martha as she hurried from the room. "Or trying to mine quotes for another story?"

Martha paused. I wanted to jam my thumb into Kimmie's chin cleft and shove her face away from mine.

"Martha," Daniel said, "the washcloth, please."

As Martha left the room, I answered Kimmie. "I'm here as a friend, not as a reporter."

"Then be a friend, and follow my instructions and leave."

I opened my mouth with a retort but instead nodded and let myself out of the house. I wasn't a close enough friend to Martha and Mrs. Pridgen to insist on staying against Kimmie's orders, and since Daniel had the situation under control, nothing seemed left for me to do.

On my way back to my family's house, my stomach felt uneasy. If I had been to the Pridgen's home only as a friend, I wouldn't have followed my curiosity, tiptoed down the stairs, and spied on the conversation. If I had been there as a friend, and as a friend only, I wouldn't have felt the pang inside, the yearning, to immediately broadcast to the world the news that Abby's death officially was caused by another person, to plead to anyone who had any information about the homicide to report it. I knew I wouldn't release this information before it was made public—that wasn't even a question—but I still felt the gnawing inside me that wished I could write the story and have it published in tomorrow morning's newspaper.

On an impulse, instead of going inside the house where I could see my father's silhouette in front of the flickering colored lights of a baseball game on television, I walked to the back porch and grabbed the lattice. After a few hard tugs, it gave way, and I shifted the lattice panel to the side. I crouched low and squinted my eyes into the cool darkness beneath the porch. I couldn't believe it—she was still there— my old surfboard. I pulled her out and wiped off dirt. Under the grime, despite all the years, she remained beautiful. The white board faded to blue at the nose and tail, and featured a thin yellow wing design that looked like a curved lightning bolt mirrored at the left and right edges. At nine feet, she sported a concave bottom and rounded rails. She was light but strong and shaped for versatility.

I knew what I wanted, what I needed. Not caring that I wasn't wearing a bathing suit or that the bit of makeup covering my bruise would wash away completely, not caring that I wasn't a teenager anymore, that I hadn't surfed in years, I walked my surfboard quickly across the island to the beach. I needed the release. I needed the ocean waves. I needed to wash away the turmoil of the past couple of days.

The evening was spectacular. No clouds marred the deepening blue-purplish horizon, and gentle swells rolled steadily inland. No one was in the water. Rarely in this gated, aristocrat community did anyone swim past dinnertime. I flipped off my shoes, strapped the board around my ankle, and paddled out past the breakers, feeling the cool water crash over my head. My tank top and Capri shorts would do for a swim and surf. In the calm, deep water, I straddled my board and sat upright, face forward to the open water and back toward the world, and I let the tears fall.

Abby was dead. She had been pregnant! And she and her baby had been killed. They were gone. But someone—the killer, Abby's murderer—was back there, loose. And here I was—alone, with a ghost family, with my closest friend a stepbrother whose loyalty to me conflicted with his allegiance with Kimmie, barely surviving paycheck to paycheck, leaving burned bridges in my wake, depending too much upon a job that was as stable as a stack of ice cubes in my father's glass of sweet tea. And the way Daniel and Kimmie treated me, they acted as if I were guilty of killing Abby. Yet I was drawn to Daniel, and he seemed attracted to me as well. I couldn't take this.

Sliding off my surfboard, I sank underwater. My body stretched prone under my board; and I pushed against its bottom to remain submerged, the cool water numbing my face like drunkenness, as if I could escape from everything, as if my problems would lose me before I was forced to resurface for air.

But my problems, my myriad of problems, paled in comparison to Abby. She was dead. She couldn't have any more personal problems. I banged my forehead softly against the bottom of my surfboard. I needed to fix my life. I wanted to find Abby's murderer. I needed a plan for both. I surfaced for air. There was no hiding beneath the water.

Some problems I couldn't control: my family and the way they acted, my past. Freelancing at the *Tribune* was the best I could manage in terms of a job, so I'd stay with it. But some problems I could influence. I could prove myself worthy of a salary and benefits at the paper. I could actively try to make amends with my family. I could remain open to a new romantic relationship, if it found me. I could investigate Abby's death and do my part to try to discover who killed her and her baby. I owed it to Abby for all the times she was good to me, for all she taught me, for being there for me when my father was busy and Vicki and Kimmie turned up their noses at me. Loyalty and friendship didn't die, even if Abby and I had lost touch. As I paddled to shore, the sky darkened overhead.

CHAPTER 15

"If that building doesn't say 'municipal institution,' I don't know what would," Stu said as I changed gears for the fifth time in front of the Wilmington police station in an effort to squeeze my truck into a space. Parking was not tallied on my list of strengths. Stu's arm, which kept rubbing against mine since he was sandwiched between Jason and me in the cab of my truck, only irritated me more.

Jason and I were teamed up to cover the press conference about Abby's death at the police station. Since Stu drove the previous day and Jason's tires were being rotated, I volunteered for chauffeur duty. However, for the amount of time it took me to maneuver into a parallel parking space between two news vans, we would have been just as well off had we walked.

Inside the station, dreary florescent lights buzzed overhead, giving the white linoleum flooring a yellowish glow. Reporters and cameramen from the local television news stations crowded the small station conference room. Jason and I split up, figuring we'd have a better chance of getting more of our questions answered apart than together. Stu separated from us to shoot photographs, and I watched his plum purple shirt push into the crowd. At least he had chosen a milder outfit than yesterday's ensemble, though I wouldn't have partnered a brown pin-striped tie with the shirt.

A sudden tightness gripped my neck. I wasn't looking forward to the announcement that Abby's death was a homicide. What didn't help my nerves was an impending lunch appointment. Jason had cornered me after the staff meeting and told me I was to have lunch with him and Lee— a newcomer's ritual. Jason earned compliments at the staff meeting for our job of putting together a short article on Ballings' vandalized lab. Nothing had been reported stolen from the university, and the case was under further investigation. Jason was unable to reach Ballings for comments.

At least this morning I had managed to schedule an interview with the elusive Ballings for later in the day. Ballings hadn't picked up his phone the first several times I called him during his early office hours, and I half choked on my coffee when he finally answered.

"Ballings here," he had said in a clipped, bored tone that simultaneously conveyed impatience to hang up the phone and annoyance at being bothered.

I introduced myself. "I was calling to see if I could set a time to come by and interview you about Abby and the research she was doing with you."

There was a pause. Ballings didn't fill it.

"I came by the other day during your office hours," I said, "but you weren't there."

"My office was vandalized."

"Is that why you weren't there?"

"What's that?" He was stalling.

"Were you not in your office because it was vandalized?"

"No." Another long pause. I decided to wait this one out. "Do you want to come by today?"

I decided to let the diversion go. I could pry answers from him in person. We set an interview time. Before leaving the newspaper office, I tried to jot down a list of questions to ask him, but with the press conference heavy on my mind, I only managed to write a few phrases.

Through a side door in the police station's conference room, a woman with hair the color and apparent texture of steel entered the room, followed by a man in police uniform—most likely the chief—and another woman in a business suit with a university pin on her lapel. The first woman stepped up to the podium, greeted everyone, and introduced herself as the spokeswoman for the police force. She also introduced the police chief and the university spokeswoman. Looking over my shoulder, I noticed Daniel and Kimmie against the back wall near the conference room's double doors.

The police chief set a sheet of paper on the podium and began reading. "The Wilmington police force is investigating the death of Abby Pridgen. Ms. Pridgen was an associate marine biology professor at the Ogden University Cooperative Center for Marine Biology. Evidence leads us to conclude that her death, and the death of her unborn child, was a homicide."

A collective silence quickly broke as reporters began breathing again. I searched the crowd for Jason. His attention was on his notepad, but his pen was frozen in his hand.

The chief glanced up before submersing himself again in his recitation. "As you all know, Ms. Pridgen was found dead roughly 48 hours ago. The approximate time of death was several hours before that, in the very late evening. We have determined her death was a result of a tree trunk puncturing her left lung with hemorrhaging restricting air flow to the point of asphyxiation." He looked up again, like a swimmer competing in the breaststroke, before returning to his statement. "Based on the evidence, we also have determined that her death was not an accident. We are ruling it homicide. As this is an ongoing investigation, we are not at liberty at the present moment to delve further into the details of this case or our findings." He again raised his head. And this time his eyes remained on the crowd of reporters. "Solving this case is the top priority of our investigators and of our entire police force. We feel confident that this case will be resolved soon."

The police spokeswoman stepped up to the podium. "Are there any questions?"

Several reporters spoke simultaneously.

"One at a time." The spokeswoman pointed her finger at a reporter.

"The unborn child—approximately how far along was Ms. Pridgen?"

"About 10 weeks," the chief said.

"Do you know who the father was?"

"We cannot comment on that at this time."

"Do you have any suspects?"

"We currently are looking into several leads," the chief said.

"I cannot say more at this time; to do so could jeopardize our ongoing investigation."

The spokeswoman pointed her finger to another reporter.

"Any ideas on motives for killing Ms. Pridgen? Do you think her pregnancy and the murder are related?"

The chief fielded this one. "As I said, this is an ongoing investigation, and we are not at liberty to go into more detail."

"What's the evidence that made you rule this as a homicide?" Jason shouted.

"We cannot discuss evidence at this time."

"When do you expect to make an arrest?"

"I can assure you we are working very hard on this case. Again, solving it is our top priority. However, we are conducting a thorough investigation and will not be rushed."

The spokeswoman pointed at me.

"Are there plans to beef up security at the university?"

The chief nodded to the spokeswoman from the university. She stepped up to the podium.

"The university police routinely patrol the center, along with other university property," she said. "The Cooperative Center for Marine Biology and the university at large are relatively safe places for our students. Our doors are locked after hours, and keys are restricted to faculty only. Outside we have bright lighting and a number of red-light phones, phones that are a direct line to campus security and are easily spotted. We are looking into measures to make the center safer, but in the meantime, we are confident that this is an isolated incident."

"Did the campus police on duty at the time of the homicide see anything?" a reporter near me asked.

The chief stepped in front of the university spokeswoman. "We cannot answer that publicly at this time."

Reporters blurted out more questions.

"That will conclude our press conference," said the police spokeswoman. "We will be available individually to answer questions for a very short amount of time."

I looked at Jason. He gestured for me to talk with the university representative. He pointed at himself and then at the police chief. I nodded and elbowed my way forward into the semi-circle of reporters in front of the university spokeswoman.

"Who do you think killed Abby Pridgen?" a reporter asked as I neared the university spokeswoman.

"That's a question for the police chief," she said.

"What about the boardwalk?" I said. "Are there any plans to strengthen railing or to remove hazards from below the walk?"

"I can assure you that our facilities, including the boardwalk at the Cooperative Center for Marine Biology, meet and go beyond required safety standards. That being said, there are no measures we can take that will completely eliminate injury by accidents or especially malicious conduct."

A cameraman knocked into me.

"Was Abby liked by fellow faculty and students?" a horsy reporter asked, shoving a mike in the spokeswoman's face.

"Yes. Ms. Pridgen was smart and charming. She consistently was available to assist students in their schoolwork. Her conduct and professionalism were unmarred. She was clean-cut and—" The spokeswoman's cell phone rang. She glanced at the caller identification. "I have to go. Thank you."

The camera crews near me shuffled over to join those surrounding the police chief, who continued to field questions from reporters, Jason included. I stepped back and looked around. Daniel still leaned against the back wall. Today, his polo shirt color was a deep maroon that brought out a slight blush in his face. I could see Kimmie through the windows of the doorway, cell phone buried underneath frizz so thick she probably didn't need her hand to keep the phone in place. I approached Daniel.

Daniel smiled briefly but voiced no greeting. He appeared to be watching the police chief.

"I had the impression you didn't like reporters, yet here you are at the press conference. Can't you keep away from us?"

"Notice I'm at the back of the room."

"Mind if I ask you a few questions?"

Daniel chuckled. "Doesn't mean I'll answer."

"The chief didn't mention Abby's broken nose." I paused, hoping he would elaborate, strike up a monologue on his thoughts.

"That's not a question." His mouth curled.

"Can you tell me more about the other signs of a struggle?"

"I can't discuss an open case freely."

"Off the record?"

Daniel shook his head.

"What about the printout of my article in her car? Have you checked it for fingerprints?"

"Every time I see you," he said, his voice barely audible above the zoo of reporters and a warm smile revealing white teeth, "you have more questions."

"I'm a reporter." I took a deep breath and summoned the guts to ask the question that had been brewing in the back of my mind since the interrogation at the crime scene. "Am I a suspect?"

Daniel finally gave me his full attention, his gray-blue eyes staring directly into mine, making me feel like nothing else existed but him and me. "What do you think?"

"If I am, why?" I swallowed and determined I would not break his eye contact. "I'm just doing my job. That's all I've ever been doing. I'm a reporter. And I was Abby's friend."

"You're a reporter who was found with the body at the crime scene, who received an untraceable call from a person who you claim invited you to find the body, a reporter with a freshly bruised cheek, whose phone number and article were found in the victim's car, who seems to have been spying on a private conversation last night at the Pridgens. We have to consider all of this as part of our investigation."

"I wasn't—this isn't about me. It shouldn't be," I said a little too loudly. "I didn't—" I lowered my voice. "I had nothing to do with Abby's death."

Daniel crossed his arms. He had a job: to detect the truth. We both had jobs to do.

"How come the news tip call is untraceable?" I asked.

"It's the main line of the paper. Do you know how many calls came into the *Tribune's* main line during the timeframe you gave us? We can't trace which phone line within the *Tribune* they went to. We just know the numbers that called, and since the conservative window we're looking at is about an hour—"

Kimmie opened the door. "Here for the press conference, are you?"

"Hi, Kimmie," I said, disappointed I couldn't continue my discussion with Daniel alone. "So why don't you trace all those calls?" I asked Daniel. "Maybe it'd take a while, but so what?"

"Assuming there was a caller," Kimmie said.

Daniel shook his head. "Kimmie—"

"Assuming somehow, miraculously, this supposed caller knew you were just beginning work there that day," Kimmie continued, unabashed, "assuming we could figure out who made each and every phone call from the various persons who had access to all those different numbers that phoned in, who's to say the caller is the killer?"

"It's something. It's a start."

"Hello," Stu said, saddling up beside me and grinning at Kimmie.

Jason remained a step behind him. Compared with Daniel, Jason looked boyish, almost geeky.

"Officer Wyeth," Stu said, "Kimmie, a pleasure." He winked at Kimmie. "Don't let me interrupt."

"We were just leaving," Kimmie said. She glared at Stu, pinching her lips to reveal a canine, before spinning on a heel and storming out the doors.

Daniel's eyes found mine. He nodded and followed her.

"Oooh-lala," Stu murmured after they rounded a corner. "Ready to go?"

Jason held the door open.

"What's eating at you?" Stu asked, glancing at me.

"Nothing." I flattened my pink short-sleeved dress shirt against my stomach and tugged straight my khaki skirt.

"Then why are you stomping around like you're trying to crack the flooring? You know they could arrest you on a property damage charge if you're successful."

I turned on him, prepared to chew him out, tell him to mind his own business and stop drooling at Kimmie, but the genuinely concerned expression on his face stopped me.

"If it's being paired up with Jason, you know you're only stuck with him for a couple of weeks, and then we can be together, just the two of us."

Jason smiled at me.

I huffed out a sigh and nodded toward the doors that led outside. We resumed walking. I was hesitant to tell Stu and Jason how close I was to Abby, how we had a personal relationship years ago, how I had visited Martha and overheard more than I should have, and how my information was found in Abby's car—any one of which would be sure grounds for me to be taken off the story—so I only told them about my concerns about discovering the body.

"That's bogus," Stu said. "I mean, I know my reassurance means diddly, but you're taking matters to an extreme level. You're not a suspect. Just consider the way that Detective Wyeth looks at you. That's got me suspecting something else entirely."

Jason cleared his throat. "Suspecting you would be like suspecting me of vandalizing the lab yesterday because I was there when we found you in it. I'd never even seen the inside of that room before."

I then told them that the news tip call was untraceable.

"No dice," Stu said. "Just say you did kill her. I've only known you a day or so, and I already can tell you're not stupid enough to off someone and then return to the body during broad daylight in front of a school full of students."

I felt nauseated.

"No offense," he said. "But you're being irrational. Hey, if it ever came to an indictment, you can count on Jason to report it with only the slightest bias in favor of you. I'll wear my powdered blue '50s tux with the frou-frou collar to the trial, if it comes to that, and take some really great shots that will make you appear like an angel, if they allow me in. I have a lens that makes lights look like stars."

I fought to restrain a smile. I was beginning to realize why Stu seemed to be liked by everyone he knew. Still, both he and Jason were speaking from ignorance. They didn't know even half of my connection with Abby's investigation.

CHAPTER 16

"How did the press conference go?" Lee asked, setting down his pint-sized draft beer with a thud. I supposed since he was the editor, he was allowed to enjoy a drink with his lunch.

Lee, Jason, and I were dining at the Platinum Canteen on Front Street, a posh restaurant featuring overpriced plates and a loud, open-air dining area. Lee had opted out of the salad even though it was included with his lunch.

I glanced at Jason, who was busy chewing and using his fork to search his salad for olives, before speaking.

"The press conference was short, very much to the point," I said, spearing a ziti noodle off a glossy beige platter with scalloped edging, "and packed with television reporters. The police announced that Abby's death was a homicide and that she was 10 weeks pregnant. They wouldn't say much more than that."

"The police called and asked about the news tip you received in my office," Lee said. His eyes looked owlish behind his thick glasses.

"Did they ask if you believed that it was what I said it was?"

"Something to that effect."

"They're acting like tracking down that caller isn't a big deal."

"You think the caller killed the girl?" Jason asked me. He pushed at a rolled-up sleeve that had lost its characteristic crispness after battling the midday humidity on our way to the restaurant.

"I think the caller has something to do with it. It's suspicious, not calling the police but calling the newspaper instead, and asking for me."

"Yes, asking for you," Lee said. He took a swig of beer and considered me.

The din of the restaurant, coupled with my tension from the press conference and now this lunch meeting, where I felt like I was under scrutiny, was giving me a headache. I needed a shot of caffeine, or a beer.

"I can't believe Abby is dead," I said, immediately wishing I could slap my forehead without drawing more attention to my slip-up.

"You knew her?" Lee asked. He frowned.

Jason looked up at me with a slight jerk.

"In high school, we were acquaintances," I said quickly, playing down our relationship. "You must remember her, too, don't you, Jason?"

Jason shrugged, flushing slightly.

Abby hadn't been a cheerleader—she was too involved in soccer and track—but her popularity and beauty pushed her up the high school social cliques. Few students wouldn't have known who she was.

Lee rubbed his mug's glass handle. "Was she around when you did the story on that visiting professor at the university last fall? What was his name—Bells? Bellings?"

"Ballings," Jason said.

"You wrote a story on Ballings?" I asked, surprised he hadn't mentioned it.

"Just about Ballings joining the center."

I remembered Jason saying he hadn't seen the inside of Ballings' office before it was vandalized. Maybe he did a phone interview, I thought.

"Are you going to Abby's funeral?" Jason asked before I could press him for information.

"I'm planning on it."

"So you could cover it? I can't make it." Jason shifted his eyes to his salad, probably trying to avoid revealing hints of his real motive for wanting to duck out of the story. No doubt he wanted to avoid the hostility that existed still between him, Kimmie, and myself.

I took a bite of my meal and chewed it over. I felt hesitant to write about a ceremony in which I would be participating as a mourner. I would have to split myself again between friend and reporter. Still, I wanted the article. No other reporter knew Abby, could pull from memories the essence of Abby as a person. Besides, the television reporters would be there, waiting just outside the grounds to nab funeral-goers once the ceremony ended, trying to suck quotes from their lips. And maybe this story would win back some honor between me and Kimmie, and between me and Martha and Mrs. Pridgen.

I finally nodded. "I could do it better alone."

"You don't like Jason?" Lee asked, his voice light but his eyes still observing.

"No," I said, feeling my cheeks burn. "I like him."

Jason glanced up at me, a smirk stretching his lower face.

"I also like my space," I said. "And having known Abby, I just think—" I paused to consider my words, "I could do a better job, incorporate more of the emotion of the funeral, without having another reporter there, right beside me."

Lee glanced at Jason and leaned back into the booth cushion. "Montgomery, the publisher and owner of the *Tribune*, has been in contact with the Wilmington police chief, and the chief has told him that you are a person of interest in the case," he said.

I opened my mouth to speak, but Lee held up his hand, silencing me.

"Montgomery says the police chief told him one of his officers says you somehow keep popping up in unexpected and suspicious places during the investigation. He said the chief thinks it's extremely fishy that you were discovered in the vandalized lab, especially since you also were discovered with Abby's body."

"That's ridiculous," Jason said. "Jonie found Abby because of the news tip. And Jonie couldn't have done that much damage to the lab when we were separated at the center. Even if she had tried, we would have heard it coming in the lab to join her."

"I'm completely innocent," I said.

Lee held up his hand again. "The chief accused Montgomery of trying to make news by having you create it."

"That's bull—"

Lee held up his hand once more. I ignored it.

"I know there are a couple of coincidences tying me to the case—coincidences that seem beyond ironic. I admit it. I have no doubt Kim—" I cut myself off. "I have no doubt the police are suspicious of me. But I didn't do it, any of it, if that's what you want to know. I didn't kill Abby. You were there, Lee, when that call came in. And I didn't ransack the lab. The police can investigate all they want, but since I didn't commit any crimes, I don't know how they can hold anything over my head or over the paper's head. If the chief has accusations, let him bring them to my face so I can refute them."

"Jonie," Lee said, and the way he said my name, somehow sternly and sorrowfully at the same time, silenced me. "I believe you. You didn't write that story in Tennessee, a story of the caliber that makes the law run you out of town, by sitting back and taking shit or by writing articles based on card castles." Lee took another swig of beer. "But Montgomery said if you further compromise his relationship with the police chief, which is basically, as he said he sees it, the paper's relationship with the city authorities and those who support the city authorities, he will gladly let you go, regardless of your innocence."

I closed my eyes. The publisher-slash-owner was in charge, and I was a contract employee. As fast as Lee could fire me for poor workmanship, Montgomery could fire me for political reasons or for any trifle or on any whim. And he could do so despite my innocence, despite an article's newsworthiness, despite anything. Politics reigned here, same as anywhere. I opened my eyes and glanced at Jason, but he remained stoic, not looking at me or Lee but at his fingers.

"Watch your step, Jonie," Lee said. "Not just from this paper's standpoint, but from your own."

CHAPTER 17

I had expected to find Ballings at his desk as scheduled, but the lab was vacant when Jason and I walked in. The office, while it hadn't appeared large on my first visit, seemed more spacious now with the mess having been cleared. Gone were the broken flasks and shattered test tubes. The black counter tops were, for the most part, bare and completely cleaned of oozing specimens. A couple of large boxes full of what looked to be the remnants of ruined instruments sat on the floor beside the counter tops. Several stacks of papers sat along one wall, as if waiting to be re-filed. The smashed computers had been removed. Ballings' desk sported a replacement computer which was running a screen saver resembling an aquarium. But even with the lack of clutter and straightened shelves, a slight stench of rotting chemicals remained. After waiting ten minutes to see if Ballings would show as he promised, we gave up. I left one of the *Tribune's* tacky business cards with the paper's name, address, main line, and website address typed on it and blanks where I'd used a pen to fill in my name and cell phone number.

I suggested to Jason that we walk around the building and see if we could find the professor. A few minutes later, I spotted Ballings through a shaft of glass in a classroom doorway. Busted, I thought. While waiting for Ballings' class to end, I listened for the professor's deep voice, catching segments of words he spoke with languid authority. Other students joined us in the hallway, waiting to enter the classroom. Finally, the rumbling of dozens of wooden chairs scraping against linoleum flooring sounded, and students began filing out.

I pushed toward the door and into the classroom, which seated about fifty and tiered downward toward a long, dusty blackboard. Ballings stood at a wood podium, wearing a preppy suit that gave him an all-American look. He was talking to a curvaceous brunette wearing a tight, cropped top, daisy dukes, and pink flip flops. With Jason following close behind, I slowed my approach to examine Ballings. His silver-black hair topped a handsome, soft-featured face. He had sad eyes, like dog eyes silently pleading for a treat, and a five o clock shadow that, despite his GQ-caliber suit, gave him an almost shabby appearance. He nodded his pepper-haired head to something the student said and looked at a paper the student held. Ballings rested an arm on the student's shoulder and gave her a quick squeeze. In a flicker, I thought I saw his eyes shift from her paper to her chest. But when I looked again, he was smiling into the student's face and had released her, making me wonder if my mind misperceived a simple gesture of reassurance. I hadn't forgotten Dean Kipling's 10 p.m. appointment at the center the night of Abby's death and wondered if Ballings knew anything about it. Ballings looked like a lady's man, and Kipling was a lady. The student walked away, and Ballings shuffled some papers on the podium. He still hadn't noticed us.

Despite my fermenting anger about Ballings missing the interview and not calling to reschedule or at least alert us that he would be late, I decided to approach him amicably.

I forced a smile. "You weren't in your office for our scheduled interview, so since I was in the neighborhood, I thought I'd walk around and see if I could find you."

"Jonie, *Tribune* reporter, right?" He chuckled, crinkling the corners of his eyes and showing off a row of very white, unnaturally straight teeth. His eyes found Jason behind me. "Good to see you again, Rossini."

"I just wanted to ask you a couple of questions about Abby and the research you were doing together," I said. "And I wanted to talk to you about your lab. Do you know who vandalized it?"

"Now is not a good time to talk. I'm filling in for a colleague, taking on another class in a few minutes." He gathered the papers on the podium. "I would have called, but it was an emergency."

"Just a couple of minutes—" I began.

"I really must prepare myself for this next class right now." He turned his eyes to the papers in his hands and cleared his throat.

"Fine. I'll just wait until this class is over, and we can do the interview then. I've stored a good book I've been meaning to read in my truck."

"I can't do an interview after the next class, either. I've scheduled an engagement."

"So you're avoiding me. Why?"

"No, I'm not avoiding." He chuckled but kept his eyes on his papers. "I'm simply busy."

"I don't see what the big deal is. It's a straightforward article about Abby and her research. I'd just take a few minutes of your time."

He frowned and scratched the back of his head, perhaps in an effort to ruff his hair—a look I imagined he thought was charming.

"Professor, if I must, I'll interview other sources, and I'll have no qualms making it clear in the article that you refused multiple requests for interviews, which will make you and the university, but especially you, look callous. And it'll make it look like you're hiding something."

His fingers twitched into a clench around his papers. "I'm—don't threaten me!"

I paused. He was indeed hiding something—why else the allegation that I was threatening him—but what? Did he have something to do with Abby's death? Did he know something? Was he involved somehow? I needed to know.

"I'm not threatening you," I said. "I'm just saying that I'm working on a deadline, and I'm going to turn this story in, whether or not you talk to me. And if you won't talk to me, I'm going to find out why."

I turned to walk away.

"Tomorrow morning. My office. First thing. 8 a.m."

I turned again to face him. At least his eyes were meeting mine now; perhaps he actually would make this appointment. "8 a.m. Your office. Thanks."

The corners of his mouth jerked back in what could have been a smile.

"You're quiet," Jason said, leaning back in his chair, so he could see me through the cubicle opening to my area. His olive complexion looked yellow in the office lighting.

I grunted, interrupted from mulling over the depressing reality that already the amount of time I had spent trying to meet with Ballings made the money I would be earning for the story less than minimum wage. I'd been wondering why I bothered coming back into the newspaper office at all, since I could have traveled home to daydream about stapling Ballings to his office chair and getting a night job as a bartender. At least then I'd have a steady salary. If I bought some more makeup and a push-up bra, who knew what I could earn in tips? I rubbed the heels of my palms on my forehead.

But the source of my irritation at being postponed in interviewing Ballings was more than monetary. I wanted to learn about Abby's research because it seemed to be related to her death. Abby was killed outside her lab, and then the next day her lab was ransacked. Something was going on. The two events were connected in my mind.

I pulled up the center's website again and examined Abby's research information: *Pseudopersistent Pollution and its Effects on Marine Life*. What was pseudopersestent pollution? Did Abby find what pollution caused dead fish to wash up on the banks of the Cape Fear River? What were her preliminary findings? If Ballings kept dodging interviews, I would need to get the information from someone else. A name came to my mind: Martha. She was a scientist. Since she and Abby had lived together recently, she might be able to tell me more—that is, if she could get over my foiled eavesdropping incident. My cheeks reddened at the memory of the vase clanging against her stairwell as Mrs. Pridgen fainted. I'd have to face the Pridgens sooner or later, I reminded myself, picking up a phonebook and looking for their number.

Mrs. Pridgen answered. She didn't immediately hang up on me after I introduced myself—a good sign.

"I wish there was something I could say to let you know how sorry I am to hear about Abby's death being a homicide," I said, uncertain if I should segue into apologizing for overhearing the conversation the previous evening. Since Mrs. Pridgen didn't respond, I continued. "I was hoping to speak with Martha."

"She's at work." Mrs. Pridgen's voice sounded slurred.

"Work? Of course, Martha must find the routine comforting." I spoke quickly in an attempt to cover up my shock. Again, Mrs. Pridgen didn't speak. "Is there any way you could pass along a message to her from me? I really need to speak with her."

"I can give you her cell number."

I hastily agreed and copied the number. We hung up, and I dialed Martha. If Martha was surprised to hear from me, she didn't let on.

"Your mother gave me this number," I explained. "She sounded—" I didn't want to say that Mrs. Pridgen sounded sedated, so instead I asked, "Is she okay?"

"She's coping, just as I am."

"I was calling because—first of all, I wanted to apologize for the way my visit ended. I didn't mean to—" If I said I didn't mean to overhear, I would be lying. I didn't mean to get caught spying.

"You didn't hear anything you wouldn't have heard at the press conference."

I ignored the sharpness of Martha's tone. "I also wanted to talk to you about Abby's research," I said. "I'm having trouble getting Abby's research partner, Professor Stephen Ballings, to speak with me, and I thought you might be able to give me some insight."

"I doubt I can be of much help there, but I want to talk to you, too."

I offered to drive to Prestol immediately. Martha gave directions to her office building. We hung up, and I packed my laptop. Jason leaned through the cubicle opening again.

"Where are you headed?" he asked.

"I'm visiting an old friend."

"Work or pleasure?"

I tried to gauge how much of my conversation with Martha he'd overheard. "I'll meet you tomorrow morning at the marine center for our interview with Ballings," I said.

Jason frowned at me before speaking. "If you're off to interview someone for a story, I need to be with you."

"I'm not two years old; I can drive myself. Besides, I'm cleared to cover the funeral on my own." I smoothed my hair, grabbed my bag, and stood up to leave. "And this is a personal visit."

Jason shook his head and opened his mouth to argue, but he seemed to have second thoughts and scooted forward to allow me to pass.

CHAPTER 18

As I followed an intern through the labyrinth of hallways to Martha's office inside a three-story building with a footprint that seemed to be as long as a city block, I admired Prestol's campus from the windows. In the dead of summer, the company's grass was lush, the landscaping immaculate. The sprawling campus was more like a mini-city. I had needed Martha's directions to find her building. Quiet four-lane streets were divided by medians with mature trees. Asphalt trails cut into nearby woods, and directional signs pointed to a cafeteria, gymnasium, and daycare, among the two dozen or so business buildings.

When we stopped to wait for an elevator, the intern smiled at me. A shaggy haircut hung in wisps over his pimpled forehead. He shook his head to push dangling strands out of his dark eyes.

"Don't I know you from somewhere?" he asked.

"I just got into town."

"What brought you here?"

"A job. I write for the *Tribune*."

"Are you here to do an article on IEC?" He pronounced it 'ice.' "Intravenous ethanol chemoembolization," he explained. "Martha's the team leader of the IEC development group."

"I'm here on a personal visit." I had no idea what intravenous ethanol chemo-whatever-he-said was.

"I've been interning under Martha since the spring. Couldn't have come at a better time." The elevator opened, and we boarded. The intern punched the button for the top floor. "Of course," he continued, "Martha's been working on IEC since the beginning, but we're about to tie up our major research push and move on to mass manufacturing." His chest was pushed out. He grinned at my reflection in the elevator door.

"What does IEC do?" I asked.

He looked at me as if I might have been joking. "IEC is producing unparalleled success in fighting liver cancer in our test cases."

I nodded. It made sense. Abby's and Martha's father died of the disease when they were children.

As we again walked through hallways, he talked on, explaining that the IEC treatment involved injecting an intravenous sponge containing a chemical that blocked blood flow to the tumor. Ethanol was slowly released to kill the tumor, and this was followed by a chemical called an efflux-pump inhibitor that prevented the tumor's cells from being able to filter out the drugs. My head was beginning to swim with all the technical jabber. Because of the inhibitor, the mechanism in the animal cells that was designed to filter out alien material became less effective, so the ethanol had a better chance of killing the cancer cells.

"We're breaking new ground with the efflux-pump inhibitor," he said.

The intern reminded me of Stu, but a Stu with an exponentially greater IQ and multi-syllabic vocabulary. I stifled a yawn, but he talked on, oblivious.

"Our inhibitor is cutting edge. It's not like others already on the market, and it's what makes our treatment so effective. It's like putting a drunk into a boxing ring with a heavyweight; the way cells respond to ethanol after being hit up with the inhibitor, they're hopeless. KO."

So Martha had helped develop something miraculous. Good for her.

We finally arrived at Martha's office, which wasn't as sparse and impersonal as Kipling's but felt similarly utilitarian. A couple of trays cluttered with paperwork lined her desk, along with a computer monitor and a photograph of her family when she and Abby were girls and their father was alive.

Martha dismissed the intern and greeted me. "Did you find my building without much difficulty?" she asked.

"A map would have helped."

"There's a reason we don't supply maps. We take security seriously. A while back, some PETA fanatics protested for a couple of weeks outside the security gate to our headquarters. Had they breached security, we wouldn't have wanted them to use a map to find our animal testing facility."

"You do testing on animals here?"

Martha eyed me to gauge my reaction. "It's necessary."

Looking across the small desk into her dark, sleepless eyes, she looked deflated. The light from a nearby window illuminated half of our faces, leaving the other half in shadow, and refracted off the shiny Prestol badge Martha wore clipped to her blouse. Though I had come with an agenda of learning more about Abby's research, Martha seemed to be summoning strength to talk about something more, so I let her have her time.

Martha cleared her throat. "You said you found her body. Abby's body. I haven't seen her. Since. Her body. There's not going to be a viewing."

"Oh."

"What did she look like?"

"Abby looked—" I thought for a moment, wanting to find the right words, and a chill traveled up my spine as I remembered the crabs. "Abby didn't look like herself." I wasn't doing a good job explaining. "I mean, that wasn't Abby."

"I just wanted to know if she suffered, if she seemed—"

"No," I said. "It didn't seem like she suffered. It looked fast."

Martha took a breath and looked away from me. She seemed lighter, as if imaginary strings holding her shoulders taut had relaxed. I noticed she still wore her father's gold Rolex as it glinted in the sunlight.

"I know you're going through a lot," I said, "but I wanted to ask, do you have any idea who would want to hurt Abby?"

"That's the thing. Abby was so—she was Abby. You know. Who could help but love her?"

"Do you know if the police have any ideas?"

"They said they were looking into a couple of suspects, but who—they didn't tell us. Kimmie did seem interested in you, though. She asked what you were doing at my house last night."

"I think she suspects me. But I swear I have nothing to do with Abby's death."

Martha shook her head. "The police, especially Kimmie, said they were curious about how you came upon the body."

"The news tip that came in." I could almost hear Kimmie's nasal voice tattling to Martha and Mrs. Pridgen about the call. I supposed the Pridgens had every right to know how I found Abby's body, though.

"A news tip coming in to you, on the first day of your job, a tip that leads you to Abby—it seems suspect, like Kimmie said." Martha frowned.

"I agree, but that's what happened. The caller was a man, and he was disguising his voice."

"A low voice? High-pitched? You're sure you didn't recognize—"

"No."

"I can't help but wonder if the caller was Abby's ex-fiancé."

"Mark, right?"

"Mark Listlen. He wasn't anything special. Sometimes I wondered what she saw in him to begin with. He's creepy. Let's just say Mark always had a way of turning up unexpectedly, saying things that seemed uncanny, and if he knew Abby was pregnant—"

"Do you think he killed her?"

"When Abby broke up with him, he gave her a hard time. Actually, he wouldn't leave her alone. He would call her cell phone day and night, sometimes every ten minutes for hours on end. He even called our house phone and, when I picked up, asked me to talk to Abby and intervene for him. Of course I refused. He sent her flowers, left little gifts for her on the doorstep until I alerted the island bridge tender to keep him away. He was obsessive."

"Do you think he fathered the child?"

Martha shrugged. "Who else could it be? But if he wasn't the father and found out she was pregnant, there's no telling what he would do."

I was silent a moment. "Can you think of anyone else who might have held a grudge against Abby?"

Martha shook her head. "I just hope the police reach the bottom of this. It's terrible not knowing who," she closed her eyes, "killed my little sister."

I felt an urge to wrap my arms around Martha. She suddenly seemed frail instead of driven. She now had lost both her father and her sister—a shattered piece of a broken family broken once more.

"You wouldn't happen to have any idea who would want to wreck her lab, would you?" I asked.

"No idea."

"Do you think maybe whoever did it was looking for something?" I asked. "Did you know if Abby had something to hide other than her pregnancy—not that she was hiding that, but—" I stopped talking before I said anything worse than what had already escaped.

Martha shook her head.

"What about her research?" I asked.

"All I know about Abby's research project was that it seemed pretty mundane, testing water samples for contaminants."

"Don't other agencies test for contaminants?"

"Of course. Municipalities and state agencies monitor discharge in waterways, as do volunteer agencies. I think it's federal law that every agency that discharges into a watershed has to attain a permit and monitor its pollutants."

"So what would pseudopersistent pollution have to do with it?" I asked. "What is pseudopersistent pollution?"

Martha allowed a small smile.

"What's funny?"

"Pseudopersistent pollution. To put it in layman's terms, an example of pseudopersistent pollution is a toxin being released on occasion over a long expanse of time into a river like the Cape Fear. Because the river pushes the pollutant away, out to sea, the pollutant doesn't stick around long like toxins caught in slow-flowing, small creeks. But because the pollutant is being discharged now and again, supposedly it's consistently present."

"But you laugh at it?"

"With all the pollutants that attack the Cape Fear River— overflowing hog waste lagoons, untreated sewage spills, muddy sludge from clear-cut construction sites, all the chemicals, herbicides, and insecticides leaching into the water from all the riverside golf courses, my little sister goes after pseudopersistent pollution."

"So Abby was worried about it."

Martha shrugged. "We didn't talk about her research much." Martha moved her hands to her lap and closed her eyes again. "We were—it was a constant—not argument, but point of contention, perhaps, between us—her going into environmental science when I advised her that her brain could be used to greater benefit elsewhere." She cleared her throat. "Silly argument when I think about it now, when she's not here anymore. But at the time, when she was deciding what to commit her life to, I couldn't understand why she would dedicate herself to studying cold-blooded fish when there are so many human causes." Martha shrugged. "Our father's death didn't affect her as it did me. Abby was so young, she didn't remember how he suffered. She didn't remember having to choose between two tortures: taking a drug that would make him deaf while it did the liver's job of filtering toxins, or not taking the drug, keeping his hearing, but losing his sanity while he waited to die. In the end, he lost everything, anyway."

"But your intern says you've developed a new liver cancer treatment, IEC."

"Did he tell you much about it?"

"Too much," I said. "After discussing chemoembolization and efflux-pump inhibitors, I think they were called, somewhere around highlighting chromatograms, I lost track."

Martha clucked her tongue. "He'll be revealing our secret recipe next. Keep what you heard to yourself, if you don't mind. We can't have our competitors creating copycat drugs too soon and profiting off our years of research before we have the chance to recoup our expenses."

"Sure."

"I'll need to have a word with him."

"He made it sound like, for the people you're testing IEC on—"

"Animals. We test on animals first."

"—IEC is effectively treating the cancer."

"IEC is resulting in unparalleled success." She echoed the phrase her intern used earlier.

"Congratulations."

Martha nodded and smiled. "We're going to save lives."

"You don't discharge into the river, do you?"

"No." Her voice echoed in the small office. "No. All our chemical waste gets deposited into containers and shipped away by truck." She looked at me as if to gauge how much I believed her. "Come on. I'll show you."

CHAPTER 19

Martha shrugged on a white lab coat that had been hanging over her chair and walked across the hallway. She swiped her badge over a remote entry. A beep sounded, and I heard the door unlock. We entered a laboratory. A handful of scientists wearing lab coats and safety glasses attended large machines that dotted the room. The intern who had ushered me in was stationed at what appeared to be a metal hood that sucked away gases, like a fan above an industrial oven.

"Welcome to our primary IEC development laboratory," Martha said. "We're in the final stages of testing: testing the drug's stability and how it responds to storage under a variety of conditions and for varying lengths of time after manufacture."

As she led me through the lab, she pointed out different instruments—something called an HPLC "for quantitative analysis," a centrifuge, dissolution baths. We stopped at a series of three translucent white drums about waist high and so wide my arms couldn't fit around the diameter. Martha tapped one of the drums with her foot.

"These are our storage drums where we dump all the chemicals we use. Whenever we do experiments—across the board, even in divisions other than IEC—we dump our chemicals into a waste container like this one. Even after the chemicals are deposited into the waste container, we rinse the glassware with water. She pointed to a nearby sink. We dump that wastewater into the waste container. Then we rinse again, and that water also goes into the waste container. Nothing's left to go to the sewage treatment plant when we send the glassware to the washer."

"Nothing goes to the river?"

She shook her head. "Everything is dumped into a drum. Two or three times a week, our disposal company brings their trucks around and replaces full drums with empty ones."

"What about your sink drains?"

"Our wastewater goes to the Wilmington sewage treatment plant."

I frowned.

"We don't pour the chemicals down the drains. I suppose it's remotely possible—highly improbable—it really doesn't happen. No one is that clueless. Not only is it standard policy; it's common sense."

"But if someone wasn't following policy?"

"The waste would end up going down the drain and to the treatment plant, true. But the way our lab is set up—" she gestured around at the openness. From where we were standing, we could see the entire room. "I cannot see anyone getting away with dumping chemicals down the drain for long before someone else noticed what was happening. Even if that ever occurred, the chemicals only would have been going down the drain for that little while."

I nodded.

Martha checked her watch. "I should be going. I've left my mother alone all day." I followed Martha back to her office, where she pulled a blue handbag from a drawer.

"I'm sure the police have leads they're not revealing to you or the media," I said.

"Let's hope. In the meantime, I'm not taking any chances." Martha fanned open her bag to reveal a flash of silver, a gun so small it looked dainty, before pushing the fabric closed again. "It belonged to my grandmother. She used to carry it around, loaded, in her purse. I can't help but wonder, if Abby had been carrying this gun, if she could have—" Martha wiped her eyes and took a couple of deep breaths. She turned off her office light and closed the door behind us.

CHAPTER 20

The next morning, after overestimating Wilmington rush-hour traffic, I arrived a quarter of an hour early for my interview with Ballings. Two marked Wilmington police cars were parked in front of the building, and I didn't see Jason anywhere.

I contemplated my options. I wanted to climb out of my truck and see what the police were up to. Though Jason and I were planning on meeting outside and entering the center together, if I idled in my truck and they found me waiting around, I would look suspicious. If Daniel and Kimmie weren't wrapping up Abby's case and were at the center on some other related crime, Kimmie wouldn't hesitate to report my presence to her chief, who would tell my publisher I was somehow linked with whatever was going on at the center again—not good for me. So my other option was to turn around and hightail it out of the parking lot, but that would mean missing my interview again with the professor and looking like a complete loser for yet again not having the story—also big trouble. Every option attached itself to a negative, so I settled on a compromise.

I squeezed into a parking space between a couple of SUVs that shielded my truck from view. I decided to walk as inconspicuously as possible into the center, seeing if I could determine what was happening on my way to the professor's office. With any luck, Jason would spot my truck in the parking lot when he arrived and figure out where I went.

I grabbed my notebook and camera, jumped out of my truck, and walked between cars toward the building. I could see down the side of the building. Daniel and Kimmie, along with another officer, stood at the far corner of the building near the pier, far enough away that they might not recognize me if they caught a glimpse of me. Kimmie was squinting at the upper story of the building. I followed her gaze to Kipling's office window that overlooked the garden. From the distance, I couldn't tell what she was examining. Daniel was looking back toward the woods and the path that wound through the garden. Patrick emerged from the trees.

I ducked behind a trash can, thankful my slacks and vest were a soft gray that wouldn't attract attention, and powered on my camera. Using the trash can to hide me, I disabled the flash and took a few photos, one showing both the building and the woods with the officers standing around, another a close-up of Daniel and Patrick talking. I then zoomed in on the dean's window. Even with the zoom, I still needed a couple of seconds to find what Kimmie was looking at. A small pockmark was centered around a spider-web type pattern of cracked glass. I returned the camera to my pocket. Students were trickling into the center—a good sign, I thought. If the situation was serious, surely no one would be able to enter the building.

I figured I'd better interview the professor and leave the center before the police noticed my presence. When I turned down the hallway that led to Ballings' office, I caught a glimpse of his peppered hair and another designer suit whipping through the door to the stairwell, the heavy metal door swinging shut behind him. I cursed under my breath. I wasn't going to allow him to dodge this interview again. I ran to the end of the hall and followed him upstairs, hearing the upper story door close as I turned a corner. I wrenched the second story's door open just in time to see Ballings slamming the door to the dean's office.

I sucked in a breath and glanced around. The hallway lights were on, but most of the offices that linked to it either had closed doors or were still dark. I checked my watch. It was ten minutes until 8 a.m. The dean's secretary hadn't appeared yet. I walked to the end of the hallway, figuring I could wait for Ballings to emerge and then pounce on him. I couldn't help but hear the raised voices in Kipling's office.

"And I want to know the truth!" Kipling was saying. "With all these other crimes, did you think I wouldn't report this? This isn't funny, Stephen."

"You're being irrational."

"I told you I put in the application for your supplementary funding, but this shenanigan is not going to speed up the budgeting process. I told you it's out of my hands."

"You can't believe I'd do anything like this for funding."

"What are you going to do next—kidnap the fish from the downstairs aquarium and hold them ransom? I thought since your little apprentice was doing all the work on the pseudopersistent project, now she's—" Kipling paused— "unavailable, you'd want to drop the project straightaway lest you actually have to roll up your sleeves."

"I pull my own."

"Remind me how much research you've published since taking credit for Tracey Miles' work 20 years ago."

"We were co-researchers."

"Too bad Tracey can't set the record straight about your role in that research. The offer to join our staff still stands," Kipling said, "but only if you quit screwing around. If you don't stop, I will make a point to tell the police what you won't, and withdraw funding, and withdraw the job offer."

The door was snatched open, and both Ballings and Kipling gaped out at me.

CHAPTER 21

"I'm here for our interview," I said, pretending I hadn't heard any of Ballings' conversation with Kipling. "When you weren't in your office, I figured I might find you up here."

Ballings ignored me and stormed away, and I looked into the dean's office. Kipling stared out at me, not bothering to greet me. Against the backlit window, her hair disappeared into her black business suit. I looked at the damaged window, the hole surrounded by spiraling cracked glass that glistened in the morning sunlight.

"Is that a bullet hole?" I asked.

She shrugged, then nodded, her shoulders sagging in the gesture. She seemed more fragile than usual, as though the argument with the professor shrank her from a seamless concrete barricade to a mere a speed hump.

"Any explanations for it?" I asked, remembering the fluid gleam of Martha's tiny gun from the darkness inside her handbag.

"Sometimes hunters on the waterway drift too close to our property." She straightened her phone on the corner of her desk. "Is there something I can do for you?"

"I was here to interview Ballings, but a bullet through a window sounds like a story to me," I said. "Hunters shooting a university building?"

"We're not sure if that's who it was."

"So you think that there's a possibility that the shooter wasn't a hunter?"

Kipling glanced at me before looking down at her desk again. She was taking her time answering my question, but I was going to be patient.

I heard steps on the carpet behind me. I turned, hoping to see Kipling's secretary but expecting to find Kimmie and Daniel at my back. Instead, Jason frowned at me.

"Ballings said you were up here." Jason noticed the hole in the window. "Is that—that's why the cops are here?"

"Dean Kipling was about to tell me why someone who wasn't a hunter might be firing a bullet through her window."

"I really should refer you to the police," she said, looking me in the eye again. Some of the dark fire that smoldered in there was back. "Yes," she said. "The police will answer questions of this nature."

"Fine," I said. "But after I speak with the police, I will have some follow-up questions. We'll call you."

I turned again to the door. Behind Jason, Daniel blocked it. He had arrived undetected. He must have followed Jason upstairs. He smiled briefly at me, and I couldn't help but notice his clean-shaven jaw line, that razor-thin scar emphasized by the angle of the morning light. He noticed where my eyes had wandered, and the corners of his mouth twitched.

"We were just about to find you and ask some questions about what happened here," I said to Daniel.

"Good morning to you too." His voice sounded weary, but his eyes twinkled at me from where he settled in a chair near Kipling's desk.

"Blame my lack of greeting on my perplexity at seeing you here at the marine center for yet another crime," I said.

"You show up so consistently whenever suspicious incidents and the marine center intersect, I've ceased to be perplexed."

"Suspicious incidents?"

"Right now, we're coding this as property damage."

"So tell me about today's suspicious property damage incident, if you won't call a bullet through a window a crime."

"You're playing hard ball."

I paused, waiting for him to fill me in. He leaned back in his chair almost lazily and looked me over. I resisted the urge to tug my fitted vest straight. After a few seconds, I said, "I'm not playing; I'm working."

"As am I."

"So?"

Daniel raised his eyebrows.

"I can ask the questions one at a time, or you can give me a summary and cut out the games. Either way, we both know I'll end up with the same information for the *Tribune*."

Daniel stretched his fingers. "I'm not the type to volunteer information, so shoot. Ask a question and I'll answer it."

"Fine. Who reported the crime and when?" I began.

"Dean Kipling called the non-emergency line of the Wilmington police shortly after 7 a.m."

"And what did she say?"

"She reported a hole possibly made by a bullet in her office window."

"And then what happened?"

"We arrived on scene to check out her claim."

"And?"

Daniel again raised his eyebrows, grinning like a cat in the sun.

"What did you discover?" I asked.

"It is, indeed, a hole made by a bullet."

I sighed. Daniel needed prompting again.

"Can you tell where the shot was fired from?" I asked.

"Exterior of the building."

"From how close?" I asked.

"We're going with about 50 feet, give or take."

"And the type of gun used?"

"I'm guessing a revolver. One of our guys is about to search the attic for the bullet. As you can see, the bullet traveled through the window at an angle and passed through the ceiling panel."

I looked up. Sure enough, the ceiling exhibited another hole as clean as if someone drilled into the paneling.

"Is it possible a hunter came too close to the building and made an innocent mistake?"

"It's highly doubtful."

I glanced at Kipling, whose face looked pale.

"Hunters aren't allowed on university property," Daniel continued, "and the university has posted signs along the waterway and along the property's entire perimeter warning trespassers to keep out. Besides, nothing is in season."

"So, no suspects, no motives?"

Kipling jerked slightly.

"We're working on it."

"Dean Kipling," I said, "are you sure you don't know why someone might have taken a shot at your window?

She stiffly shook her head once, not giving anything away. From what I overheard, I suspected Ballings fired the shot, or at least Kipling thought so.

"Am I correct in assuming the shot was fired sometime last evening or before dawn this morning?" I said.

"My window was intact when I left my office yesterday afternoon, and it was like this today when I arrived."

"What about campus security?"

Kipling looked to Daniel for help.

"No witnesses of the shooting have come forward thus far," he said.

I turned my attention back to Kipling. "So you weren't in your office last evening?"

"No."

"Do you ever have occasion to be here at the center in the late evening?"

Kipling gave her head another quick shake.

I held her gaze for a moment, wanting to press further but knowing to do so would require me to reveal that I had dug through her trash and found her appointment book page. I turned back to Daniel.

"Was this shot accidental?" I asked him.

Daniel hesitated. "It's inconclusive."

"Can you expound on that?"

"No. This is another open case that we've just begun investigating."

"Do you think this case is linked to Abby's homicide?"

"None of the evidence suggests that."

"But you do admit that there's been a rash of crime here recently—first the homicide, then Ballings' office is torn apart, and now this."

"All of these are separate incidents," Daniel said.

"Separate but linked?"

"Doubtful," he said. Now his eyes looked drained. "Sometimes you find a chain of unrelated crimes in the same vicinity by mere coincidence or unrelated circumstance."

"But sometimes they're linked," I said.

"Can I speak off the record?"

I lowered my pen and notebook.

"Often in my experience, I've found you people—sorry, I mean reporters—try to make a story when there really isn't one."

Angry blood pulsed in my head, my heart beating hard and fast in my chest. He acted as if the "you people" jab was accidental, but I wasn't buying his charade. "You don't think a bullet shot through a dean's office window is a story?" I asked, my voice coming out low and cool with only a slight tremor.

"What you're trying to get us to say about the crimes being linked isn't a story."

"How can the crimes not be linked?"

Daniel exhaled slowly. "Remember, the lab wasn't vandalized until the day after—or the night after—the homicide, and nothing was overtly taken from the lab. If the killer wanted to destroy the lab and had half a brain, he would have ripped the lab apart immediately following the homicide rather than risk returning to the center on a separate occasion. This shooting comes days after the homicide. So it could just as easily be an accidental discharge from a weapon one of the students was carrying as anything else."

"Or, it could be a message," I insisted.

"No one wants to jump to conclusions. The only link I see at the moment is your involvement in reporting and your presence—at the best, very early on—at each and every one of the incidents you just mentioned."

I tried to think of a civil response.

"Jonie," Daniel said, his voice pitying, "are you suggesting that Abby's killer is sticking around, tearing apart labs, and shooting through windows, doing everything but pleading with us to capture him face-to-face? Try to see it from that perspective."

I held Daniel's gaze for a moment before allowing myself to check my notes, my cheeks burning. I wanted to ask Kipling what Ballings wasn't telling police, but I knew she wouldn't reveal anything. I already gave her the chance. I looked at Jason to see if he had any additional questions. He shook his head, so I formally thanked both Daniel and Kipling for their time.

As Jason and I walked down the hall and to Ballings' office, I quietly told him about the conversation I overheard between Ballings and Kipling.

"I always felt like he was insincere," Jason said. "Even when I interviewed him when he first came to the university, something seemed plastic."

We reached Ballings' office, and for the first time, peeking through his open doorway, I saw him seated at his desk.

CHAPTER 22

Ballings' motley-colored hair again looked unkempt, like he'd worked out since I'd seen him with Kipling. His slacks were wrinkled. He noticed Jason and me staring in at him.

"You want an interview?" Ballings' voice was almost belligerent. "I don't know how much you overheard, but Kipling thinks—" His mouth opened and shut like a fish sucking air on the sand, like words formed in his mouth but he was restraining himself from ranting. His breathing slowed. "It doesn't matter." He waved his hands toward the doorway as if wafting away stale air. "I'll be on to bigger and better things soon enough."

"Kipling thinks what?"

He shook his head once and crossed his arms.

"When you say 'bigger and better things,' are you referring to continuing the research you and Abby were conducting?"

Ballings considered me for a moment and then brightened. A sudden smile full of teeth stretched across his face, the transformation as distinct as a change of clothing. "The fish kills. Pseudopersistent pollution. It's a big issue, of state importance, and beyond, possibly international importance. That's what you're here to talk about—I'll give you your interview."

"Our interview," I agreed.

He gestured to Abby's old chair and another metal chair set near a new microscope swaddled in bubble wrap. "Might as well become cozy."

I settled into Abby's fabric seat, taking up the space she used to fill, there in the worn dip in the cushioned chair in front of what used to be her desk. Jason refocused my thoughts by dragging the metal chair near mine with a shrill squeal as it grated against the flooring.

"Let me begin," Ballings said, tugging his tie undone and unbuttoning the top of his wrinkled shirt to reveal graying chest hair, "by saying how sorry I am that I haven't been able to meet with you until now."

I focused on removing the cap from my pen, opening my notebook, and tucking my hair behind my ears.

"As I'm sure you know, a professor's life is more than busy. And with all the—all the happenings that have transpired in the past week, my life, my work, it's all been put on hold because of this series of setbacks I'm not sure I've yet recovered from."

I waited for him to finish his sorry excuses, mildly stunned at his change in nature from his former standoffish interview avoidance to his now gregarious unprompted narration.

As Ballings babbled on about the nature of a professor's life, I tried to overcome a growing irritation. One of my pet peeves as a reporter was interviewees who attempted to run the show, a maneuver common in politicians who would drone on and on about what they wanted me and the public to hear and then end the interview by saying they had a telephone call coming in or a scheduled meeting to attend, fully expecting no further questions.

Finally, the professor paused for a breath.

"Alright, then," I said. "Let's get to it: Abby's legacy, her research, the fish kills. What did Abby think was causing the fish kills and how was she going about proving it?"

"We were studying pseudopersistent pollution, looking at toxins not typically monitored. These pollutants are in such small amounts, one part per billion, that many people believe they don't affect the environment, especially not in a fast-flowing river like the Cape Fear."

"So why study those pollutants?"

"We thought they actually were influencing the environment."

"Were they?"

Ballings leaned back in his chair and stroked his stubbled chin. "Typically, I don't like to release my theories until the research proves—"

"You can generalize. What did Abby find?"

Ballings' hand dropped to his lap. "Chemicals in the water. That's what we—I—believe to be causing the fish kills. I was out to prove where the chemicals were coming from: runoff from the city or other developed areas, non-point source pollution, or perhaps farmland runoff. Also, we were considering if just one chemical or if a combination of chemicals was causing the kills. Of course, narrowing findings down is very difficult because the chemicals we were looking at were in such small quantities and in combination with who knows what other substances—a nightmarish number of possibilities. We were studying water samples and fish samples from a number of different sites in a 40-mile area at the base of the river."

"What were your preliminary findings?"

A student with wavy brown hair, pouting lips, and very tan legs knocked on the door, and Ballings glanced over.

"Professor," she said, "I wanted to talk to you about making up my lab work?" I cringed at the way she phrased the statement as a question.

"Can you come back in a few minutes, Trish?" he asked, winking at her. Ballings turned back to me, a lazy grin on his face.

"Your preliminary findings?"

"Well," Ballings twiddled his thumbs, and then sat up straight. "The particular chemicals we were looking at seemed to be most concentrated around the Wilmington area."

"And what would those chemicals be?"

"We're talking about a number of variables taken from a number of different sites from which we've pulled water samples and examined numerous components within the water. It's not simple."

"Try me."

"I really would rather let the research speak for itself."

"Fine. What does the research show?"

"I told you, it's not complete, and I don't want to release our findings until research is finalized."

"So you can't tell me anything about the research, really, is what you're saying?"

"Not until it's all done, no."

I threw my pen on my notepad and raised both my hands in the air, huffing out a sigh. It was a risky move, acting out my exasperation, as it could turn Ballings against me instantly and permanently, but I didn't know what else to try.

"Well, okay, off the record?"

A second request to relay off the record information in one morning? Usually, I despised getting information off the record. Most times something anyone wanted to say off the record was a fact no one actually would have cared enough about if it was said on-record, anyway. And then, if I wanted to use the off-the-record information, I had to find some other source and goad that source to come up with the information all over again.

"Fine," I said, despite myself. "Off the record."

Ballings lowered his voice. "Our research identified a handful of different chemicals found in pharmaceuticals in very minute amounts in the waterway. We're talking parts per billion and trillion, such a small amount it was detectable only by using gas and liquid chromatography and mass spectrometry. But Abby's—our—theory was that the pharmaceutical chemicals—one of them, or a combination of them, or a combination of them coupled with a combination of other toxins—caused the fish kills."

"Pharmaceuticals in the river?"

Ballings nodded.

CHAPTER 23

"Pharmaceutical pseudopersistent pollution is a growing study area," Ballings said. "More than 20 years ago, the EPA documented aspirin, caffeine, and nicotine in water being released from a sewage treatment plant. A more recent EPA study found about 80 percent of 139 streams in 30 states contained trace amounts of pharmaceutical contaminants. Another study found pharmaceuticals—sex hormones, anti-convulsants, antibiotics, mood stabilizers—in the drinking water supplies of at least 41 million Americans."

"But how do the pharmaceuticals get into the environment?" I thought of the Prestol campus just a few miles upstream from Wilmington. But Martha had shown me that they didn't dump waste into the river or treatment plant. I decided to ask anyway. "Would they come from manufacturers, or a scientist dumping chemicals down a drain?"

"No, actually. Manufacturers have strict guidelines on disposing their wastes. The way the pharmaceuticals reach the river is much more banal: excretion!" Ballings clasped his hands and wriggled his fingers. "Some research shows that up to 90 percent of a consumed drug can be excreted. Sewage plants don't remove the pharmaceutical toxins before releasing treated wastewater into streams. Abby believed, per my encouragement, of course, that minute quantities of excreted drugs pose a threat to the wellbeing of the environment. Just think about how many drugs Americans use, especially popular drugs like aspirin, which, theoretically, continuously trickles out of the treatment plant and into the river."

"What chemicals were you looking at?"

Ballings' smile wavered. "There was a handful, like I said. Er, aspirin was one of them, along with a drug used during X rays, and a few others. Abby was in the process of running tests on fish using the isolated drugs when—when she passed.

"So you haven't determined which drug was responsible for the fish kills?"

"That's the million dollar research grant question, isn't it?" Ballings smile was now a sheepish half-grin. He ran a hand across his chin again. "No, I have no idea which, if any, drug was responsible. See, I'm the type of professor who allows my ducklings, like Abby, to pretty much run the show. It's my philosophy that scientists do their best work if unfettered by the demands and particularities of an overbearing advisor. Of course, I oversaw everything, acted as the invisible artist behind the canvas, if you will. Abby was more than competent, more than adept." He shook his head. "I knew I should have kept closer tabs on her. You know about my lab being vandalized. When that happened, Abby's computer was knocked off her desk, probably kicked around, and all of our data was destroyed. Sorting out the printed paperwork that was scattered is a Herculean task I haven't begun. Not that Abby had given me any indication that she was anywhere near completing the research, but it would have been nice to know what direction the preliminary results were—well, a professor's life, you know. Busy, busy. Details inevitably get away."

I understood. Lazy, skirt-chasing Ballings was using Abby to write his research. He wanted the credit.

"Abby knew—I told her—to make a backup disk of all our data," Ballings said. "I just haven't found her disk yet amidst the rubble. I've got a whole box of enigmatically labeled data CDs to load and sort through." Ballings kicked a large box of jumbled CDs. "The research is bound to be here, somewhere. Damned vandal."

"So who exactly do you believe destroyed your office?"

"No idea." Ballings shook his head and scowled, but the expression looked feigned on his face.

"It wasn't you?"

"Be serious. Probably some student."

"But why would a student target your office and no one else's?"

"Must have been on drugs. High on drugs by the look of the place. Papers scattered everywhere, computers and microscopes smashed to oblivion, testing samples ruined."

"What happens if you don't find the disk?"

Ballings flicked his wrist and rolled his eyes. "It's here. You saw the mess. If it's not in this box, it was thrown in one of the boxes of ruined equipment. Once I find my backup disk with all the data, if there's anything significant on it, you'll be the first to know, I promise."

I doubted I'd be at the top of Ballings' list, but I let his fib slide. I had gathered enough information to write a vague description of Abby's project, so I moved on to a touchier issue.

"Did you know about Abby's pregnancy before her death?"

Ballings paled for a heartbeat before color flooded his face. "No."

Jason shifted in his chair, as if he thought I was prying too far and was trying to tell me to curtail my inquiry nonverbally. I ignored him.

"She didn't confide in you?"

"Not about that type of—no."

"And you didn't notice any symptoms of pregnancy, morning sickness, or—"

"No."

At a loss for ideas for probing more out of the pregnancy vein, I changed the subject. "Who was Tracey Miles? I heard Kipling mention the name."

"Tracey was—she assisted me in research a long time ago."

118

I remembered Kipling had accused Ballings of taking credit for the work and inferring that Miles wasn't defending herself. "Where is Miles now?"

"Dead."

"I'm sorry," I stuttered, trying to regain my composure. Were the deaths of two of Ballings' research partners coincidences? "Was it recent?"

Jason shook his head, a slight tic, another warning

"No."

"What did she die of?" I pushed.

Jason coughed loudly.

"A severe asthma attack. Ah, Trish!"

I looked over my shoulder. The student who needed help had returned.

"Just one more question, professor," I said. "Is there something you're not telling the police about Abby?"

Ballings' hand jerked out of his pants pocket, scattering change on the floor. By the time he retrieved the coins, his aloof smile had returned. "Of course not." He was looking at Trish when he spoke. "Let's meet in the lounge. I need to stretch." He stood up, and I followed suit. Ballings bid Jason and me a hasty farewell as he followed the student's tan legs from the room.

I watched Jason, who admired the student's progress down the hall. He muttered something in Italian beneath his breath and turned to me. "How exactly do you suppose that girl is going to make up her work?"

"Focus, Jason. Did you hear anything Ballings said?"

"Everything."

"Don't you think it's peculiar that he doesn't know the direction Abby's research was going? They were supposed to be research partners."

"You heard the man: 'busy, busy.'"

"Ballings spoke so specifically about other studies on pharmaceutical pollution but could hardly put together a coherent sentence about Abby's research."

"He's busy, alright," Jason said.

"Do you think he was busy in that way with Abby?"

"What kind of question is that?"

"A valid one." Instead of continuing to dwell on the possibility that Abby and Ballings might have been romantically involved, I said, "He seemed overly evasive about Tracey Miles, too."

Jason shrugged. "I liked when Ballings said 'excretion.'" He mimicked Ballings' hand gesture. "Speaking of excretion, I'll be right back."

I sighed and plopped back down in Abby's chair to await Jason's return. My mind wandered. I thought about Lee's warning about Montgomery. My first visit to the center, I found Abby's body. The next visit, I was discovered in the vandalized lab. I wondered if Montgomery had heard about the bullet through Kipling's window yet. Would Kimmie exaggerate my involvement to the police chief again? I imagined what Montgomery would look like—hulking, grumpy, wearing nice clothes that were rumpled from scurrying to overbooked good ol' boy meetings at different established country restaurants. Possibly he smoked a cigar. I could visualize his fat fingers pinching that cigar and repeatedly jabbing it at me. While every feminine bone in my body despised fools like who I imagined Montgomery to be, my brain kept me in check, reminding me that the good ol' boy system still ran the South, most places, and that Lee's warning had been sincere. I thought back to my troubles with the law in Tennessee. If I lost this job, where would I go?

I ran my fingertips across Abby's smooth desktop. There was nothing but barren wood to look at, so I glanced out the window. A butterfly with yellow wings batted around just outside. I tracked its progress as it fluttered up and down, admiring the wings' pure yellow color inside the intricate black pattern. I noticed something dull glinting nearby against the window's track. It was a silver key, propped inconspicuously in the track's metal notch just below the lip of Abby's desktop.

I fished out the key. It was heavier than it appeared and made of cheap metal. The key was thick and scratched with square ridges instead of the sharp peaks found on house and car keys. Abby's desk drawers, which were unlocked anyway, featured tarnished gold locks. I walked to the cabinets below the laboratory countertops. Most had black locks; the ones with silver locks fit significantly thinner keys. The door lock to Ballings' office was too thin and flimsy for a match. I slipped the key in my pocket and decided, for now, not to mention it to Jason when he returned.

I focused on my breathing, forcing my attention away from the burning in my thighs. I was enjoying the cool, early Sunday atmosphere, my favorite time for jogging and taking advantage of the lack of morning commuters traversing the streets of downtown Wilmington. I felt strong and sleek in my most beloved jogging outfit, a tight, black tank top and silky, skimpy, practically weightless jogging shorts, well-deserved spoils from a not-too-distant shopping indulgence.

I had begun my jog by warming up, traveling downhill to the Cape Fear. I increased my speed along the riverfront boardwalk and weaved along a few of the lower streets parallel to the river for a couple of miles. Now I pushed up the Market Street hill, my goal the tall concrete fountain with the horned faces in the center of the roundabout on Fifth Street where the bluff finally levels off.

With the rest of the world sleeping in, no speeding cars broke my pace. I accelerated, sucking air in through my nose and breathing hard out through my mouth, pumping my arms. I saw another runner ahead of me on the opposite side of the road. He was running slower than me. I stepped up my pace again with a new goal, beating him up the infernal hill to the fountain. As I neared him, out of the corner of my eye I saw him glance at me. He then increased his pace. He didn't want a woman to beat him, I imagined. I sped up even more. From my peripheral vision, I could tell he had followed suit. One more block until the fountain. I unleashed myself, going all out. He looked to be going all out, too. I lost sight of him as I went around the fountain, but saw him reach the opposite corner of the road a hair faster than me.

I stooped over my knees, panting, legs on fire, lungs stinging, arms trembling, sweat soaking my collar. I straightened up and shook out my legs.

"Nice try!" he yelled.

I glanced across Market St. The runner was Daniel.

CHAPTER 24

"What are you doing here?" I asked.

"Racing you. I won."

"You had a head start."

Daniel looked for traffic and then jogged to my corner. Sunlight glinted off beads of sweat in his hair.

"And I meant, where did you come from?" I asked.

"It's Sunday; take a break from the questions." He gave my ponytail a light tug and smiled. "I live just over there." He pointed in the vicinity of my apartment. "A few doors down and on the corner across the way from you. Want to come over for some juice?" With a shrug of a shoulder, he wiped a bead of sweat from his jaw with his loose T-shirt.

"What happened to not fraternizing with reporters? And according to you, I'm not just any reporter, I'm the reporter who shows up at suspicious incidents. Are you supposed to be inviting suspects to your house?"

"No one could prove you visited my home. If it came down to it, it would be your word against mine. But you're not a suspect."

I sucked in a breath. What? Not a suspect?

"You're connected to the case, but I don't suspect you."

"Good."

"And I'm not on duty."

I crossed my arms. I wanted to trust him, to go with him, to learn more about him. Undeniably, I was attracted to him, but something like a twitch inside me held me back. I couldn't place where the nagging suspicion was originating.

"And you're off duty, too," he said. He smiled and tucked his chin slightly so his eyes teased mine. "When you come over, you're not going to be asking any questions about anything related to what I do while I'm on duty."

His mischievous smile was melting my resolve. It was a fair deal, I thought, or at least too tempting to turn down. And I was intrigued.

We walked to his house talking about how far and where we jogged. The distance between our homes wasn't more than a block. If I leaned out an upper story window in my apartment, I could see into his yard. Daniel's two-level brick house was built during the same era as mine, the early 1900s. Like my house, Daniel's sported few frills other than ornate trim and offered a generous front porch. I followed Daniel up loose brick steps, through the door, and into a hallway that ended at the kitchen. The house smelled fresh with an underlying woody odor. Carpet began halfway up a staircase on the right. The bright yellow-brown hardwood floors on the lower half of the stairs and in the downstairs hallway looked ancient.

"Original heart pine," Daniel said. "I refinished them myself."

"They're beautiful."

"I'm restoring the house one room at a time. The downstairs is done. The stairs are a work in progress."

The kitchen, though compact, shined with cleanliness and displayed stainless steel appliances. A door on the left led into a spacious den with a large screen television beside a chipped brick fireplace. I stepped into the room. A woven beige rug covered most of the flooring, and two couches and an armchair lined the walls. An antique wooden table was set in front of one of the couches. I carefully set my apartment key on a glass coaster.

"Apple, orange, or cranberry juice?"

"Cranberry," I said.

As he poured the drinks, I continued my inspection of his den. The two walls with windows were brick. Daniel hadn't hung anything on the interior walls. The only knickknack in the room was a long, intricately carved wood box on the fireplace mantel. The reddish wood of the box blended in so well against the bricks I looked twice to make sure the box wasn't an illusion. I unlatched it and pried it open. Inside a sharp piece of black metal rested against the felted green bottom. The metal looked like a fragment of something, its edges seemingly chipped on both sides. The piece was nearly a foot long and would have made a menacing knife blade if its jagged edges weren't so irregular. It didn't shine in the light.

I heard a shuffling step behind me, and I looked around in time to see Daniel walking toward me with a couple of glasses of juice. He noticed I'd opened his box. His brow furled, but his expression wasn't of anger. It might have been one of confusion.

I shut the case and returned it to the mantel. "What's that inside the box?"

He handed me a glass, backed away, and sat down in the armchair. I walked to the matching leather couch opposite him.

"It's personal," he said. "Otherwise, I wouldn't have put it in a box, out of sight from people I didn't want looking at it."

I turned my eyes toward my glass. I supposed opening the box qualified as snooping.

"You have a knack for stumbling on things," he added after a moment. "Dead bodies, vandalized labs, shattered metal."

I wanted to ask what shattered metal.

"Is that why you took up tae-kwon-do, to work grace into your predisposition to stumbling?" Daniel teased before I could ask. His eyes were smiling again.

I thought back to that moment in my life, walking into the neighborhood dojo, bargaining down the price of lessons.

"I took up tae-kwon-do to learn how to defend myself."

I remembered my ex-boyfriend's temper, stinging slaps so sudden the shock hurt worse than the physical pain, the nagging ache of pulled hair, the daily selection of my clothing based on the location of a purple bruise.

"Tae-kwon-do grew into an outlet for my frustration and for my stress. It didn't hurt my grace, if that's what you want to call it, either."

"What's your favorite move?"

"Roundhouse followed by an axe kick."

Daniel clapped his hands. "Will you show me?"

"I'll make you a deal. You tell me what makes metal shatter, and I'll impress you with my tae-kwon-do prowess."

"No." Daniel snapped. "What's in the box is personal."

"Sorry. I'm pressing you. I shouldn't—"

"I'm sorry," Daniel said. "I just don't—I've never told—It's something from my time overseas." He spat out the words. "I was with the Army Special Forces."

Curiosity gnawed at me, but the set of his jaw, the way he stumbled over his words, pained me.

"I don't talk about it, generally," Daniel said, "ever, at all, really." He pinched his forehead. "There was a—" Daniel closed his eyes. Swallowed. "I had—"

"Stop. You don't have to talk about anything just because I pushed or opened something I shouldn't have. Tell me about it when you're ready."

Daniel nodded.

"In the meantime, I'll still give you a preview of my skills."

Daniel grinned. I set down my glass, and we moved to the center of his den. I felt awkward, standing there in the morning sunlight in my jogging shorts and tank top, getting ready to attack a man whose build and demeanor so vastly surpassed my own in potential for ferocity.

I cleared my throat. "Ready? I'm not going to do it hard."

He beckoned me forward. "Try it," he said. The light in his eyes was dancing, daring me.

I raised my eyebrows.

"Go for it." He chuckled.

I planted my left foot, twisting my hips and bringing my right foot forward to his face. He ducked the kick, and my right foot landed. I spun on it, raising my left leg, flexing my foot, and bringing it back down in a chopping motion toward his neck. He blocked it with his forearm. He then caught my calf and pulled it forward. My other foot slid on the rug. Off balance, I fell backward and hard onto the floor. I looked up at him towering above me, his hand outstretched to pick me up. I wasn't taking it. I used my legs as scissors and clipped him around the ankles. He fell, too, toward me, but I twisted out of the way and stood up. He smiled when I offered him my hand. He grabbed it and pulled me down, catching me before I could land on him, and rolling me over so he was on top, pinning me with his legs. I squirmed, trying to escape, shift his balance. It was pointless. I gave up, panting. He was panting, too, his hands on my wrists, our sweat intermingling, his face so close to mine I could feel his breath on my lips, the cool silver cross he wore around his neck resting on my breastbone. I felt like I would never be able to catch my breath.

"You give up?" he teased.

I squirmed again, and he pushed his body even closer.

"If I could gain any leverage, I could knee you in the groin, and then you'd be the one giving up."

He instantly let go and sat to my side. I sighed, disappointed.

"I wasn't expecting you to attack me." I pushed myself up so I was sitting next to him. I rubbed my wrists.

He grinned. "So that's passable for a frontal attack. But I was expecting more from a black belt."

"You want me to show you more?"

Daniel pulled me up to a stand, holding onto my arms, holding me close enough to kiss. "What if you were trying to take me down and my back was facing you?" He turned around. I saw his muscles tense, as if he was expecting a hard hit.

I frowned.

"Go ahead. Try me."

I felt awkward again. He was standing so close my knees almost touched his legs. And he wanted me to attack him again. I considered my options. I could try to trip him.

"I don't know," I said. "This is a weird angle for starting a fight."

"Just see if you can get a kick in."

The situation felt wrong. I wasn't trained to attack someone when his back was turned.

"Humor me."

I wondered if he was playing a trick on me.

"I'm ready, Jonie."

I could start out striking a sensitive area, like his kidneys. Or I could knock the wind out of him and then go for a harder punch. But he stood so close; it would be like I was attacking someone who trusted me, like a friend. Then it hit me—what he was trying to sucker me into doing.

CHAPTER 25

"You're trying to see how I would've taken down Abby!" I said.

Daniel turned around. The look on his face, like a boy caught trying to glue back together a china vase his baseball shattered, told me my suspicion hit dead on; and he hadn't expected me to realize it. I wanted to kick him for real. Then I wanted to kick myself even harder.

"So that's what this was all about?" I felt violated. My fists were clenched, and I could feel my face heating up. I was shaking again. "You said I wasn't a suspect. I didn't attack Abby. I didn't kill her. You can test me all day long, hook me up to a lie detector—whatever it takes—but I didn't do anything to Abby."

I sidestepped around him and walked to the kitchen. I spun around to face him. He remained in the middle of the room, and his face had changed from chagrin to another clouded expression that I couldn't read.

"If the killer attacked Abby from behind, that's—" I tried to hold my eyelids open to prevent tears from falling. I failed. "It takes one bastard to know another. Or maybe you killed Abby! That makes just about as much sense as—"

"Jonie," he said, his voice a shade louder than a whisper. "I'm sorry. I never thought it was you. But—someone else—I just wanted to eliminate suspicions."

"What? Someone else?"

Daniel looked away.

"Someone else?" My voice broke. "You can tell that someone else to—"

My arms were still shaking loosely, and I didn't trust myself to respond further. I stormed out of the house and slammed the door. It was only when my feet stumbled on the sidewalk two houses down that I realized I'd left my apartment key on Daniel's table. I considered climbing up the porch and breaking into my apartment like Phaser, but I turned around. Daniel answered his door with my key in his hand.

I grabbed it before he could say anything, turned, and promptly tripped on a loose brick step, falling to the walkway. Blood trickled from a cut on my knee, and my knuckles were scraped from where I'd clutched the key and hit the pavers. I bit my lip and fought off tears of humiliation.

Daniel dropped to his knees at my side.

"I'm sorry," he said. "Are you okay? Come inside, and I'll clean that up. I need to fix those bricks."

"Get away," I cried, pushing his arm off mine and shoving myself away and up. Despite the stinging scrapes and weakness in my joints from my morning run, I jogged off— the faster I distanced myself from him, the better—still fighting my shame at falling for him, for falling for his game of play-fighting, for falling for yet another man whose intentions were not what they should have been. *Jonie moves back to Wilmington only to find nothing has changed—nothing about her family, nothing about herself or the situations she continuously puts herself in*, I thought, maliciously racking my brain for other self-deprecating headlines that could sum up my life. *Jonie: 'Kick Me' sign on forehead visible to all but herself.*

Phaser stood outside his apartment, painting the trim around his door and wearing baggy, threadbare denim coveralls. Flecks of white paint contrasted with the freckles spotting his face.

The sign on the door to Phaser's apartment read "PC Physician" and showed a cartoon of a computer with a frowning face on its monitor, and sizzles and sparks sprouting from it like hair. A cardboard square painted red hung from the door handle by a piece of green yarn and read, "The Disk Doc is IN." Most of Phaser's computer repair customers were his old school pals and others who found out about his business by word of mouth.

Phaser saw me coming and caught my arm, smearing white paint on my skin in the process.

"What happened to you?"

He steered me inside, released me at his dilapidated plaid couch, and disappeared into his kitchen. I plopped down on the sagging couch and wiped my tears, trying to regain control by distracting myself with an examination of his apartment.

Computer parts littered every flat surface of his den: counter tops, the mantel, the top of the television, the floor, but I knew Phaser could recall exactly where he had placed anything on demand. A disco ball near the window refracted light as it lazily rotated in the slight breeze the ceiling fan created. A poster of a voluptuous model in a swimsuit that looked tailored for a toy doll was tacked to one wall. Though Phaser was my age, from the appearance of his room, he seemed stuck in early adulthood.

Phaser returned with some wet paper towels and a brown bottle.

"Not hydrogen peroxide," I moaned.

He pressed a towel against my knee, mopping up blood. Then he doused another towel with the peroxide. I squirmed at the fizzing sensation as he dabbed it on my wound.

"What are you crying for?"

I felt ridiculous. I was behaving like a child. "I was jogging, and I tripped." It wasn't exactly a lie. I noticed an ironing board in the corner that hadn't yet been smothered with computer parts. A black suit on a hanger darkened a doorway.

"Are you going to Abby's funeral?" he asked. "We can go together, if you stop crying and bleeding. I'm taking the Harley."

"You don't want to take my truck? Sure, it doesn't have air conditioning, but it too makes a statement."

Phaser shook his head. "I'm driving. Don't you need to get all fussed up? Down here, proper ladies need at least three hours to prepare to set foot outside a doorway, and six for an important event, so—"

"Thanks." I stood up, at once thankful to have a reason to dismiss myself, relieved to have someone to be with at Abby's funeral, and dreading what the ceremony would bring.

CHAPTER 26

Abby had been cremated. The outdoor ceremony, presided over by a minister, was surprisingly brief and more sentimental than religious. The funeral had been a popular event. Even though no chairs had been set on the bluff, lush with grass so healthy it looked wet beside my once black flats, I felt crowded by the standing funeral-goers. The bluff fell steeply to the Cape Fear River where Abby had focused her research. The river looked blue at a distance, but close up I knew it to be clouded and chalky brown. The tide was falling, so the water hurried out briskly, as if trying to purge the city of some transgression hidden in the water's depths. Only a couple of blocks south of the downtown tourist section where Nun St. plunges to the river, and just north of the port where cargo ships docked to unload truck-sized containers, the bluff offered a view of an ancient tugboat slowly decaying beside the wild, forested acres across the river.

The funeral ended with Martha and Mrs. Pridgen solemnly releasing Abby's ashes into the river. Then after a pause, the bluff came to life slowly, beginning with somber hugs and swelling into giggles and even laughter. If the bystanders weren't dressed in black, the gathering might have been mistaken for a large picnic or a high school reunion. I noticed my family nearby. Vicki was whispering something to my father, probably complaining about the ceremony's lack of religious pomp. I thought the funeral provided just the right combination of humanity and holy conviction, not that I was in any shape spiritually to be a divining rod.

I recognized roughly half of the hundred or so persons gathered, even if I couldn't remember names. They had been Abby's friends—ahead of me in school. Then there was a smaller group of older adults, Abby's family and their miscellaneous friends, and a group that looked like colleagues from the university, including Ballings and Kipling, her waist-length black hair remaining strangely straight and untangled.

It was as if some cosmic switch had been flipped. Most everyone gabbed away as if one of the best of us had never died, as if Abby hadn't been killed, as if the killer wasn't at large. Phaser wandered with Kimmie to a group I knew from high school. Vicki and my father went to talk to the group from the university. I stayed rooted, my cotton skirt hugging my hips and thighs in the late-afternoon breeze, watching the swirling mirth around me and feeling distant, almost invisible, existential, as if I weren't really there, and the funeral hadn't really happened.

Near the water, Martha spoke with a short, muscular man with pasty skin that looked too smooth, except for the crinkles around his eyes, as if that texture of skin belonged on a child. His eyes were squinted, but the sun on its descent to setting had long since hidden itself behind a low cloud.

. Martha pushed her finger into the man's chest, and with each poke, the man seemed to inflate a bit. First his fists clenched, then his arms fanned out, then the veins on his neck bulged. I stepped closer, within a few feet of them, ready to defend Martha if she needed assistance.

"...full of tact as usual, Mark," Martha said.

"Tact? Look who's wearing—"

"Waiting until now, until Abby's funeral—"

"When else would I see you to—"

"That's not the point." Martha turned away from him.

Mark grabbed her wrist. My leg muscles instinctively tensed, ready to pounce. Martha slapped him with her free hand, and he released her. She stumbled into me. I caught her and noticed Abby's diamond ring on a long necklace. I helped her regain her balance and glared at Mark. He backed a step away.

"Are you okay?" I asked Martha.

She nodded and tottered slightly, then walked away, toward the crowd. Mark took a step in an effort to walk around me and catch Martha, but I blocked him.

"What was all that about?" I asked.

"Move." Mark's lips were drawn tight, almost frowning, his face so taut I couldn't picture a smile on it, ever. I tried to match his voice to the news tip caller, but my memory of the call was too fuzzy.

"I don't appreciate your attitude toward Martha."

"I'm Abby's fiancé."

"Abby broke it off with you."

He flinched as if a horsefly bit him. "We were working things out."

"Where were you the night Abby died?"

"How is that your business?"

"I'm a reporter covering the investigation."

"You're Jonie Waters?"

"You know me?"

"I saw your byline on the story."

"So where were you the night Abby died?"

Mark moved his mouth, but no words came out. After a moment, his voice returned. "I was drinking at the Dirty Bird Lounge downtown."

"Can anyone confirm that?"

"Ask the cops. They ought to know."

"The police are questioning you in relation to her death?" At least Daniel was following another lead, I thought.

"I didn't do it, if that's your next question." He took a step toward me.

I held my ground. "Who else would have motive to kill her?"

"'Who *else*,' did you say? I didn't have any motive to kill her." He took another step toward me; our bodies were almost touching. "I told you, we were getting back together. I loved Abby."

My heart was pounding, my fingers nearly pulsing in rhythm. Mark looked dangerous, sinewy, pent up, explosive. I could see the clogged black pores on his nose.

"Screw you," he whispered and walked away.

The hairs on the back of my neck were standing up, despite the balmy air. I watched him stride up the bluff toward the street, through the bystanders still congregating, still hugging and laughing. I saw a group of women who looked as polished as senior sorority sisters. A couple of them gave each other a handshake that included snapping, clapping, and bumping hips. Kimmie stood among them and laughed. Martha was standing there, too, not smiling or even watching what the women were doing, just looking vacantly into the distance. I walked toward them. Kimmie said something to the group. As one, they turned like a school of fish, grabbing blank-faced Martha, all walking away from me across the bluff, with the exception of Kimmie. I couldn't help but note Kimmie's black, short-sleeved blouse with puffy shoulders and a long black satin bow tied at the base of the v-neck collar. At least the shirt distracted focus from her hair, I thought.

"Nice of you to stick around, Jonie," Kimmie said.

"What were you saying when I walked up?"

Kimmie smiled, which meant she wouldn't answer. "You know," she said airily, cocking her head at an angle, "I look around and I think to myself, as a detective, I think that whoever killed Abby probably is here on this bluff. This is the cast of characters, the inner circle."

"I'll quote you on that."

"Don't tell me you're prostituting Abby again, taking advantage to earn a couple of bucks."

"If I weren't reporting about this funeral for the *Tribune*, someone else would be. And you'd better be glad it's me, Abby's friend, doing the reporting."

"That's the modest Jonie I know."

"I'm just saying that, as her friend, I can do—want to do—a better job with this article than a total stranger."

Kimmie shook her head and walked away. I resisted the temptation to stick out my tongue at her back.

I located Phaser sitting halfway up the bluff amid a throng of his aged high school buddies and walked up to him. His relaxed, square face smiled at me, and I wondered again how a sister and brother could be so different.

"I'll meet you at your bike," I said.

Phaser jerked up to join me, but I gently patted his shoulders.

"Whenever you're ready," I said. "I want to be alone for a while."

I was in no mood to be around others, least of all anyone who would want me to hold up my end of a conversation or be pleasant, so I quickly climbed the bluff. When I reached the top, I caught a movement beneath a nearby live oak. It was Daniel, dwarfed by the shaded trunk, almost camouflaged against its wood. I caught my breath. He held my eyes and took a step toward me. My heart continued its heavy hammering, and I hoped it wasn't because I was attracted to him; he wasn't watching me because he was attracted to me. He was watching me because I was Jonie, the suspect, one of Kimmie's 'cast of characters.' I let the breeze blow my hair to hide my face and quickened my pace until I reached Phaser's motorcycle, parked parallel to the curb next to a 10-foot stone wall so ancient that ferns, leafy weeds, and vines grew from its cracks. I sat down. Phaser's bike shielded me from the view of passing pedestrians. I tried to slow my breathing, calm myself. I concentrated on watching the shadows climbing the wall as the sun set, the sky turning to blue-gray, then pink, then purple. I listened to mourners steadily leaving the cemetery, their footsteps scraping the rough pavement.

I thought about Abby's funeral, about the spectators who could laugh and goof off as if nothing had happened. I thought about the fight between Martha and Mark. I wondered if Martha would give Mark the engagement ring back. Mark was intimidating. His hesitation and resistance made me doubt he was really at the Dirty Bird the night Abby died. I had learned the hard way not to trust men with violent tendencies. Had he fathered Abby's baby? Had Ballings? The professor seemed too friendly with Trish. What had he been like with Abby, with whom he had shared a tight office? What wasn't Ballings telling police? Did he shoot Kipling's window? Was Kipling's accusation about taking credit for Tracey Miles' work true? And what about the key I found in Ballings' office? What did it unlock?

"Have you been sitting here, hiding behind my motorcycle, all this time?" Phaser asked, his voice making me jump.

I dusted myself off. "Have you forgotten I'm less of a social creature than you? Being here alone was good."

"Prepare for some togetherness. I accepted an invitation to a family dinner for you. We're meeting the folks and Kimmie at Jonah's Restaurant. Since I'm your ride, I figure you don't have a choice."

Dinner with my family had the potential to be more depressing than Abby's funeral. I contemplated walking the 20 minutes home but knew the blocks would drag by, the way I was feeling. I consented and squeezed on Phaser's spare helmet.

On the way to dinner, my arms wrapped around Phaser's waist, the wind flattening my clothes against my body, my mind swirled while my stomach felt heavy. I wouldn't be able to eat. I was alive and Abby was dead. And work still awaited me tonight. I had an article to write—the article about Abby's funeral. How could I begin to put into words the hollowness I felt inside, the loss of Abby and who she was, what her death meant, what her funeral meant; something that words could never capture, anyway?

CHAPTER 27

The Waters clan was halfway through dinner at Jonah's Restaurant, and I was on my third glass of sweet tea before I began to consciously loosen my tense shoulder muscles. The gesture was a mistake; I should have kept my fight-or-flight reflexes at the ready. Despite feeling as if my stomach was full of rocks, I tried to at least enjoy the atmosphere. I had joined the rest of the family around a table hidden beneath a spotless white cloth at one of the downtown restaurants which were strategically placed along the riverfront in order to suck in hapless tourists and charge them nearly a six pack's price for one bottle of beer. I would have ordered one of those over-priced beers—or, better, a refreshing cosmopolitan—but figured Vicki's denial that her saintly family had anything to do with alcohol—despite her uncle's several unsuccessful stints in various rehabs—would remain best unchallenged.

Dinner had been civil enough, quiet enough. As typical, my family ate in silence intermittently interrupted by brief spells of small talk on nothing remotely personal. Kimmie was pretending like I didn't exist, a courtesy I graciously returned, and my father and Vicki were acting as if they didn't notice our estrangement. What I despised almost as much as them refusing to confront us, or at least acknowledge that they knew we were at odds, was that my father's lilac tie and handkerchief matched the sash on Vicki's dress perfectly.

Phaser simply concentrated on shoveling food into his mouth.

Then my father asked Vicki about her plans for the upcoming week. Apparently, she and Kimmie were attending a mother-daughter tea at a neighbor's home on Figure Eight Island. Vicki droned on about the house they were to visit. It was one of the island's largest beachfront homes, recently remodeled with the addition of marble flooring throughout the downstairs, fireplaces both upstairs and down, an upper deck that included a lap pool and views of both the Atlantic and the Intracoastal Waterway, and other various amenities that made the residence sound more like a mansion than a quaint, southern beach house.

I imagined what attending the tea party with my own mother would be like, if she was around. We'd giggle at our failure to comply with the etiquette, secretly compete over whose pinkie finger extended the furthest from the cup, and slurp only loud enough for each other to hear. Of course, the mother in my fantasy was sober, and she wasn't too lethargic to leave the house or too greedy to give up an afternoon of painting. She was my mother from my earliest memories, not the woman she became before she left.

"Didn't you say the woman who owns the home is one of your customers, mom?" Phaser asked.

Vicki nodded, her stiff bob wobbling smugly in the motion.

"Who else is going?" my father asked.

"Just mothers and daughters of the island," Vicki said, listing a few of the mother-daughter pairs. "The Pridgens are attending, too." She went on to explain how the menu would include the hostess' renowned homemade biscotti.

"Biscotti with tea?" I asked.

"Why don't you bring along Jonie?" my father said.

Vicki put down her fork.

"That's okay," I said quickly. "I—"

"Do you have other plans?" my father asked.

"No, but—"

"You should go. It would be a way to say you're back, reacquaint yourself with our neighbors."

"They're not expecting her," Vicki protested, an edge to her voice. "RSVPs were required a month ago, and the tea is next weekend."

Kimmie shook her head.

"I'm sure there's more than enough tea to go around." My father leaned back.

My stepmother began to protest but then pursed her lips and nodded once, her nose almost crinkling as if she smelled rotting meat. I wondered if my father realized the extent of our mutual discontent. Instead of revealing it, Vicki picked up her fork again and turned her attention to her daughter.

"How is your work going, Kimmie?"

Looking from mother to daughter, their red hair and unusual height matched, but I wondered how Vicki truly felt about Kimmie's choice of profession, which contrasted so wildly with how Vicki spent her days at her spas, coifing and manicuring, buffing and pampering.

Kimmie smiled, like her face was a once shadowed field suddenly showered in sunlight, like she had been waiting for Vicki's question.

"My work is—" Kimmie paused for effect— "interesting. You know how the Cooperative Center for Marine Biology professor's lab was found torn apart? We classified it as vandalism, but it looked like an ape attacked it. We took fingerprints off the desk and found a very, very interesting match that was already on file." She looked at me, her eyes sparkling familiarly.

"Whose file did they match?" Vicki prompted, cocking her head in mock ignorance.

"The prints were Jonie's!"

I had been prepared for this. I knew my prints would be found among others in the lab.

"I didn't vandalize the room," I said, keeping my voice steady. "As you know, Kimmie, I merely looked around the desk to see if something obvious had been taken."

"Of course you didn't have anything to do with the crime," Kimmie said. She smirked at me. "It's just what I find interesting is that when we ran the prints, you were already in the system."

I glared at Kimmie. I hadn't been expecting this. I knew my fingerprints were on record, but Kimmie teaming with Vicki to dramatically unveil it was a new low.

"Why would Jonie's prints be in the system?" my father asked.

"Do you want to tell them, or do you want me to break the news?" Kimmie asked.

CHAPTER 28

I was speechless. Phaser had stopped eating.

Kimmie used the pause to take the initiative. "After Jonie's prints were found as a match, I looked to see why they were in the system. Apparently, a couple of years after moving to Tennessee, Jonie assaulted the boy she ran away to Nashville with. She put him in the hospital."

Vicki quickly dabbed her mouth with her napkin.

My father stared at me as if he expected me to expound, but the words weren't even lost between my stomach and my throat; the words simply weren't there. I thought back to that night. I remembered the icy, concrete outdoor stairwell, dim lighting beside the long faded third-story apartment door, hands tightening around my throat, me twisting to break away, smashed eggs and scattered apples from my plastic grocery bag on the landing, me clawing, kicking, and the blur of a heavily jacketed figure jittering down those dozen steps to the lower landing.

"I don't understand," my father said.

"She beat up her boyfriend so bad, he had a broken collarbone, a concussion, and a number of other injuries. He had to suffer through 32 stitches, once it was all said and done, right Jonie?" Kimmie took a swig of her ice water. "Jonie was arrested, taken to jail, fingerprinted, everything."

"It was self defense!" Phaser shouted, banging his fist on the table, silverware jangling.

I jumped. I rarely had seen Phaser angry, or choosing to take sides between me and Kimmie. Diners surrounding us turned and stared.

"You knew about this, Philip?" my father asked.

I noted the use of Phaser's formal name, a telltale giveaway of my father's rising anger.

"I asked Phaser not to tell you," I said. "It was my problem, my life."

"Fantastic." Vicki fanned her face with her fingers. "You're making me invite a convict to a mother-daughter luncheon."

"I'm not a convict. The charges were dropped. It was self defense. And it was years ago."

"You broke his collarbone, gave him a concussion—"

"He fell down a stairway," I said.

"She was lucky he didn't die," Kimmie said. "Then she would have a murder rap to contend with. Involuntary manslaughter at the least."

"I was lucky I wasn't kicked down the stairwell first," I said.

"Bless your heart. That poor boy," Vicki mused. "He was always so pleasant. His mother was PTA secretary and sold the best pies at the Wrightsville Lutheran bakery sales."

"What would you know about him?" I asked. "Did you ever ask me about my life while I was living with you? And just because someone is churchy and well-to-do, or makes good pies, it doesn't make them or their offspring nice. You ought to know that from personal experience." I glared at Kimmie.

She still was smirking, calm and cool as the ice water she was using to hide her amusement from my father. She had procured exactly what she wanted. She had revealed one of my most personal secrets, riled me to anger, all the while remaining collected and distant. It was Kimmie's MO, that well rehearsed teaming of her and Vicki on one side and me on the opposite. I pushed up from the table and found the restrooms before I overcame my self-restraint.

The bathroom's heavy wood door swished shut behind me, muffled the noise of the restaurant, and left me alone. The white bathroom felt clean. I didn't know whether I should

144

lock myself in a stall and cry, or scream and break something. Why was I so frequently roused to such anger against Kimmie? Had I not matured at all? I thought I was ready to forgive, if not forget. Why couldn't I move on, rise above? Soft classical music played from a speaker hidden behind a glass vase of fake day lilies so realistic I felt the petals to confirm my hunch. I leaned forward on the sink counter and frowned at my reflection in the mirror.

Remembering that night in Tennessee somehow tired me. Gray circles ringed my eyes. My head ached. I found the old scar that twisted up from my lip and wondered why I hadn't ended my relationship with the man who had punched me so hard my skin ripped when I had been the one to visit the emergency room, months before that icy evening. I consoled myself by telling myself I wouldn't do the same again, would dump any boyfriend who even hinted at signs of abuse, that I was stronger and smarter now, but I also wondered—even though I knew it was a moment of extreme self-pitying—what was wrong with me, why I wasn't loved. Despite knowing in my brain these thoughts were false—that nothing was wrong with me and that I was loved by Phaser and by my father at the very least, in my soul, the feelings seemed true at moments like these. Where was my mom when I needed her?

I ran hot water over my hands, shook them dry, and reentered the restaurant.

"I'm sorry," I said, after I settled into my seat at the dinner table. "I shouldn't have said that last bit."

"There's a lot that shouldn't have been said tonight," Phaser said. I noticed that he still had not resumed eating.

"Now, now, Philip," Vicki said. "Kimmie was merely answering my question about how her work was going."

"It's you, too, mom," Phaser said. "Going on about a mother-daughter tea as if Jonie wasn't sitting right here."

"She's not my daughter," Vicki said, "per se," she quickly added for my father's benefit.

"She's a part of this here family," Phaser said.

"And she's invited." Vicki forced a smile.

CHAPTER 29

"Fancy meeting you here at this early hour," Jason said.

Finding him behind me in line at Port Java House, I was so groggy I could only muster a sleepy hello. "I typically would reply with a catchy comeback, probably something to do with you missing us Waters sisters in action at the funeral yesterday, but I didn't sleep so well last night," I said, noticing Jason also appeared tired.

"Don't tell me the *Tribune's* brew isn't savory enough for aspiring reporter Jonie Waters."

"I see you're in line, too, though."

Jason smiled grimly. The sleeves of his crisp dress shirt were rolled up as usual, and a light blue tie hung loose, begging for tightening already. Not that I modeled business wear in my slightly wrinkled light green, silk button-down top with my hair pulled back into a low ponytail. I simply was glad the bruise on my face from fighting Phaser my first night in town had disappeared, finally.

The coffee line inched forward. After the dinner fiasco with my family last night, I had stayed up writing and rewriting the story about Abby's funeral, e-mailing it to the layout designer just before the deadline. I then stayed up because I was so disheartened I couldn't sleep. When I forced myself to climb into bed, I caught only snippets of slumber. Finally, I decided to start my day early. I wanted to find Jason's article on Ballings and find information on the professor's old assistant,

Tracey Miles. I planned to search the internet and look in the newspaper databases after ordering the largest-sized mocha Port Java offered, complete with the works: whipped cream, rich chocolate syrup, and a chocolate-coated coffee bean.

"I read your article." Jason waggled a rolled-up *Tribune* at me, a hint of cologne momentarily overpowering the coffee smells. "It was hard to read."

I looked at him. Was that a criticism or a compliment?

"It was more emotional than I expected," he said, bouncing on his heels.

I frowned; that didn't clarify his comment. The article was written in third person, as detached and unemotional as any other news article, I thought, but I had typed through tears, squinting to see the screen. I wanted to ask Jason what he meant, but I also felt thankful my turn was up to order coffee, and in the time and confusion between multiple registers and jostling to take the correct cup, Jason and I were separated. I weaved my way out of the store and fished the coffee bean out of the whipped cream before it sank to the bottom. On the sidewalk outside, Jason was on my heels. He chuckled as I used the back of my hand to wipe whipped cream off my lips.

"You're not worried about your waist," he said.

"What did you order? Black coffee?"

"It's simple, straightforward, journalistic, and conventional in a Hemingway-esque fashion, like me."

I nodded, remembering how a younger Jason had been drawn to Hemingway, progressing from reading *The Old Man and the Sea* to reading *A Farewell to Arms*, *The Sun Also Rises*, and the author's collected short stories. I had stopped at the required reading. Any more than that and my surfing schedule would have been adversely impacted.

We stepped in pace toward our building.

"It was a good article," he said, "about a bad event. A tragic event, I should say."

"Thanks. Do you think this means I pass?"

"Pass?" We stepped onto the elevator.

"Do I graduate from the sidekick-to-Jason status at the paper?"

Jason shook his head. "It's just going to be a few weeks with me. Look at it more as a way of integrity and quality control than writing school, a way for the *Tribune* to do everything possible to ensure we're getting a solid reporter. Not that I can't already vouch for your journalistic integrity, having witnessed your budding years and the shockingly frank documentary you aired the evening you left."

My face instantly flushed. So there it was—the past—dredged up, no longer an avoided issue. I was spared a response, not that I could have conjured one, because the elevator pinged open at our floor. We silently walked to our desks.

As I booted up my computer and logged into the *Tribune's* system, I downed my mocha as if it were an antidote to all the different emotions: my shame and confusion, anger and glee, and terrible sorrow and emptiness, that I had saved from that distant night. Emotions so visceral I felt as though I stored them, corked inside me, like a vial of poison slowly leaching. Finally, even the dregs of my coffee drained, I focused on my computer screen.

I looked up Ballings again on the internet, this time limiting my search to *Tribune* articles. Jason's previous article appeared, along with a photo of Ballings in his laboratory, his arm draped around a microscope. Behind him, the counters were clean and orderly. In the opposite corner from Ballings, I noticed a tennis shoe. The person—I couldn't tell if the shoe was masculine or feminine—wearing the shoe was cut off, probably leaning away from the camera's angle of view. Was that Abby? Was it Jason? Though Jason had said his first time in Ballings' lab was when it had been vandalized, Ballings recognized Jason when we cornered the professor in a classroom. Stu's name was on the photo credit. Perhaps Jason had interviewed Ballings somewhere other than his office. I scanned the article and learned little I didn't already know. Ballings began teaching at the center last fall and had signed on for a two-year stint. The name of his decades-old saltwater parasites study was given, and I ran another internet search using its title.

That search brought me to a one-paragraph synopsis of the study, listed as one of a number of research studies conducted at a New Jersey university. In the synopsis, Ballings was listed as a co-author of the study, along with Tracey Miles. I then searched for Miles on the internet.

Surely, if Ballings' claim to fame was the study, the same study had granted Miles celebrity as well. But after multiple searches, none of the Tracey Miles links that popped up were related to the parasites study. I pulled up another search engine that accessed newspaper archives across the nation, narrowed my searches, and finally got what I was looking for—Miles' obituary and an accompanying newspaper article.

Her full name was given, along with family and personal information, and the dates of her life. Miles had died weeks before she would have finished her graduate degree. She died at age 25 after a severe asthma attack. Ballings hadn't lied about that. But a related news article gave me information Ballings had failed to reveal—that the two were housemates and that Ballings was driving Miles to the hospital for treatment for the asthma attack when Miles lost consciousness, never to recover. The article also stated that the attack may not have been fatal if Miles had reached the hospital earlier.

I leaned back in my chair. Even if Kipling insinuated Ballings was taking Miles' credit for the research, that didn't mean Ballings had killed Miles. The newspaper article didn't say Ballings had postponed driving Miles to the hospital after realizing his partner needed care. I wondered if Ballings had known more about the research he had conducted with Miles than he knew about his research with Abby. Were the relationships similar?

From my desk drawer, I picked up the key I found at the center and slowly twirled it between my fingers. I wondered what the key opened, if Ballings knew about the key and would miss it, and if I should have taken it in the first place. Now that I had the key, I couldn't turn it over to the police without rousing their suspicions against me again, which would result in Kimmie ratting to the police chief, who would tattle to my publisher, Montgomery. I'd be fired. So determining what the key opened was left to me. I ran my fingers over the square ridges. And then it hit me.

The key looked exactly like one my father used to own for a safe deposit box. Could this be Abby's safe deposit key? What bank would Abby have used? Dozens were located in the area. I could call Mrs. Pridgen and ask where Abby banked, but then I would have to explain why I wanted to know. Mrs. Pridgen probably would want the key returned to her before she told me where Abby banked. So I decided to tell a little fib, to disguise my voice and lie to Mrs. Pridgen. I looked up the Pridgens in the phone book, waited until Jason left his desk, took a deep breath, and wished my office chair had a seat belt.

"Hello, Mrs. Pridgen?" I used a nasal voice. "This is Callie Burgess from the Ogden University Finance Department."

"Yes?" Mrs. Pridgen's voice sounded bone weary.

"Our records show that we have a remainder of an equipment deposit from Abby that we need to return. Since Abby cannot claim the check in person, our policy mandates that we make the check out to the bank that holds her account, and I needed that name, the name of her bank."

"Live Oaks Bank off College Street," she said automatically in her deflated voice. I cringed with guilt.

"Thank you so much; we'll put that check in the mail right away."

I was evil, I thought, hanging up the phone. Keep Hell's gates open wide, I thought. I was well on my way and continuing my trajectory. Now I needed to determine if the key fit the bank's safe deposit boxes. I decided to visit the bank later in the day.

After the morning staff meeting at the office, the day seemed almost dull. Jason was contacting the police for an update on Abby's death investigation. The following day, the university was holding a memorial service for Abby in the marine center garden that both Jason and I would cover. But today, with only the article on Abby's research to assimilate, I felt utterly unexcited about writing, assisted no doubt by my lethargy from a sleepless evening. I leafed through the notes I had taken in Ballings office, skimming for a good lead-in quote and bemoaning how evasive he had been about the research.

I decided to procrastinate writing the article, at least until the afternoon. I wanted to learn more about Abby's research first. I'd exhausted internet research tools, Ballings' meager knowledge, and Martha's scientific background. I stood up and straightened my skirt, as usual checking my handbag for my notepad and pen, cell phone and camera.

"Going somewhere?" Jason asked. "You know you're obligated to take me with you if you're going on an interview for an article. In addition to the resultant pleasure my company brings, do I need to remind you about the newspaper's policy?"

"Jason," I began, realizing the impending conversation would be lengthy. I sat down. "I know what Lee said. I know about the *Tribune's* policy for new reporters. I'm not breaking any rules or stepping out of line." I didn't broach the subject of his company.

"So where are you going?"

"The Wilmington wastewater treatment plant. I want to see if anyone there can shed new light on Abby's research, but I'm not writing an article about it, so you can back off."

"Why would you think you could find information about Abby's research at the plant?"

"I don't trust Ballings."

"Do you think Ballings had something to do with Abby's death?"

"The other day, before our interview with Ballings, I overheard him arguing with Kipling. There's something Ballings isn't telling police."

"Like what?"

I shrugged. "But there's that, there's the trashed lab, and he was so vague during the interview. Something's out of whack," I said. "And you also should know I'm going to Southern Skillet tonight. Remember that crumpled page I found in the trash from Kipling's appointment book? She listed a meeting at Southern Skillet the night of Abby's death. I'm going to lie low and see if Kipling has a regular weekly meeting there, and if so, who she's seeing. It could be Ballings. And if it is, I'm going to see if I can overhear anything, but not for an article; so there's no need for you to be my shadow."

"You're seriously going beyond reporting. This dedication borders on harassment—or detective work."

"Don't you trust the police to do their jobs?" Stu asked, popping above the cubicles. He lacked only a tall yellow hat to pass as Curious George's caretaker. He grinned at Jason's and my surprised faces.

"Oh, hello, Stu," I said, feigning politeness.

Stu nodded and repeated his question.

"Of course I trust the police," I said, though my stomach disagreed with my tongue. Kimmie was busy spreading rumors that I was a suspect and a boyfriend-abuser. And both Daniel and Kimmie seemed to be checking into the wrong person—me. "But following up on leads also is a reporter's duty."

"I'm just saying, you're like one of those little terriers."

I gritted my teeth. Jason shook his head and returned to the story he was writing on his computer.

"Yipping and running around, all this energy going out all these places, looking in trashcans, second guessing your sources. Right, Jason?"

Jason glanced at me, and the creases on his forehead made him appear concerned. "I go about things differently, definitely a lot less disbelieving of authorities and subjects whom I've interviewed, but that doesn't make Jonie's methods wrong, necessarily."

"I just want Abby's death resolved," I said. "If I can do anything that helps figure out why she was killed or help identify her killer—" I cut my ranting short as another fellow reporter passed nearby. I stood up again. I'd had enough of basking in the fluorescent office lighting. It was time for fieldwork.

CHAPTER 30

"It ain't no botanical garden," said a man as broad as two Phasers put together and easily taller than six feet. George Tyson was Wilmington's wastewater management director, friendly and jocular, showing me around the city's wastewater treatment plant with pride that rivaled a Yellowstone park ranger narrating a sightseeing hike.

The smell of Wilmington's sewage wasn't as awful as I anticipated. Though I could smell the underlying odor heavy on the air, the stench wasn't overwhelming.

"The stink varies day to day," he said, "depending on weather and how many citizens eat Mexican for dinner." He chuckled.

One of the benefits of being a reporter was learning—constantly learning about whatever subject an article covered—so I wasn't surprised that I enjoyed discovering more about how wastewater was treated. Tyson's enthusiasm for his plant and thorough explanations made him an excellent educator.

First, the plant filtered out solids from the wastewater using a screen and then again using a large circular vat that also generated greasy scum. The water then moved to another tank where bacteria removed organic materials and nutrients, "sort of like how your body digests waste," Tyson said. The waste again was transported through filter beds that removed the bacteria before the water was released to pipes that emptied into the Cape Fear River.

Having completed the tour, the time for asking my controversial questions arrived. I asked if the plant treated the wastewater for pharmaceuticals.

"Not specifically. I know there's been hype about pharmaceuticals in wastewater lately, but there ain't been no solid evidence showing it has any effect on anything."

"But the treated wastewater flows into rivers and lakes, and some of those are drinking water supplies."

"Public Utilities also treats water they take in to make it safe for consumption."

"What about fish kills?" I asked.

"You think there's been fish killed by pharmaceuticals in treated wastewater?"

"I don't know. I'm just asking."

"Pharmaceutical fish kills. That's a new one." He laughed. "I'd be more worried about coliform bacteria from human waste spilling into the water—or nitrogen and phosphates from fertilizers, which can cause algae growth that sucks out oxygen from the water. It's raw sewage spills that can kill fish, not pharmaceuticals."

I thanked Tyson for his time, tallied another dead end to my research, and headed to Abby's bank. On the way, I considered my options for finding out whether the key opened one of the bank's safe deposit boxes. I didn't want to present Abby's key, only to find out that, since I wasn't Abby, I couldn't open the box. I didn't want the key confiscated.

Entering the bank with its cushioned carpet, plush chairs, and tile flooring so polished it reflected, I was struck by how comically opposite it was from the purely functional, metal warehouse-feeling wastewater treatment plant I'd just left. I walked up to the bank's customer service counter, hoping the stink of the wastewater treatment plant hadn't followed me.

"May I help you?" Though balding, the employee behind the desk had a thick, neatly trimmed mustache.

"Hello," I began. I smiled.

The employee allowed a perfunctory smile.

"I'm sorry to bother you," I continued, "but my ex-roommate had a safe deposit box here a while back. She left, and I found a key when I was cleaning, and I couldn't figure out what it opened. I just was driving by and had the thought that maybe the key I found belonged to her box here."

"Do you have the key with you?"

"No, unfortunately," I lied. "But I was wondering if I could see what one of your safe deposit keys looks like."

"Let me check with my supervisor."

The man left and returned a minute later and displayed a key in his hand. I frowned. While both the bank key and Abby's key had square ridges and a silver coloring, the bank's key was twice as long and made of a higher grade metal.

"No?" the man asked.

"No," I said, explaining the differences.

"Your key sounds like it might open a breaker box," the man said. "Or, ask your roommate if it fit a cabinet of some sort."

"Thanks," I said, trying not to sound too dejected.

I climbed into my truck as stumped as ever. At least I had gained a new idea. Perhaps the key fit a breaker box, not that I had seen any breaker boxes at the university. Of course I hadn't been looking for them either and probably wouldn't be allowed to check the key against any boxes on the center's property openly, anyway. Nor did I have any inkling why Abby would hide a key to a breaker box. Probably it just fell into the window track during the vandalism. I drove home for a shower and change of clothes.

Though Southern Skillet dishes were undeniably Southern cooking at its best, I had trouble picturing Kipling at one of the pockmarked tables. While the Skillet wasn't necessarily a dump, the house-turned-restaurant fell a tick shy of homey. Its wrap-around porch now slanted precariously in places, especially when more than one person walked on it. A couple of cats with matted fur prowled around the parking lot. I remembered a past occasion when a meal was interrupted by a cook chasing one of the cats through the eating area and out the door. Inside, a thin layer of dust coated the petals of the fake flowers stuck in cheap glass vases on the mismatched tables. Ancient, colorless photos of persons long dead hung from the food-speckled, yellowing walls that most likely were last painted when the portraits' specimens were alive. The portraits' solemn black eyes looked eternally hungry, I thought, which made me feel self-conscious. I didn't know how the restaurant passed its inspections, but the food tasted delicious enough that customers always packed the dining area and, like me, didn't mind overlooking a little grime and fur.

I wondered why Dean Kipling, a middle-aged English woman—a woman wound so tight that I expected her to spin off like a tornado any moment and so proper that her business suits looked like they were ironed while on her body—would come to run-down, low-down Southern Skillet. I glanced around the restaurant, searching for an inconspicuous location to set up my post. Southern Skillet's policy was to seat yourself and hope the one waitress servicing the entire floor noticed you before you had to flag her down and receive a dirty look and poor service in exchange for your impatience. I was glad for the crowd and hoped Kipling wouldn't spot me when she arrived. I chose a corner table under a conveniently burnt-out light bulb and looked at the daily specials on a chalkboard over the door to the kitchens.

I heard the door slam shut again and glanced over. Stu had arrived. I didn't know whether to smile or groan.

CHAPTER 31

Stu headed straight for my table. "I couldn't let my number one lady friend dine alone."

"What about Kimmie? I thought she was your lady friend," I kidded.

"Cool down. I only meant to say that dining alone is depressing." Stu slid into the seat opposite mine. "Plus, I want to be a witness if anything goes awry."

"Like?"

"Like the restaurant gets torn apart, vandalized, or Kipling ends up dead. I can vouch for you, or at least give Jason an eye-witness interview from the experience."

I was working up a snappy retort when Kipling walked through the door. I moved my face so that Stu's blonde-white curls hid my face.

"Is Kipling here?" Stu whispered.

I nodded and peeked around him. Kipling was walking away from us. She settled at a table near the other side of the room, far enough away that she most likely wouldn't notice us beyond the dozens of diners between us.

"She just sat down over there." I tipped my head in her direction. "No! Don't look! I don't want her to see us."

"She doesn't know you dug through her trash and her appointment book. What do we do now?"

"We wait," I said. "Wait and see who else shows up. And eat."

The waitress paused by our table, and Stu asked for sweet tea and a dinner plate with chicken fried steak, mashed potatoes and gravy, macaroni and cheese, and blueberry cobbler. I ordered the same, substituting fried okra for the macaroni.

Stu looked like he was trying to come up with something to talk about, which was surprising for him since his mouth always ran. I leaned back and watched him think. He looked like he was chewing an enormous wad of bubble gum.

"You dating anybody, Jonie?" It came out as almost a tease, but his voice also sounded tense.

I frowned and hoped he wasn't working up to asking me out. While Stu had made some screwball comments that suggested he could be interested in me, he also had shown attraction to every other female he had come across while we worked together, especially Kimmie.

"Can't you come up with anything better to talk about?" I asked.

"It was just a question."

I knew better than that. "I don't date colleagues."

"I'm not talking about me, but even if I was, technically we're not colleagues, seeing as you're not a permanent staff member."

Now that was endearing, I thought. Really, I wanted to flick his forehead, but our sweet tea arrived. I took a big gulp.

"No offense," Stu continued, "but you're not my type. Not only are we from different generations, but I go for the pleasurably exotic. You're built for practical living—not too model-ly, not too beefy—practical, like your face. You're no Barbie, but you're no troll, either." Stu took a slurp of tea, oblivious to my reddening face. "Besides, you're too intense for me. It's like you're driven or something. I like my women loose—no, no, not like that—loose meaning able to let go and have a good time."

My teeth were clenched so tight they felt fused together. I peeked around Stu at Kipling, who still sat alone.

"Well?" Stu asked.

"My dating status is none of your business," I snapped, taking my eyes from Kipling. "And regardless of where I fit in between beauty queen and barnyard livestock, I'm hoping that very soon we'll be colleagues. In the meantime, we can continue to be friends."

Stu pawed the air as if he could wave my comment away. "What if it was Jason asking?"

I adjusted my hair barrette to stall for time. What if it was Jason asking? I didn't want to admit that traces of the old attraction to him remained, even if they were well hidden like hairline cracks in bedrock, even if years apart eased the estrangement somehow.

"Come on. I know you like Jason. Everybody likes Jason," Stu said. "Ciao! Amore! Linguini! Rossini! What's not to like?"

I glanced at Kipling, who was saying something to the waitress. I decided not to respond to Stu. Jason didn't appear to have revealed our past relationship to Stu, and I viewed Stu's ignorance positively.

"So?" He persisted.

"So what? I'm not discussing this with you."

"So you're interested in Jason?"

I contemplated flinging my tea at Stu, but the result would be a terrible waste of tea so delicious I could write sonnets about it. "I'm drawing a line, Stu. I am not talking about any of this with you. You and I, we're friends. Friends and future colleagues. Same goes for Jason."

Styrofoam plates piled high with fried delicacies saved us from further argument. I focused on refraining from drooling over my dinner. After digging in, I changed the subject to surfing by asking what kind of board Stu rode.

Stu's response took me through most of my plate, and I was grateful we moved to a safe subject. I occasionally glanced at Kipling who alternately was checking her watch, tapping her fingers on the table, and scribbling in a notebook. As I scooped up the last of my mashed potatoes, Kipling stood and gathered her belongings. No one had joined her, and her face assumed a sour appearance. The waitress came our way, and I flagged her down.

"The woman who is getting ready to leave that table—" I pointed. "Does she come here often?"

The waitress laughed. "Honey, she's a regular. Her and her beau. They come here pretty much every week, she more often than him."

"What does her beau look like?"

"A handsome fellow, like a teddy bear, black and gray hair, good smile, excellent tipper, when he shows up. She's foreign, doesn't know how to tip."

"Does her gentleman friend have facial hair?"

She looked at me curiously. Then she shrugged. "No, but he has that macho stubble thing going for him. Not like some men with hair that looks like a paper napkin could wipe it off." She glanced at Stu, whose chin looked soft, almost plush.

"Thanks." I asked for an order of apple cobbler to go and the check.

"You're getting another dessert?" Stu asked, looking me over. "Where do you put it?"

I ignored his comment. "The waitress' description sounds like Ballings. He has salt-and-pepper hair and a five-o-clock shadow."

Stu fingered his chin. "It's nice only having to shave twice a month."

"I didn't know you had hair that sprouts there," I joked. "How many hairs—four? Five?"

Stu leaned forward. "The ladies like it. It's smooth, doesn't chafe their chins after all-night make-out sessions."

The to-go dessert box arrived, and I put money on the table and bid Stu farewell.

"Same place next week?" Stu asked.

I shrugged, but I was smiling. "I can't keep you from coming."

CHAPTER 32

Students flooded the marine center garden. The overflowing parking lot was dotted with police cars and news vans with satellite dishes raised high. Even a television news helicopter, blades chopping the air with a deafening roar before the crew realized no shot was to be had beneath the trees of the garden, attended Abby's memorial. Jason cussed at the helicopter and muttered something about decency as we elbowed our way to the front of the crowd surrounding the gazebo. Stu separated from us to take photographs.

My father wore his typical crisp black suit with a university-function royal blue tie to match the school's logo. He joined Dean Kipling beneath the gazebo. Her dark eyes were hawk-like, constantly scanning the gathered crowd as if searching for prey. I gave a small start as our eyes met, and then I quickly turned my gaze to Martha, who sat erect in a chair. Her hair still missed its sheen, but her skin color looked healthier than it had at the funeral. I wondered who a vacant chair had been meant for as Kipling removed it and placed it at the side of the gazebo before stepping up to the podium and introducing herself.

After brief statements by Kipling and my father, Martha approached the podium.

"Abby put her soul into this program, into her research. She lived for it." Her voice echoed slightly off the trees. "I always have thought that the best way to live is to have a goal and strive unceasingly to reach it. That's what Abby did in her last days." A tear fell onto the podium.

I glanced at my father, his brow furled, perhaps in concentration; and then I glanced at the dean, whose eyes still darted about the crowd. Who was she looking for?

"Abby said she enjoyed this garden, sitting on its benches, clearing her mind, and getting new insight into her research. And then for her to—die—" Martha opened her mouth as if she had more to say, but then stepped back.

My father gave her a quick hug and invited students to place flowers beside the garden bridge. He and Martha led the procession of faculty and students through the grasses to the creek, roses and daisies and sunflowers limp in their hands, returning to the gazebo empty-handed, light drained from their eyes.

The program clearly over, news reporters pushed toward the stage while the rest of the crowd dispersed.

"I want to talk to Martha," Jason said.

"I'll be around." I sidestepped around him, pushing deeper into the garden, wishing to get away from the crush of the crowd. I could wait for Jason on a bench. Then I looked at the boardwalk rising above the marsh grass where Abby's body had fallen, and my feet followed my eyes.

Out past the pile of flowers, out of the garden's shade on the wide wood, I slid off my dainty eyelet blouse, revealing my blue tank top, so I could feel the sun's warmth on my skin. Abby's death below did not seem possible or real at this moment. With the body bag gone, along with the crime scene tape, and with the broken railing replaced, only the memory of her fallen, injured body remained. I walked on, above the grasses swaying in the gently running water, out past where Abby had lain, out to where the creek's current ran swift and deep. Gulls called to each other in the fresh breeze and dove after minnows beneath the surface. The head of a large sea turtle peeked out from the depths and then vanished again. Nature was callous, I thought. With Abby dead, every day should have been miserable with low gray clouds pelting cold rain.

I jumped at the sound of loud footsteps thundering closer on the boardwalk toward me. Mark, Abby's former fiancé, dressed in all black from his T-shirt to jeans that were tucked tightly into muddied combat boots, was feet from me before I had a chance to react.

CHAPTER 33

"I want to know what you know," Mark said.

I backed away a step down the boardwalk toward the unpopulated section of the garden opposite the gazebo. Mark scowled at me and circled behind me, forcing me to back away in the other direction. I tried to order my feet to stand their ground. I glanced back at the gazebo. It appeared my distress was unnoticed. I thought about how easily I could be pushed off the boardwalk. I wondered if Abby felt vulnerable like this, also, before she fell.

"I said I want to know what you know," Mark repeated.

"About what?"

"About who killed Abby."

"What makes you think I know more than you? Why don't you ask the police?"

"You're a reporter. You have access to stuff."

Mark cussed and backed a step away.

I turned my head and noticed Kimmie walking toward us.

"Look into Ballings," Mark said. "Don't you wonder why he didn't claim his on-stage seat?" He hurried off the boardwalk, past Kimmie, who ignored him.

"What are you doing out here?" Kimmie asked.

Nearly two days had passed since Kimmie tattled to my father about my incident with my ex-boyfriend in Tennessee. Hadn't she done enough damage? Why was she still on the warpath?

"Are you going to answer me?" she asked.

"I'm here for the memorial. The reporter I came with," I said, avoiding Jason's name, "is interviewing Martha. I guess I came out here on the boardwalk to—"

"Meet with Mark?" Kimmie shifted around me so that I had to turn my body to follow her.

"It wasn't an arranged meeting, if that's what you're insinuating. He is your prime suspect, right?"

"I'm not talking to you about this case."

"Mark wanted to know how the investigation was going."

"Why would he ask you?"

"I'm a reporter covering the investigation. Maybe he viewed me as less intimidating than you."

Kimmie faked a laugh and turned her head. I followed her gaze to the Intracoastal Waterway. We watched the islands across the way in silence. I thought about what I had done to Kimmie long ago, before I left town. I supposed I deserved her belligerence and tattling. I wondered when we could call ourselves even. I suddenly wanted to fill the void, to say something—about the past, about my hopes for reconciliation, possibly a relationship.

"Before I left," I began.

Kimmie cleared her throat, but I barged ahead.

"We both did things."

"Jonie—"

"We never really gave each other a chance, or even came to know each other, really—"

Kimmie flicked her hair behind her back futilely. The breeze immediately blew it in front of her shoulder again.

"And I don't know why that is. But I guess what I'm trying to say is—"

"Here comes Jason and that other guy," Kimmie interrupted.

I glanced down the boardwalk. "Jason and Stu," I reminded her, noticing they were followed closely by Daniel, light brown hair tousled but not unkempt, presence formidable but not unapproachable.

166

"Are you getting back together with Jason?" Kimmie asked quickly, before the trio could hear us.

"We work together."

"You might as well, because you're insane if you think you're getting together with Daniel. I've seen how you look at him." Kimmie lowered her voice. "Back off."

The men reached us.

"There you are," Stu said, squeezing between me and Kimmie and fiddling with his camera.

I tried not to snarl as I was forced to step to the side to make room for him. Jason patted my back. "Are you okay?" he whispered.

"I'm not sure if you noticed," Kimmie said loudly, over Jason's voice, addressing Daniel, "but our friends Jonie and Mark decided to have a rendezvous just now. I've had enough step-sisterly conversation for a year, so I'll meet you at our car." She stalked off, back toward the gazebo.

"That seemed pleasant," Jason said, after Kimmie was a few steps away.

"Kimmie's your sister?" Stu cut in. "Kimmie's your sister, and you didn't tell me?"

Jason shifted, and a short laugh escaped from Daniel. His eyes met mine, and he winked so quickly I wondered if he had actually winked at all. I glanced at Jason, who was staring back at the garden and hadn't caught the gesture. I felt my resolve melt a little, despite Daniel's behavior at his house. He nodded at me before following Kimmie back toward the gazebo.

"Come on, Jonie!" Stu was saying. "I thought we were friends."

I turned toward him. "I didn't feel my relation to Kimmie was something you necessarily needed to know."

"Can you give me her number? Please?"

I shook my head.

"Come on," Stu begged. "What will it take? I'll buy you lunch."

Though a free lunch was tempting, I was about to explain to Stu that I wouldn't give Kimmie's number even to my enemy when shouting shattered the garden's silence.

From the elevated boardwalk, I could see two men rolling on the ground near the gazebo, throwing punches. As quickly as the fight seemed to have begun, it was over. Daniel pulled Mark off Ballings and flattened Mark on the ground, handcuffing him.

"I'll kill you!" Mark yelled at Ballings, adding on a string of profanity. Daniel pulled Mark up and shoved him toward the parking lot.

Ballings pushed himself from the ground and began brushing his clothes off. Trish, the student I'd seen with Ballings during our interview, approached him, appearing to try to help, but Ballings swore and she backed away as if she'd been slapped.

"I loved Abby!" Mark yelled from the garden path. "But you—Abby meant nothing to you. You show up late to her memorial with your new girlfriend."

I noticed Kipling watching Mark's retreat silently from the shadow of the gazebo, her eyes dark as black holes.

Mark released another succession of profanity. "I'm coming for you! You killed Abby. I'm going to kill you!"

CHAPTER 34

To my surprise, Phaser accepted my narration of Mark's fight at Abby's memorial with a grim shrug. Phaser had allowed me to cook for him at my apartment, so I had prepared my much-tested pepperoni lasagna recipe in the hope of building his confidence in the limited cooking abilities I acquired since I last lived in Wilmington. We were eating the lasagna and drinking cheap wine. My apartment's windows were open to allow the afternoon breeze to push away the smoke that had resulted when the cheddar from my garlic, cheesy bread dripped over and scorched itself into a permanent grit on my oven's floor.

"Mark," Phaser said, waiving a forkful of lasagna as if he'd anticipated the fight. "The boy's unstable. I wish I'd been there. Seeing him attack the professor would have given me another chance to knock him around."

"Another chance?"

"He tried to follow Abby into the roadhouse the last time she visited, after their engagement was off; but he wasn't counting on me bouncing his butt down the alley." He took another bite of lasagna. "That arrangement is mighty pretty."

I glanced at the flowers I'd bought on sale at the grocery store. My favorite, simple daisies, joined a few delicate yellow roses, spotted pink lilies, and greenery. "Don't change the subject. What happened?"

"I told Mark he wasn't welcome, to quit stalking Abby, that they were done. And that was that."

I shook my head at him.

"I'd seen Mark with Abby at the roadhouse before as a couple, so I recognized him, and that night Abby had asked me to keep an eye out for him. "She said he'd been giving her trouble ever since they broke up."

"Like what?"

"She didn't go into it."

"And you lecturing Mark at the roadhouse—that's all it took for him to leave?"

"He jumped in my face. I punched him up a little, and then he left." Phaser shrugged. "Fights happen sometimes."

I took in the new information. "Before the memorial, I thought Abby might have been killed because of her research. Maybe she'd discovered something, and maybe Ballings wanted sole credit. Now, I think she was killed because of a personal relationship. Witnessing Mark's temper and violence, I'm wondering why the police don't go ahead and arrest him."

"I never liked Mark."

"But Ballings is no prince either. If what Mark told me is true, Ballings was supposed to speak at the memorial, but he skipped out. And he appeared to arrive late to the memorial with a student—her name's Trish—and the way he looks at her, I think something inappropriate is going on between them."

"You're not trying to play civilian detective, are you?"

"I'm just trying to gather information."

"Let Kimmie do her job. She's the detective."

"Kimmie thinks I killed Abby. She's wasting time harassing me while Abby's death is unresolved. I can't sit back and do nothing."

Phaser ignored my last comment and scooped a third helping of lasagna from the pan. Fine, I thought, avoid further discussion; just don't get in my way.

Even from the outside, the Dirty Bird Lounge's name was an obvious misnomer. Because of the darkness outside, I paused by a corner window and scanned the lounge. The bar Mark named as his alibi stood out amid other downtown stores. Bronze palm-frond fans mechanically waved from the ceiling in a constant back-and-forth motion. A few women sat drinking in the corner, and a couple flirted at the far end of the bar. Mark wasn't around. Though business was slow on a weekday night, it appeared that the lounge hadn't changed any in my absence from Wilmington. It remained an upscale bar by night and an eatery by day, frequented by lawyers and other well-groomed clientele among whom I couldn't visualize angry-young-man Mark. The Dirty Bird was anything but unclean. I entered and sidled over to the bar with what I thought might be an innocent smile.

"What can I get for you, honey?" A man barely younger than me with tan skin and curly black hair waved a furry arm. "I've got a delicious merlot you might like."

"Thanks, but I just have a couple of questions," I said. While being called honey by someone my own age was insulting, it gave me hope that the bartender was enough of a homeboy to succumb to my feminine charms, which were shaky at best. "Besides, I'm more of an imported beer drinker."

The man crossed his arms.

"You wouldn't happen to know Mark Listlen, would you?"

"Who's asking?"

"I'm Jonie." I held out my hand. "I write for the *Tribune*, but I'm also a friend of Abby Pridgen."

The bartender paused, then shook my hand. He didn't offer his name in return.

"I don't have anything to say," he said, turning his back on me and grabbing a dish towel.

"I'm not asking for the newspaper." I climbed onto a bar stool. He glanced at my reflection in the mirror behind the bar. "I promise."

He turned around and crossed his arms again.

"I grew up with Abby," I said. "We were next door neighbors. I've been living out of town and have only just come back, and now she's dead."

He untangled his arms; I was wearing him down.

"All I want is to find out who killed her. All I want is justice. I want to ask you about Mark Listlen."

"You're not going to put anything about me in the paper?"

"Nothing."

"You swear this isn't going anywhere?"

"I swear."

He shifted the dish rag back and forth between his hands.

"I don't even know your name, anyway," I added.

"I know Mark," he muttered. "He's a regular, comes here all the time." He noncommittally swiped the rag across the impeccably clean counter.

"All the time?"

"He works a couple of blocks over and comes in during lunch breaks and on weekends. Always drinks Woodies." He pointed to an elegantly shaped bottle containing golden-brown liquid. The label read Woodcroft Reserve. A smaller label identified the bottle's contents as Kentucky straight bourbon whiskey. Potent stuff, I imagined, and from the looks of it, the drink did not come cheap, either. But the drink fit the bar and its clientele.

"Mark doesn't really seem like the kind of folk this bar caters to," I said.

The bartender shrugged.

"So how did you come to know Mark?" I asked.

"I'm friends with Abby. Was friends. Acquaintances, really. So Abby and Mark came by for drinks here. I gave them free tokens to play table soccer upstairs in the rec room."

"Did they seem like a good match to you?"

"Good as any, I guess."

"Mark treated her right?"

He nodded.

"And when they broke up?"

"Mark kept coming here; I haven't seen Abby since." He scowled.

"I bet you wished it was the other way around."

"Who wouldn't? You knew Abby."

"Were you working the night Abby died?"

He stared at me a moment before speaking. "I know where you're going with this, but he didn't kill her."

"That's not what I asked."

"It's what you're getting at."

I nodded. "So Mark wasn't here that night."

"I didn't see him—and yes, he always makes it a point to say hello when I'm working and he comes here—free tokens. That was your next question, right? That's what the cops asked me."

My heart skipped a beat. Mark had lied about his alibi! Mark had lied, and Daniel and Kimmie were checking into him, too.

"Look, lady, I'm telling you, Mark didn't kill her."

"I'm no longer 'honey?'"

"He didn't kill her."

"How would you know?"

"Because Mark loved her. He was crazy about her."

"Crazy can be good, but it can be just as bad." I certainly knew that from experience.

"I've come to know Mark, and he's a decent guy."

The bartender seemed sincere, but I rolled my eyes. My action achieved the desired effect. The bartender threw his rag on the counter. The couple at the end of the bar looked over.

"Mark's—he's—he wouldn't do it. He's, first of all, he's in love—soul love, the kind that's your heart and mind and everything. Second, he doesn't have it in him. He's—it's not shy—but he—he just couldn't have killed her." He sucked in a breath and let it out slowly. "You either believe me or you don't."

"Alright," I said. He had given me all he could. "Thanks."

I slid off the bar stool and exited into the muggy, salty air. I felt guilty at prodding the bartender to anger, but it was the only way I knew to ensure an entirely honest assessment. Despite the bartender's opinion, I believed Mark was capable of killing. I felt it.

CHAPTER 35

Where a cup of hot coffee and a couple of scones could take me was amazing. The police receptionist directed me across an open office area to Kimmie's desk and said she'd page Kimmie while I waited.

With Jason as my warden, I was set to cover an evening fundraiser at the marine center, some celebratory black-tie event for the Young Alumni Association, a group comprised of graduates aged below forty. The unsettlingly formal press release presented me with another problem: finding a dress. Since newspaper business was slow, and I needed caffeine, and since Kimmie had blown off my attempt at a reconciliation on the boardwalk at Abby's memorial, I thought I'd bring coffee to the police station and try to force the conversation with her. Maybe the effort would convince her I wasn't all bad, that I hid nothing, least of all any involvement in Abby's death. Maybe I could make her feel guilty for embellishing my relationship to Abby's case to the police chief and for filling in my father about the incident with my ex-boyfriend in Tennessee. Maybe we could call a truce.

Kimmie's desk sat near a window overlooking the bleak humdrum line of old but not antiquated buildings across the street. I put the coffees and bag of scones on the worn-bare wood and glanced around Kimmie's tidy desktop. A cup with pens, a stapler, a dish of paper clips, and in and out trays were lined up next to a flat screen computer monitor. Past the monitor, I spotted a plastic cube with photographs on every side. I picked it up and looked at the snapshots.

There was Kimmie, rock climbing up the side of some lichen-spotted mountain boulder. There was Kimmie again, arms around a dark-haired man and generously-breasted woman, all wearing form-fitting black short-sleeved shirts with "POLICE" scrawled in gold across the busts, all laughing. There was Kimmie in another photo, in dress uniform, holding one hand on the Bible and another up in oath, being sworn into the force, my father and Vicki beaming beside her. There was Kimmie, standing amid a bunch of men, all wearing police softball uniforms. The Kimmie I remembered would have sooner allowed herself to be seen with her hair wet—a surefire sin for a true southern belle—than climb a rock. When did Kimmie stop worrying about breaking a nail and learn to play softball?

As I reached over to set the photo cube back in its place, I noticed a stapled stack of paperwork on Kimmie's chair. I glanced around. Other officers seemed busy; no one was looking at me, so I held the photograph cube over Kimmie's chair, pretended to study the photos some more, and instead scanned the top sheet of paper. Right away, I saw that the paperwork was an incident report for stalking charges. I searched for a name. The paperwork listed the reporting officer's name, the dispatch officer's name, the place of the incident, Siler Ridge, Illinois. And then I found the name of the suspect: Mark Listlen! I scanned down the page for more information. I found a short description of the incident at the bottom of the page:

"Responded to call from residence on stalking allegations. Found suspect behind large tree in back yard with half-empty whiskey bottle. Suspect detained overnight. Case closed; prosecution declined."

I looked for the date. The report was several years old.

I frowned. If the victim wouldn't prosecute him, were the stalking charges serious or just a way to run off a pest?

Already, the vibe I felt around Mark told me that if I saw him hanging around my backyard in the dark, I'd call the cops. At Abby's memorial, Mark had been arrested for disorderly conduct; communicating threats; and resisting, delaying, and obstructing an officer. Were these arrests symptoms of something worse, the stalking arrest a stepping stone down the pathway to murder and the disorderly conduct arrest an aftershock? Suddenly, the incident report was swiped from the chair.

Kimmie slapped the report face down on her desk and shouldered me as she plopped into her chair.

"Just admiring your photo cube," I lied. "Where did you go rock climbing?" I pointed to her photo.

She grabbed the cube from me and slammed it on the report. I noticed a few of the officers in the room, Patrick included, looking at us. I walked to the chair beside Kimmie's desk and sat down.

"What are you doing here?" Kimmie asked.

I nodded to the coffee. "I had some spare time and thought I might drop by and say hello. Would you like some coffee?"

Kimmie picked up the cup closest to her and sniffed it.

"What did you put in it? Syrup of Ipecac?"

"I didn't poison it."

"I wouldn't put it past you."

I shrugged; in high school, pouring Syrup of Ipecac into Kimmie's drink would have been something I might have done. "Fine," I said. "Let's switch cups."

Kimmie shook her head.

"Perhaps you're thinking that's what I was going to say," I joked, "so this cup is the one you actually don't want to drink from." I wriggled my eyebrows.

Kimmie crossed her arms and squinted her face into the expression I used to call the hissing cat.

"Kimmie." I sighed. I wanted to tell her to grow up. Instead, I said, "I'm sorry for what I did to you in high school and college," and I couldn't help but add, "just as I'm sure you're sorry for what you did to me." I leaned forward. "Why don't we finally start fresh? A toast to new beginnings." I raised my coffee cup.

"I'm not going to be seen toasting a suspect in the biggest homicide we've had this year."

My smile sagged. "I'm not guilty." When Kimmie didn't respond, I added, "Is that all I am to you now? A suspect?"

"You're not my sister," she hissed. "You never have been."

"You've never been my sister, either," I said amicably. "But we should try, right? Why not begin just by acting friendly, like reasonable adults, now?"

"Do you ever say anything that ends in a period, or is your whole life one big interview?"

"Good morning, Jonie," Daniel said as he slid into a neighboring desk and shuffled some papers. "What brings you here?"

"She was just leaving," Kimmie said.

"I brought Kimmie some coffee and scones, but seeing how she thinks I poisoned them, you're welcome to them instead."

Daniel laughed, but stopped short when he saw Kimmie's face. Kimmie noisily exhaled and twisted in her chair so that her back faced us. I passed him the coffee and bag of scones, but he hesitated before reaching for them.

He said, "I'd like to apologize again, Jonie."

Daniel lifted the bag from my hand, his fingers brushing against mine for so long the gesture could only have been intentional. The way Daniel said my name, smooth and soft, filled my chest with warmth.

Kimmie swirled around to face him. "I can't believe this."

Daniel lowered his voice. "We know she's not a suspect; she's linked to the case, that's all."

"We?"

"Kimmie, we discussed—"

"She's still the media."

"What's she going to report about this?"

I stood up. "I should be going, tempting as it is to stay, sit back, and watch Kimmie bicker with someone else for a change. But I didn't come here to stir up anything or distract you from finding the person who killed Abby." I addressed Kimmie. "If you change your mind about starting over, you know where to find me."

CHAPTER 36

"What's up?" Jason asked, setting down the hand-held Tetris video game he played to supposedly clear his mind before writing a story.

I realized I was lost in thought at my work desk again, pondering Daniel's behavior at the police station instead of finishing a short article about a boy earning his Eagle Scout ranking. "A lot," I said. Realizing I was being rude, I added, "I just really want Abby's case solved. And I want Kimmie to give me a break." I filled him in on Mark's faulty alibi at the Dirty Bird and on the stalking report I saw on Kimmie's desk.

"Why didn't you tell me you were going to visit Kimmie this morning?" Jason asked. "I would have chipped in for the coffee, so long as Stu could have tagged along."

We grinned at each other, imagining the mismatched coupling.

"Did someone mention Kimmie?" Stu's blonde hair and pointed face appeared suddenly behind our cubicles. "Surfs up, Jonie."

"Kimmie who?" Jason asked. "So tell me more about Mark," he said, turning back to me as Stu disappeared behind the cubicle fabric once again.

"I just felt a really bad vibe, to put it in Stu's terminology, when I was around Mark. And you saw the brawl at Abby's memorial yourself. If Mark is capable of that amount of violence in front of a crowd, what's he going to do when he's alone with Abby?"

"I'm sure the police will announce they've arrested him for the murder soon."

"A bad vibe and losing your temper once doesn't mean he did the deed," I said, though I believed Mark seemed capable of, and possibly even inclined to use, extreme violence. "Still, Abby's sister, Martha, said he was stalking Abby after they broke up. I'm also wondering what's going on with Ballings."

"Not Ballings again." Jason picked up his video game.

I took the hint and turned back to my desk. I tapped my fingertips against my computer keyboard, not hard enough to depress any keys but enough to make a rhythmic beat. I still wanted to know what Ballings was keeping from the police, but even more, I wanted to know who killed Abby and why. Mark's stalking history merely added to my suspicions about him. Martha suspected him, and he acted aggressive toward both of us at Abby's funeral. Considering his behavior at Abby's memorial and Phaser's experience with him, Mark was well above Ballings on my suspect list.

"However," I thought aloud to Jason, waiting for him to pause his videogame, "you can't rule out Ballings entirely. Would Mark have yelled at Ballings at the memorial like that if Mark killed Abby?"

"Mark's psycho."

"He seemed to be irrationally angry at the memorial yet sane enough to know what he was saying."

"Mark gives you that fake Dirty Bird alibi, almost kills Ballings at the memorial, has a past arrest for stalking added to yesterday's arrest, and now you're saying he's sane?"

"Maybe."

Jason shook his head and restarted Tetris. I turned back to my computer and ran a search on Mark Listlen. In the newspaper's database, he was listed as holding a degree in computer science from a university in Arizona. His home phone and address were unlisted. An internet search for his name led me to a computer software design business in downtown Wilmington. The business' website listed his direct phone line and showed his photograph. I stared into Mark's dark eyes that were shadowed in deep sockets above angular cheekbones. Bad photo or portrait of a killer? I blinked and found his menacing stare etched into my memory—perfect fodder for at least one good nightmare. Then I searched the internet for Mark in Siler Ridge, Illinois. No matches to my information were found.

I racked my brain for any other way to find online information on Mark. Coming up with none, I decided I had exhausted the computer research tools at my disposal. I dialed Mark's business line. When he picked up, I hung up and grabbed my backpack pocketbook. Apparently, Mark was out of police custody and available to chat.

"Where are you going?" Jason asked.

"Out." I stood up.

"*Tribune* business?"

"I know the policy, Jason." I hoped the grit in my voice warned him to quit playing caretaker.

"Are you coming back to the office, or will I just meet you at the dance?"

"What?"

"The fundraiser tonight at the marine center. There's going to be dancing there, you know."

"Getting all gussied up to do a story on a fundraiser that includes dancing isn't what I call reporting," I growled.

"I suppose your idea of reporting is digging up conspiracy theories, unleashing controversies, staking yourself right up front and center so you won't miss any part of the fray."

"My idea of reporting is writing stories that matter, that affect others, that make a difference."

Jason considered me for a moment. "You turned out different from how I thought you'd be."

"You, too."

CHAPTER 37

While Mark may have looked more like a mercenary than a computer geek, the receptionist at the computer firm where he worked at least looked her role. Since lunch hour was nearing and Mark had answered his phone, I planned to catch him before he headed out. The receptionist buzzed Mark and told him he had a visitor in the lobby. I was grateful she didn't ask my name. The door of the lobby opened, but a woman walked out. I checked to see that the digital voice recorder in my pocket was ready. I didn't think I'd wrangle a confession out of Mark, but in the off chance he said something interesting, or if anything went awry, I was taking no chances of missing out on documentation. The next time the door opened, Mark exited, wearing his typical black attire, his pants sporting more pockets than bare fabric.

He glared at the receptionist, who had returned her attention to polishing her nails.

"I need some answers," I said quietly. Before he could rattle off an excuse to ditch me, I continued. "I'll buy you a hot dog. I noticed a concession stand near the riverfront."

Instead of answering, Mark walked out the front door of the office, and I followed. By the time I caught up, an unlit cigarette hung from his lips. While he paused to light it, I continued. "If you're innocent of Abby's death, you don't have anything to hide."

"Fine."

Mark walked jerkily and looked for cars three or four times before crossing the street and heading toward the hot dog stand, joining the flow of pedestrians already surging toward the river. Walking with him at my side allowed me to notice how he was diminutively built, framed smaller than me, like a jockey, but with bulkier muscles. He was not someone I would have seen Abby tied to for the rest of her life. Since he took no initiative to speak to me, I also remained silent, formulating what I would say and how I would say it, until we settled onto a concrete border that fenced in a tree and both took bites of our hot dogs.

"Mark, don't freak out," I said, hoping the shade in the heat coupled with the river running silently feet from us was relaxing him. "I want to be honest. I've done some research about you. I know you said you didn't kill Abby, but there are some things that bother me. I know how it feels to say you didn't do something and to be accused of it anyway. That's why I wanted to talk to you—to hear what you have to say for yourself, to hear your viewpoint."

Mark took another bite of his dog.

"I visited the bar you said you were at when Abby died. The bartender says you weren't there that night."

"He must be confused." Mark was not making eye contact.

I shook my head and put down my soda.

"It's none of your business where I was that night," he said.

"I want to find out who killed Abby. Don't you?"

"Ballings killed Abby," he growled.

"So help me out and tell me where you really were that night."

"I told you."

Fine, I thought; I'll move on. That was only one of the strikes against him. "You have a history of stalking."

"So what? The cops know all this. Just because I was accused of something once doesn't mean—"

"In addition, somebody called me at the *Tribune* to let me know where I could find Abby's body. It was a man's voice—a

183

man trying to conceal his identity but wanting to report Abby's death. Was that you?"

He shoved the rest of the hot dog into his mouth.

"It was you who called me, wasn't it?"

He wadded up the tissue paper that had been holding the hot dog. I needed to work fast before he escaped.

"No one knew I was working at the *Tribune* yet, to contact me there. But there was a printout in Abby's car of my article with the paper's number on it. Maybe you had been with Abby and saw the article."

Mark stood and threw his trash beside me. It skittered against me, leaving a streak of mustard on my favorite silk top before falling next to the tree.

I stood too. "Were you the father of Abby's unborn child? Or, do you know who—"

"Ballings. Balling was the father. But if you don't believe me, why don't you ask Jason?"

"Jason?" My mouth hung open. "Ask Jason at the *Tribune*? Ask Jason who fathered Abby's child? What does he have to do with this?"

"You don't know?"

"Know what?"

"He and Abby were like this." He grabbed my hot dog that I somehow still held and squeezed the bun around the dog until the bread ripped and ketchup dripped out. He chucked the hot dog into the river.

I was stuttering, my mouth and my mind trying to keep up. "How—"

"You've already made up your mind about me." Mark stormed away, down the river walk.

My attention snapped back into focus. I scurried after him. "Mark," I said to his back, jogging to keep up with his pace, "there's your alibi problem, your stalking history, your phone call to me at the paper—"

Mark stopped and turned on me, grabbing my forearms and pushing me against the river walk's metal rails. "I didn't kill Abby," he said, tightening his grip with each word. My

184

eyes watered in pain. "You and the cops, both. You disgust me. I loved Abby." He spat on the walkway by my feet before walking away.

This time, I did not follow. My arms were shaking, my forearms throbbing. I glanced around to see if anyone had noticed Mark holding me there. I caught myself feeling almost embarrassed, like in Tennessee, before my boyfriend and I split, when our public arguments became physical. I cursed silently to myself.

I had wanted to catch Mark in a lie—to have him admit to something that I could turn and use against him. So in addition to being out the money for the two hot dogs, and now sporting a stained shirt and bruised forearms, I had failed to obtain the ammo I needed to prove Mark was Abby's killer. Instead, I had even more questions: What was Jason and Abby's relationship? Had Jason been close to Abby too? Why had Jason hidden it? I cursed again—this time, out loud.

CHAPTER 38

Walking, the blocks back to the *Tribune* passed in a fury. My strides lengthened to the maximum my pencil skirt allowed. On the way, I called Jason and demanded he meet me on the top level of the parking deck that served our building. I told him that he ought to know why I needed to talk with him and that he should come alone. But when I arrived, I found both Jason and Stu standing in the back corner of the deck nearest the river. Stu was lolling against the railing looking down at the sidewalk and street two stories below, probably eavesdropping on pedestrians. One of Jason's arms was crossed over his chest. His other hand was rubbing his earlobe. When he noticed me walking toward them, I saw him tense. He must have remembered the look on my face from when I discovered that he'd dumped me for Kimmie because I was certain my expression revealed the same level of angry betrayal as it had when I'd confronted him then about his disloyalty. Why had Jason brought Stu along? Protection? Diversion? Maybe he thought I would postpone dealing with him if Stu was nearby. Guess again, Jason, I thought.

"Why didn't you tell me?" I yelled, still yards away from him, still approaching him. "Why did you lie?"

"I didn't—" Jason held up his hands in mock surrender. "I may have left out a few things."

"Is this a lover's quarrel?" Stu asked, glancing from Jason to me, finally resting on Jason's stiff frown, which must have been more appealing than my glare. "Or, should I say a pre-lover's quarrel?"

"Does Stu know about you and Abby?" I asked.

"This is about another woman?" Stu asked. "Wait—the dead research lady from the marine center?"

"Abby," Jason said quietly, looking away from us at a steamboat chopping water. "We were friends. We became reacquainted when I was doing that story on Ballings, and we started hanging out."

"Friends?" Stu asked. "Just friends or—"

"Friends, though maybe—" After a pause, Jason looked back at me. "I didn't mention it because my relationship with her didn't seem relevant."

"You lied about it," I said.

"No."

"When Lee took us to lunch and I asked you if you remembered Abby—"

"I didn't say anything. I didn't lie."

"You lied by omission."

"Telling the truth just would have taken us off the story, and there was no reason for that. Don't pretend like you haven't downplayed your relationship with Abby all along."

"You had a relationship with Abby, too?" Stu asked.

I ignored him. "Did you tell Abby I was coming back to town?" I asked Jason.

He shrugged. So that was how Abby knew I was going to be working at the *Tribune*.

"Did you know Abby was pregnant?" I asked.

"No."

"Are you the father?"

"No!"

"What about Ballings?"

"Whoa!" Stu said.

"Abby and I got together maybe once every other week," Jason said. "When she and Mark broke up, she talked about that, but she didn't say much about other relationships."

"If you were friends, why didn't you go to her funeral? Were you afraid of being recognized?"

"What are you trying to insinuate? Who would recognize me?" Jason ran a hand through his dark hair. "How did you find out I knew Abby, anyway?"

"Mark," I said, noting his change of subject.

"The crazy guy at the memorial?" Stu asked.

I nodded, but Jason shook his head.

"Abby wasn't talking to Mark after they broke off the engagement," Jason said. "How would he know we were friends?"

"You tell me, Jason."

"You said Mark was following Abby around; maybe he saw us sometime."

I supposed Jason's behavior made sense—his reactions to Abby's death and to the vandalized lab, and at the press conference, learning of Abby's pregnancy. Even shrugging off acknowledging his acquaintance with Abby during lunch with Lee could be trumped up to a journalist's desire for a story, but what about his insistence on following me everywhere? Was that just his dedication to *Tribune* policy? What about Jason playing down his knowledge about Mark earlier?

"Where were you the night of the homicide?" I asked.

"What?" Jason stuttered. "You don't seriously—"

"Whoa!" Stu yelled again.

"Where were you the night of the homicide?" I repeated.

"You can't think I had anything to do with—"

"Then tell me."

"No. You should know me well enough to know that I wouldn't—"

"Whoa!" Stu interrupted. "Are you accusing Jason of killing Abby?"

"I'm asking where he was the night Abby was killed. If he's not guilty of anything, why would that question be so difficult to answer?"

"Because of your insinuation!" Jason spat.

"Then tell me and be done with it. Answer me."

"You don't deserve an answer."

I felt like Jason had slapped me. I did deserve an answer, and not just because I was partnered with him at the *Tribune*. Not just because he lied to me. I felt he still owed me after what he had put me through—dumping me for Kimmie years ago—and so what if it was years ago?

I spun around to walk to my truck, but Jason stepped in front of me, halting my progress. I sidestepped him, but he followed me and put his arms on my biceps, holding me there. I tried to jerk away, but he clutched me harder—then with a violent yank, I broke free. I was through being manhandled by anyone. I clambered into my truck and peeled away.

CHAPTER 39

I'd thought the festive occasion and ballroom attire for the dance and fundraiser would make the marine center less gloomy. However, approaching the building from the parking lot, with the moon shining full and bright in the dark sky, the track lighting along the building's base silhouetting overeager valets, and the disembodied strains of music carried sporadically by the wind, the building just felt disorienting and foreboding.

Awkward in a dress, I tugged at the thin, clingy, dark gold material, a shade darker than my hair but brighter than my skin. The skirt fanned out slightly just above my knees, but the dress was otherwise snug. It revealed a bit more than I had hoped for with straps over the shoulders that crisscrossed down the back to join the skirt a few inches above my waist. Still the dress was a classic—not too sexy, not too formal, not too frilly, not too plain. Since it was $18 at my favorite downtown thrift store, I'd been sold. I'd even bought a small purse to match, which stretched to contain my notepad, pens, keys, wallet, cell phone, and camera. I'd brought the camera since Stu said he couldn't attend the event.

I parked in the lot, not knowing if tipping the valets was expected. I couldn't spare the money. The gritty crunching my shoes made crossing the parking lot echoed eerily, and I felt my skin tingle, as if I were being watched. I glanced around at the dozen or so empty vehicles scattered across the parking lot, and at the sharp valets, and then at the dark woods of the garden. The hair on the back of my neck prickled, and I found my pace quickening.

In the lobby of the marine center, a life-sized portrait of Abby rested, framed, on an easel surrounded by white candles. A donation box for a memorial scholarship fund sat nearby. Instead of being relocated to a happier venue, this alumni fundraiser celebration, scheduled months before Abby's death, simply incorporated her into it. In the photograph, Abby's deep blue eyes, level with mine, looked alive, especially in the flickering candlelight. The portrait was like a portal to another world, just as real as the one where I now stood.

I broke my gaze and followed the music down a staircase and into a large, open room with floor to ceiling windows that looked toward the Intracoastal Waterway. I scanned the room for Jason and for someone who might be the president of the young alumni association. A large conference table had been pushed against a back wall, making room for a dance floor. The table was hidden beneath platters of cheese and crackers, a dish of assorted olives, a large silver tray piled with fudge squares, and a punch bowl filled to the brim with a pink concoction that emitted an almost overwhelming fruity odor.

The way I broke away from Jason earlier hadn't included setting a time or location to meet at the center for the event, so I had decided to come early, having learned from experience that if I was conducting a regular interview—not digging for sensitive information or tips and rumors interviewees are hesitant to relay—but if I was just doing a run-of-the-mill interview for a mundane story, it was usually best to interview subjects when they were sober and not distracted by dozens of guests. Plus, I wanted time to look around for breaker boxes that might fit Abby's key, and if I found no fit, I wanted to reenter her office to check again for locked cabinets. Perhaps I missed something the last time I was in her lab.

I eventually found the alumni president, and by the time I'd finished my interview with him, the band had begun its second song and a line three-deep had backed up to a bar in the corner. I had about an hour before the formal ceremony when I needed to shoot photographs. The president left my side to play host, and I decided to look around the center for those breaker boxes before the party was in full swing.

I hurried up the stairs to the lobby, away from the smiling guests who were beginning to mingle and dance in tight pairs. No doubt I'd be unlucky enough to run into some old classmate who now was a successful lawyer or doctor. The classmate would bring a devoted spouse or enticing date while I clutched my notepad and camera to my thrift-shop dress to keep me company. They would ask me what I was doing at the dance or who I came with. I wasn't ashamed of being a reporter for the *Tribune*, or of being at the dance alone, but all the same, I didn't want to replay the past or relay the path my life had taken since dropping out of college. I made my way through the now crowded lobby, but a couple of steps from the door, someone grabbed my arm and pulled me toward the wall.

It was Officer Patrick! I did a double take. Dressed in a black tuxedo, Patrick had slicked his hair and smelled strongly of aftershave.

"I would whistle," he teased, "but I'm on duty and might find myself in trouble for harassment."

"I didn't know taxpayers paid police to attend parties." I gently elbowed his ribs.

"University policy requires at least one officer to be present any time alcohol is served at an event on campus, even though this isn't campus proper. So I earn a couple hundred bucks, paid by the university or, in this case, the young alumni, to break up any potential brawls and stand guard watching rich alumni get drunk all evening."

"That makes two of us." We leaned against the wall to let a large party pass. "At least the watching alumni get drunk part. I'm on duty, too. I have the privilege of writing about this oh-so-newsworthy event." I sighed. "At least it keeps money rolling in."

Patrick and I chatted for a couple of minutes. Then the last person I wanted to see or expected to show up ambled through the front door—Kimmie. And even worse, she was coupled with Daniel. My heart sank.

CHAPTER 40

I reluctantly admitted, despite my fingers itching to tear out a couple of sizable chunks of her hair, Kimmie looked good. She had chosen a pale pink gown that wrapped around her body like cellophane. Her dress was so tight I could see her underwear line through the material that angled off her hips. I smiled as I noticed the flaw in her getup; the chest clearly was padded. Behind her stood Daniel, and I clenched my jaw shut before it fell open on its own accord. Daniel was wearing a tuxedo, and I knew that even if I spent all evening looking, I wouldn't be able to find a flaw. His eyes met mine and the corners of his mouth twitched. I wondered why he was amused. But then his focus zeroed in on Patrick, and his brow crinkled slightly before he noticed the notepad I clutched in my hand.

"Jonie," he said, his voice playful. "Ever the journalist. I should have known—what happened to your arms?" He reached forward and pulled my wrists toward him, stretching my arms straight. His hands were warm and gentle, and I lost myself in his touch until I saw his frown deepen. I glanced down at the purple-black bruises striped across my forearms, Mark's handiwork from earlier in the day at lunch.

"A minor altercation," I mumbled, taking my arms back, not wanting to discuss my unsuccessful run-in with Mark. "Are you two on duty, too?" I tried to imagine Kimmie breaking apart a brawl in her tight dress. She obviously wasn't packing heat, unless her gun hid amidst her chest stuffing.

Kimmie laughed. "We're not on duty. I went to college and I, unlike you, have a degree. I'm part of the young alumni."

Daniel's face still frowned at me. "Your—"

"We'll be moving on before we block the doorway," Kimmie interrupted. "Patrick," she said as she walked past.

Daniel raised his eyebrows at us, hesitating before Kimmie pulled him deeper into the center.

"That was icy," Patrick said.

"You noticed?" I shoved my notepad into my pocketbook. "Are they a thing? Are they dating?" I tried to ask nonchalantly, though I was pretty sure the squeak in my voice revealed my true feelings.

Patrick shrugged. "They're pretty close, being partners."

I stepped toward the door.

"You're not leaving, are you?" he asked.

"Just going outside for some air. I've never been good at small talk and finger food."

Having not seen Jason inside or his station wagon in the parking lot, I walked down the sidewalk until I was out of the glare of the entrance lighting, then cut close to the building. The dampness from the grass soaked through my shoes. I searched the front of the center for a breaker box. Of course, no boxes were showing on the front of the building, so I hurried down the far side of the center and found only air conditioning and heating units. I paused at the center's back corner. The long, wide windows of the conference room comprised about half of the back of the center. I saw a breaker box near the middle of the building beside a back door. I reminded myself that from inside the brightly lit rooms, hardly anything outside the center could be seen. Not giving myself time to chicken out, I dug Abby's key out of my pocketbook, took a deep breath, and scurried to the breaker box, hoping I would be a blur to anyone who caught my movement.

When I reached the box, I grabbed the lock and tried to slide the key in, but the key wouldn't fit. I flipped the key around and tried it again. No way did this key fit the lock; the key was too bulky. I sucked in a breath and sped down the second half of the building to the opposite corner. No more breaker boxes were to be seen along the remaining side of the center. I wondered what I should do. I couldn't stand here forever. I didn't want to go into the center to encounter Kimmie again or spend a half hour making peace with Jason, if he showed. I was a few yards from the entrance into the garden, so I stepped into its shadow.

In the moonlight, the garden seemed sacred and delicate. I settled onto the first bench I reached, which was angled at a corner of the building. From the bench, I could see if the awards ceremony was getting ready to begin and if I needed to return inside. Unfortunately, the vantage also afforded me a view of the guests inside the room, including my step-sister. I felt sick watching Kimmie clinging onto Daniel. She obviously wanted more than a work partnership out of him.

I diverted my thoughts onto something constructive, Abby's homicide case. I thought about the mysterious key. What did it open? Not a safety deposit box at the bank, not an outdoor breaker box. Perhaps it opened something in Abby's house, I mused. And I could check the cabinets in Abby's lab again, I thought.

Who was she hiding the key from, if anyone? Ballings? Dean Kipling seemed convinced Ballings took a shot at her office, though he denied it. Had Ballings also ransacked his own lab? If so, why? To search for Abby's key or the backup disk? But why would he smash test tubes and ruin expensive equipment? Who else would have motive to ransack the lab—the dean? That didn't make sense, either.

And what about Mark? I supposed having a record for stalking didn't automatically make him guilty of killing Abby; I owned a record of violence, and I didn't kill Abby. If Mark had killed Abby, would he also ransack the professor's lab? If he had, why? Could he have destroyed the lab out of vengeance or rage? And who fathered Abby's baby? Mark? Ballings? Someone else? Could Jason possibly be involved?

So what did I have? Nothing. Nothing but questions. I looked out at the Intracoastal Waterway. The blue water shimmered in the moonlight, and a solitary boat motored by, its running lights reflecting off the water. Sitting on the bench, I could see the length of the garden's boardwalk. I remembered Abby's face, dead eyes blindly staring, and I shuddered. No beautiful landscape excluded violence.

After all, the earliest days of colonization on this coast were marked by countless shipwrecks, even the mysterious disappearance of an entire settlement. And nature itself, though demure at the moment, could be brutal. Hurricanes tore open new inlets and dragged away homes. Even the twisted trees of the garden showed the scars of coastal living.

My eyes followed the line of the pier from the deep water inshore, through the marsh grasses, to the marine center. Through a break in the trees, I could make out Kipling's window. The damaged window pane had been replaced. Beneath Kipling's office was Ballings' laboratory. Had someone been on this bench, watching Abby, waiting for her to venture outside before cornering her and taking her life, and later waiting for the right moment to aim a shot through Kipling's window? The shades of Ballings' office were drawn, but the lights were on. In the specks of light where the strings wove through the shades, I saw movement, something dark passing between the light and the window, repeatedly.

I crept forward, curious. Whatever the dark shape was, it seemed to be moving rhythmically, like drapery fabric swaying in time to an oscillating fan's current. I pressed my eye closer to the glass. I looked for maybe two seconds and pulled away fast. I'd seen all I needed to see. Ballings was in a tux, pressing Trish against a wall, her bare legs circling him.

I stumbled backward and squeezed my eyes closed. The crinkling of dried leaves behind me near the garden bench forced my eyes open. Mark stood where I sat moments ago, glaring at me. I turned and caught my toe on a tree root, tripped, and reopened my scraped knee. Before I could push up from the ground, Mark was on top of me.

CHAPTER 41

"Don't scream," he said. "Don't run."

I was gasping for breath, my head spinning and my heart pounding. Flattened, face against the ground, I couldn't get enough air to scream or enough leverage to kick.

"Stop struggling. I'm not trying to hurt you. Listen to me! The cops think I did it." He cursed. "You think I did it. I didn't kill Abby. You have to believe me. You have to nail Ballings for killing her because the cops have pushed their heads so far up my butt. They dragged me in earlier today, after I saw you. They snatched me from my office in front of my coworkers like I was a criminal, took me to their station, sat me down in their examination room or whatever you want to call it, tried to pick my brain and trick me into admitting to something I didn't do."

I didn't fault the police for questioning Mark. If I were Daniel, I would have brought Mark in for questioning long ago. "Why are you telling me this?" I asked. Mark backed off of me slightly, allowing me to breathe clearly. Over my shoulder, I could make out his silhouette.

"You have access to resources, as a reporter, so since the cops are on the wrong trail, and if they get to me before—I need to find someone who has a chance of revealing Ballings. I lied to you about being at the Dirty Bird the night Abby was killed because I was here—here in this garden."

I pushed up from the ground, digging dirt beneath my fingernails, but Mark caught the movement early and pinned me back on the ground. "No! You're going to hear me out. I was here, but I didn't kill Abby. I checked up on Abby from time to time, just to make sure she was okay. She always worked late. That night, I came here, sat on the bench, and watched her work. I brought along something to drink, just to keep me company, time slipped away, and, before I knew it, the sun was rising. I had passed out. I was wasted. Abby's car was still here, and when I didn't see her through the lab window, I walked around back to the boardwalk."

"How would you know to—"

"Sometimes Abby likes—liked—to take breaks and walk outside. So when I went to the boardwalk, that's where I saw her. In the water. Dead. I didn't know what to do."

"Call the cops?"

"You know I couldn't call the cops, not with my past. Just because some bitch ex-girlfriend in a whole other state thinks I'm stalking her and dials 911, years ago. But you see how it's been, even without me being the one to report finding her body."

I opened my mouth to protest, but Mark cut me off.

"So I went to Abby's car to see if—I don't' know—if anything was there, maybe her cell phone; but instead I saw this number written out across a computer printout of your newspaper article. Your name was circled. It was like a sign. I couldn't just leave Abby's body out there." He jumped off me and stood up, a couple of steps away. "Well?"

I rolled over and sat up. My arms were trembling. "Well what?"

"Do you believe me?"

I considered him. Mixed in with his aggressive attitude and clenched posture mingled a dab of something softer—true concern, perhaps—beginning to show around his eyes. But was it a trick of the moonlight, concern that he'd be arrested for a crime he committed, or genuine worry that the cops were looking at the wrong man, and that he wanted the real killer exposed? I stood up.

"If the cops don't believe you, why should I?" I asked.

"Because I'm telling the truth!" A couple of birds lit up from the garden, their furiously beating wings whistling through the air. Mark cursed.

"You're saying Ballings killed Abby."

"He was the baby's father."

"How do you—"

"Trust me."

"You said you were going to kill Ballings."

Mark smiled at me.

"Did you tear apart Ballings' lab?"

"No."

"What about the shooting into the dean's office?"

Mark froze.

"Do you know anything about that?" I asked.

He cocked his head so the moonlight gleamed off his tight, waxy skin. "All I can tell you is that I enjoyed watching that bastard run around inside that room like a fool."

"What bastard?"

"The conman. The professor, Ballings. Of course, I couldn't stay around long and watch the fool run into the walls, in case the coward called the cops. But—" Mark stepped closer to me, and I stumbled backward. "That's the thing! He didn't call the cops. Or at least not until ten hours later. I read in the article that the shot wasn't reported until the following morning."

"Right."

"Think about it," Mark said, backing away. "If he's innocent, why wouldn't he call the cops right away? He's got it coming. But if I'm arrested before I can take care of Ballings, the burden is on you." He turned and stalked into the garden, disappearing in its shadows.

Not lingering to see if Mark would reappear, I sprinted around the corner of the building. In the track lighting, I slowed to a jog until I caught a valet's attention, and then began walking quickly. I forced a smile, hoped no one would notice the blood trickling down my shin, and reentered the center. I avoided Patrick and rushed to the restroom. Washing off, I thought about how Mark and I both seemed to be at the marine center whenever something criminal occurred. The police, or at least Kimmie, suspected both of us; and we both claimed innocence. My innocence I was certain about, but Mark's alleged innocence remained dubious to me.

After a couple of minutes, my heart's pounding slowed, and the bleeding stopped. My hands clean, my dress brushed off, and my breathing almost at a normal pace, I figured it was about time to reenter the conference room and find a dark corner from which to wait to photograph the alumni fundraising ceremony.

The dance floor was busy, and the crowd's conversation competed with the band, which played a slow 90's cover song about lost love. I spotted Jason. He'd showed up after all. Still on jittery legs, I shimmied through the crowd and toward him.

"You should gussy up more often," he said when I reached him. He smiled at me, and I thought I smelled something thick and minty on this breath. "Dance with me."

I considered protesting when Jason whisked me out among the dancing couples. I felt a fluttering in my chest and a sudden warmth throughout my body. I had forgotten how a man's arms around me felt. Perhaps this was his way of apologizing to me. My body melted slightly as I allowed myself to be led by Jason, to breathe in his cologne, to enjoy the smooth rocking to the beat and firm hand on my back. Jason spun me around once and then pulled me close. Dancing with Jason but wishing I was in Daniel's arms instead, I looked over Jason's shoulder. Daniel was frowning at us, dancing with Kimmie, her back to us.

"How's your story going?" Jason asked. The words came out a slur, and I needed a moment to untangle them, to decipher his question.

"I just need a good photograph, and then I'm out of here."

"Don't hurry," he said, spinning me again and pulling me even closer.

I gasped, not ready for the sudden move. "Jason—"

"Relax," he said, moving us to a less populated section of flooring and pushing himself against me. Beneath the mint on his breath, I definitely smelled something heavier.

"Wait, Jason—"

"I'm going to teach you some moves, il mio dolce."

I tried to back away. "I'm not—"

"Watch my lead."

"No—"

Jason spun me again, then dipped me. "Not bad."

I tried to say something but gulped instead. My head was spinning, and I noticed many of the other couples, not just Kimmie and Daniel, watching us. I wondered if Jason recognized the spotlight he had placed on us, suddenly wondered if he was putting on the show for Kimmie, barely steadying myself as he spun me another time.

Jason chuckled as the song ended. While I couldn't know what he had been drinking, his actions told me he had ingested more than a few glasses of alcohol. But he held his own much better than I could have. Drunk, I would have been fumbling along the dance floor. Jason was smooth and oiled like duck feathers. A new song, a slower song, began. Using his hand that was resting on my waist, Jason pulled me closer again.

CHAPTER 42

Jason's hand that had been pressed flat on my back traced the crisscrossed straps up and suddenly raked down. By the time his fingertips reached the small of my back, I maneuvered my arms between his and pushed out, breaking his grip. I backed away. Momentarily stunned, Jason shook his head and reached toward me. One-handed, I grabbed his arm and pushed it sideways, turning him from me. I twisted the arm down and curled it by the wrist the wrong way up his back. He squirmed under the pressure, his back to me. I held him under control, close enough he could hear me whisper.

"You're drunk," I said. "Call a cab, go home, and forget this ever happened."

I released him. He sneered at me over his shoulder. His eyes flashed, as if he was pondering an insult or planning a rebuttal, but he stepped toward the stairs as Daniel walked up to me. I glanced around for Kimmie and found her glaring at us from across the room.

"You deserve better than that," Daniel said.

I looked into his eyes, which were staring into mine with a fierce intensity. "I—" I could drown in Daniel's eyes, I thought. "That was—" I couldn't speak, couldn't think.

A loud thumping on the microphone saved me from having to formulate an explanation. The awards ceremony was about to begin, and I gratefully excused myself. As I pulled out my notepad and camera from my purse, I pushed my emotions aside. I'd think about what had just happened with Jason and Daniel later.

The ceremony was brief, with the young alumni leader congratulating those gathered for raising nine percent more donations than last year. He listed top contributors. Funds would be used to purchase outdoor benches for the campus. The leader whipped a maroon cloth off a sample wood bench that bore a golden plaque honoring the young alumni association. Kipling, in a sparkling black gown, made a quick appearance and thanked the alumni.

I moved around in the crowd and shot photos. As soon as the ceremony concluded, I shuffled toward the stairs. At the back of the room, I ran into Kimmie—or maybe it was that Kimmie had sought me out, since she stood in my path to the staircase. I glanced around. Daniel now was nowhere to be found.

"What do you want, Kimmie?"

"I want to know what's going on between you and Daniel."

"Nothing."

"There's something going on. I can see it."

"Finally putting your newfound detective skills to use, are you? You're the one who came to the dance with Daniel. If there's something going on, it's between you two. I've been staying out of your way this entire evening."

"Until you got Jason to show off with you and divert Daniel's attention."

I clenched my fists. "That was out of my control." I wanted to elaborate but held myself back. A crowded room provided no place to yell at Kimmie until she thought straight.

I moved to step around her and leave, but she blocked my way. "I'm not stupid," Kimmie said.

I changed direction and attempted to step around her again, but she pushed me back a step. All pretenses at acting peaceable and reigning in my temper were lost to me. If she wanted a fight, I'd give her one. I was tired of being bullied. I returned to town in part to make amends and start again.

Kimmie, it seemed, only wanted to continue our conflict, so I decided to level with her.

"Kimmie, I'm the stupid one, to think you'd ever grow up and cooperate to resolve our conflict, move on." I couldn't stop my tongue. I shifted my purse to my left hand, clenching my right hand. "If you're after Daniel, and it sure looks like you are with the amount of padding you've sewn into your dress, then have at him, if he'll have you. Because if he's the type of guy who's attracted to a spiteful, vengeful, evil, just plain ugly—inside and out—" I searched for a word. "Person" was too kind.

I didn't even see it coming. In a swift, sudden move, Kimmie pushed me sideways into the serving table. I flailed my arms to try and stop the collision, but the enormous punch bowl took up the entire table space before me. My left arm and purse crashed into the bowl, which wobbled violently, sloshing punch down the front of my dress and splattering down the wall onto the floor. I managed to keep my camera, which was wrapped around my other wrist, safe from the deluge. Kimmie clutched my shoulders, her nails digging into my flesh, and pulled me back from the bowl.

"Jonie!" she cried to the gathering onlookers. "Are you okay? You tripped into the punch bowl! Are you okay?"

I couldn't believe it. Kimmie again was manipulating events, trying to make me look like a clumsy oaf when she was the aggressor. I needed to leave before I tackled her.

I shrugged off her claws and grabbed my purse bobbing in the punch. I left the room and the building as fast as my shaking legs would carry me, not stopping until I reached my truck. I threw my dripping purse on the hood and rested my hands on either side of it, focusing on calming my trembling arms. I felt like hitting something until it broke or at least kicking a truck tire, but I knew if I did, I'd break a toe in my dress shoes and just hurt myself more. After a moment of trying to collect myself, I unzipped my purse and assessed the damage. My cell phone had shorted out. I slammed it into my truck bed, not nearly pleased enough at the resounding bang.

My good writing pens were sticky but could be salvaged. I flipped through my notebook. A few of the pages toward the back were soggy, but the pages on which I had written notes were legible. I fished my keys out of the bag. If I was looking on the positive side, at least my truck didn't have a remote to unlock the doors, which surely would have been ruined from the punch. I tried to force a laugh. I heard footsteps on the pavement behind me and spun around, praying Kimmie or Mark or Jason was behind me. I wanted a fight and to unleash the adrenaline overwhelming my blood.

Daniel was striding toward me. "Are you all right, Jonie?"

"My ego may heal eventually, but my cell phone won't." My voice came out a harsh staccato too loud for the darkened parking lot. I wanted to warn Daniel about the cretin he had for a partner. I wanted to blurt out all of my thoughts about Kimmie. I wanted him to throw his arms around me and melt everything else into oblivion. Instead, I asked, "Aren't you supposed to be with Kimmie?"

"She's not the one who tripped into the punch bowl." He took a step closer to me, a soft smile on his face.

"I didn't trip." As I said the words, I knew Daniel wouldn't believe me over Kimmie. "Look, I appreciate you checking on me, but—"

Daniel took another step closer and brushed a wayward strand of my hair behind an ear, which burned like hot candle wax from his touch. My legs were so shaky I thought they might collapse.

"Look," I stammered again. I wanted to step forward and kiss Daniel. But part of me wondered if my desire wasn't partly because Kimmie was attracted to him. I couldn't stoop to her level and make an advance on a man just because she was interested in him. But, no, I really was genuinely attracted to Daniel. I shook my head, trying to clear my thoughts. "You better go back in to your date. She just told me she thinks something's going on between us."

"Isn't there?"

"What—you mean—you're asking if there's something going on between us?"

He nodded. Shivers tingled up my spine, and they weren't caused by the cool night air on my punch-dampened skin.

"Daniel?" Kimmie called from the sidewalk of the center. "Oh, there you are!"

"Go on and be with your date," I muttered.

I opened my truck door and awkwardly climbed into the cab, my sopping dress sticking to my torso.

Daniel held the truck door open.

"She's my partner, my work partner," he said. "That's it."

"Then you need to tell her that."

He closed the door, and I drove away.

My mind whirled as out of control as a leaf careening down river rapids. Half of me tingled, giddy with excitement. Another huge chunk of me burned at Kimmie. And I felt angry and confused at how Jason had treated me. Should I shrug it off and attribute his actions to the alcohol and our history?

When I stopped at the light at College Street, I glanced into the vehicles as they passed me, turning. The city overflowed with cars carrying normal, smiling couples who weren't sopping wet with punch, who were out enjoying the evening. A jolt of shock hit me as I recognized one of the drivers, Professor Ballings! In a flash as he passed, I saw his arm slung around Trish, who was leaning toward him from the passenger seat. They were laughing. And in the car that followed them was Kipling, black raven eyes narrowed, body hunkered behind the steering wheel. And then both cars were gone, speeding away from me.

CHAPTER 43

The minutes passed slowly the next morning, and I kept glancing across my shoulder, waiting for Jason to show for work. Because of the cubicles, the newspaper headquarters appeared vacant. The telephone calls and murmuring conversations jumbled together in a kind of white noise. I picked at my keyboard. At the staff meeting, Lee had said Jason was coming in late. Part of me had wanted to call in sick also, ask for a three-day weekend, or hunker down in a dark corner at Port Java House to finish my coffee and then order another one and another one, until my brain shivered, caffeine-fried beyond repair; but I decided I needed money more than I needed to escape. Working at home would give my mind too much freedom to wander, and besides, I hoped to catch Jason and discuss yesterday's events enough to regain a functional, professional relationship.

Since last night's alumni fundraiser wasn't urgent news, my deadline for the story was later this afternoon. I'd have the rest of the day to write the story, not that I was enthralled with the prospect. I found myself stuck, trying to pull together an interesting lead paragraph. If I were to face a hurdle in writing a story, that first paragraph always presented itself. Once I got a lead down on the computer screen, the rest of the story seemed to flow naturally. Between Mark's confession and Jason's behavior, Kimmie's confrontation and Daniel's concern, my mind refused to focus on the fundraiser.

I found myself wondering what to say to Jason about his behavior and how to say it tactfully because boundaries needed to be reinforced. Being drunk was no excuse.

The padding of footsteps across the carpet alerted me to Jason's arrival. He looked hung over, I noted, with pasty, wan skin and dark rings beneath his eyes. Maybe he already was paying for his bad conduct. I hoped he at least remembered it. I waited until he set down his coffee.

"Afternoon, Jason."

He merely nodded at me, unsmiling, and began digging in his briefcase. I looked back at my laptop, twirling a lock of my hair with my fingertips and wondering if he'd be mature enough to apologize first or if I'd need to state my case. Jason leaned toward me and threw some papers on my keyboard.

I picked up the paper-clipped stack and leafed through copies of canceled airplane tickets, bills for a hotel and rental car, and a couple of pages of restaurant receipts.

"Proof," he said.

"Of what?"

"I figured you wouldn't believe me if I told you where I was the evening Abby died. So I spared you the trouble of having to conduct research behind my back. Here's proof I didn't kill Abby. Airplane tickets to Jackson Hole with dated receipts. Almost a week's worth of expenses. Notice the dates."

Jason spent a week in Wyoming and didn't get back into Wilmington until 10:30 p.m. on the day I discovered Abby's body.

"Why did you save the receipt and the tickets? Who does that?"

"I do." Jason tossed me a magazine.

I caught it against my body. Beneath the magazine's banner was the header, "Trekking the Tetons" and a photograph of a backpacker on some rocky ridge overlooking a pure, glacial blue, heart-shaped lake. In smaller lettering, I read, "Story and photographs by Jason Rossini."

"I save them so I can get credit for my travel expenses. Satisfied?" Jason grabbed the paperwork and magazine, shoved them in his briefcase, and strode away.

I turned back to my laptop, eyes still not seeing the words. Jason had an alibi—good, I thought, but he didn't have to fling it in my face. He still owed me an apology for his behavior at the dance, and an explanation. Maybe I had driven him to drinking with my questions about Abby. But that was no excuse for how he'd treated me.

"Good afternoon, twinkle toes," Stu said, his voice melodically ringing out over the cubicles. From the staff meeting, I knew Stu had been out all morning shooting dredging photos on one of the boats spitting sand out at the end of a nearby island.

I looked up and found Stu's toothy smile grinning down on me from over the cubicle. "Good afternoon yourself."

"Did you have fun last night?"

"Not particularly."

"Don't give me that! You and Jason at a dance! Jason would have called me if he got home before midnight. So how'd it go?" Dissatisfied when I merely shook my head, he continued. "Where is Jason?"

Lee knocked on the gray cushiony cubicle fabric at the entrance to my section, sending a sheet of dust flying from the material.

"Sorry to interrupt," he said. He kept his mouth open at one side, and tobacco-yellowed teeth dully shined. "You need to come with me, Jonie."

I glanced toward where Stu had been peering over the cubicles, but he'd already shrunk away. I sensed trouble. Sure enough, a minute later, having followed Lee's brittle frame down the hallway, I was sitting in front of the publisher's desk in between Lee and Jason. On the other side of the long, glazed wooden surface sat the publisher-owner himself, William Montgomery. And he looked exactly like his name suggested.

Montgomery was wide with thick, wrinkled, tanned skin, like a human rhinoceros, and brown eyes that would have appeared vacant if not for a calculating chill emanating from them as he made no attempt to hide his examination of me. While the desktop that separated us was empty, the working desk behind Montgomery was sparsely decorated with a computer monitor, a copy of this morning's *Tribune*, and the obligatory family photograph. Montgomery had a petite wife, a grown son, and a Dalmatian. He was leaning back in his broad, leather swivel chair; and I thought I could smell cigars, though I couldn't be quite sure because I also smelled something tangy, like aerosol disinfectant, and that was in addition to Jason's cologne. The way Montgomery allowed himself to lounge in the chair and freely survey me without speaking for much longer than could be considered polite, in addition to the plaques and certificates from local clubs adorning his walls, suggested that he was an established member of the local good ol' boys alliance.

I glanced at Lee, who sat stiffly perched, not making eye-contact with me. Jason looked unduly tense, too, his hands clenching his chair's armrests. I looked at Montgomery again and tried to swallow a sour taste in my mouth. Montgomery was the only person who appeared relaxed. He was moving his tongue back and forth inside his mouth against his lips. I was certain we had been seated at least a minute by now.

"So here's the situation," Montgomery said. "I hear from my people at the police—I golf with the chief—that one of my new reporters is under investigation. It seems this reporter has turned up as part of a homicide case and keeps surfacing wherever there's an incident—and there seem to be a lot of incidents—at what used to be a quiet research center. Sure, this reporter is there where the action's at, breaking news, but that's the problem. She's the one who's always breaking the news. I can see how a tip possibly could lead her to find a dead body. I could even chalk it up to coincidence that she's found in a vandalized lab. But now I hear she's there when a bullet is discovered shot through the dean's window." His eyes continued to bore through mine. "Again I hear more. She's talking to some suspect minutes before he's arrested at a memorial—a *memorial* for cryin' out loud—for criminal conduct. Now I hear she's making a big scene at some fancy university event, dancing loose and landing in a punch bowl."

My teeth were locked together so tightly they hurt, my ears were on fire, and my nails were digging into my palms. Despite every instinct, I decided not to say anything, to wait for the question. Montgomery also waited, patiently bobbing in his chair, and I recognized this as an intimidation tactic. He was waiting for me to break. I decided I wouldn't. Maybe half a minute passed, him staring at me, me staring back, me wondering who Jason and Lee were looking at. No one shifted in their seats. The air seemed weighted. My eyes watered from focusing so intently on Montgomery's eyes, and I was struck with the sensation of being back in an elementary school cafeteria, locked down in a staring contest with another child.

Montgomery sank back deeper in his chair and crossed his arms. Finally, he cleared his throat. "I don't know what you're playing at, girl, but I don't like it."

"I'm not sure what you mean."

Montgomery sighed. "What do you have to say for yourself?"

"About the series of stories surrounding Abby Pridgen's death? I've been in the right place at the right time," I said. "There was the initial news tip which led me to the body, but since then I've gone to the university for follow-up stories assigned to me. So I'm there, on assignment," I emphasized, "when I notice the crime there. As for the dirty dancing allegation—" I glanced at Jason. Without looking at me, he shrugged slightly. A large part of me wanted to point blame at him. But if he had been the one to tattle to Montgomery, he wouldn't have bothered with the gesture. Even after what he had done, I didn't need to cause anyone more trouble. "Respectfully, Mr. Montgomery, please consider your source and how facts get muddled when they're passed from person to person and between biases."

Montgomery stood and strode the couple of steps to the window. I followed his gaze to the river. A tugboat pulled a barren, flat-topped barge past the retired battleship up the river.

"Upsetting the punch bowl," I continued, pausing. I didn't think Montgomery would believe me if I told him I'd been pushed by his police chief's informant. "I tripped. I wasn't dancing when I stumbled into the punch bowl. I was moving around the room and taking photographs."

"Normally, I don't involve myself in personnel matters," Montgomery said. "But this one affects business revenues. If you're out there looking like a loose woman and a clown, if you're caught creating stories for the newspaper and I ignore warnings, not only will this paper look ridiculous, but the good men and women of this city will yank their support of the *Tribune*. The pressure's on us."

"The only person who is insinuating that I'm creating stories, according to you, is the police chief—who is getting the facts wrong, by the way—and it seems to me that the pressure ought to be falling on him. He should be pushing his detectives to solve this rash of crimes instead of blaming the newspaper for covering the truth."

Montgomery turned and looked down his nose at me, his mouth slightly agape. I imagined not many reporters stood up to him. "I've talked with the chief, and he seems to think there are a few too many coincidences for even the nosiest of reporters to happen upon."

I thought of saying something back, but Montgomery continued speaking before I worked up a response.

"While I'm tight with the chief, the good news for you is that I also know your daddy."

I couldn't envision my father fraternizing with Montgomery, nor could I believe that my father was the reason behind Montgomery second-guessing the police chief.

"But if I hear of any more funny business that makes me think for the tiniest fraction of a second that you're fabricating stories, you're gone. Gone without warning. Fired! No loss to us. You understand me?"

"Yes," I said, my voice coming out like a croak. Then I realized Montgomery was waiting for something more. "Yes, Mr. Montgomery," I said, trying to keep the bile out of my answer.

"You're all dismissed."

CHAPTER 44

Jason and Lee joined me in the hall outside Montgomery's office. Lee nodded his head toward his office next door, and we walked inside. He closed the door and filled a stained *Tribune*-logo mug with coffee from his own personal coffee maker, but he didn't offer any to Jason or me, which suited me just fine. I didn't trust my hands to be steady enough not to spill more coffee down my shirt than into my mouth. Lee gestured for us to sit. After we obliged—I moved a stack of green filing folders from my chair to the floor first—Lee retrieved a packet of headache powder and a metal spoon from his desk. He stirred the powder into his coffee, studying the white granules as they clumped, sank, and dissolved. He then tapped the spoon on the lip of his mug and returned it to his drawer unwashed.

"I wanted to make sure you heard Montgomery's message loud and clear, Jonie."

"Selling advertising space and keeping his buddy, the police chief, happy is more important than reporting news?" I shook my head.

"That's not his message, as you know very well." Lee's voice sounded sterner than I had heard it yet, like he had snapped his fingers at me to bring me to attention. "Are you fabricating stories?"

"No!" I felt my eyes tearing.

"I know you want to be on your own, become a staff reporter here."

"I believe I can achieve that without having to make up or embellish news."

Lee held my gaze through his bottle-bottom glasses.

"In the end, the police will find out who the perp is," Jason said.

"And it won't be me!" I said, still looking at Lee as I said it.

"Here's what we're going to do," Lee said. He set his mug on newspapers stacked on a cabinet beside his desk. "We're going to take you off this homicide story and put you onto something else. No more writing about anything else to do with the case, or any other crime or event that's happening at the marine center."

"No!" I said, before I could stop myself. "That's not fair. You're punishing me for something I didn't—unfounded accusations meant to—"

"Do you want to be fired?" Lee overrode my voice.

"No."

"Then don't give Montgomery cause. No more writing about anything that's even remotely related to the marine center."

"What about the fundraiser story from last night? I'm nearly done."

"Finish up that story, and after that, no more," Lee said. "Understand?"

I paused, but Lee's glare demanded an answer. "Yes," I said, suddenly feeling like a wet cat.

"Jason, give her some of your rainy day assignments to complete." Lee nodded his dismissal.

In the hallway on our way back to our desks, Jason gently tweaked the crook in my nose. Maybe he thought he was being comforting. Maybe he thought I'd forgotten about last night. I turned on him.

"Did you know about that? Since when did you know I was going to be called in to Montgomery's office?"

"Since Lee pulled me in there just before he came to get you."

"How did he know about the dance?"

"I didn't tell anyone," Jason said. "What's this about landing in a punch bowl?"

"Kimmie." I didn't need to say more. Jason's past dealings with Kimmie should allow him to surmise what happened.

We reached our desks, and Jason began sifting through a stack of old press releases. I was certain I couldn't begin to imagine all the boring, meaningless stories Jason had been saving for a slow news day and that now were about to be bestowed to me.

I plunked down in my office chair, which gave a threatening lurch to one side before I centered my weight. I knew I should be grateful simply to still be a freelancer at the *Tribune*, but my teeth were gritted in anger, and my eyes were moist with frustration. I hadn't expected to be rewarded for good journalism by being taken off a story, chewed out by my publisher, snapped into chains by my editor, and consoled with a slew of shabby press releases to be converted into birdcage lining.

I buried my face in my hands. As a reporter, I didn't want questionable integrity. But neither did I want to be stuck permanently converting fat press releases into filler stories. If the crimes weren't solved, this was where I was going to stay.

What if the police never found Abby's killer? How long would the *Tribune* keep me if the only writing I could do was to transcribe frivolous press releases? The paper exploited unpaid interns for that.

No, the only way to prove myself here was to actually prove myself. I'd stay away from the marine center, but somehow I'd work the real story, the only story that now mattered to me, finding who killed Abby. When I did, I'd write a news story that would make Montgomery and Lee realize what blind fools they were for doubting me in the first place. I recognized my resolve. The feeling was similar to when I worked the Cheatham County sheriff scam. There too, I was pushed aside, scoffed at, told to mind my own business by the men in charge—the sheriff and his goonies—but in the end, I reached the truth.

"I heard about the fireworks in Montgomery's office."

I opened my eyes. Stu was again peering over the cubicles.

"There weren't fireworks, really," I said, looking around my desk and hoping Stu would take a hint and back off.

"Sounds like Montgomery has his eyes on you," Stu said, "and not in a good way."

"How do you know this?" I glanced at Jason's chair, but it was vacant.

"News travels fast in the newspaper business."

I paged through the news releases Jason had slid on my desk when my eyes had been closed: *Local girl advances to state Little Miss Pageant, Wilmington gardener publishes book:* Composting 101, *Lecture and slideshow on Picasso to be given at art museum.* I tried not to shudder. Even if something that halfway captivated my brain cropped up in the pile of press releases, it still wouldn't divert my attention. The only story that interested me was one about Abby's death being resolved.

"Actually," Stu continued, "I listened to the tail end of the meeting from the conference room. You can hear right through the wall."

I dropped the press releases and stood up. I wanted to shake Stu by his neck, or at least slap some tact into him, but he jumped back before I made my move.

"At least Montgomery didn't fire you outright. At least you're getting another chance," Stu said. "Hey, Jonie? Montgomery didn't mention my name, right?"

"No, Stu, it's all on me."

"I've only spoken to Montgomery once, and it was pretty intense. And I wasn't even under suspicion for doctoring up stories, or photographs, in my case."

My frustration about being taken off all marine center stories, my irritation at the lack of progress on Abby's investigation, my fury at Jason for groping me publicly, my rage at Kimmie pushing me into the punch bowl, pretending as if I tripped, and then ratting me out to the police chief—everything welled up inside me suddenly, like blistering paint before a raging fire, uncontrollable.

"Stop smiling!" I shouted. I grabbed the press releases and my laptop computer. I'd finish my work from home.

With the click of a button, I sent the alumni fundraiser story to Lee, and my last officially assigned article even remotely related to Abby was out of my hands. Now I was completely on my own initiative to pursue answers about her death. So now what? My research into Abby's life and the crimes surrounding her death had so many holes, I didn't know where to begin. I decided that my brain needed a fresh perspective. My emotions needed a release. I shut down my laptop and pulled my guitar case from under my bed.

Hours later, I still sat on my bedroom window sill with one foot on the shaded patio and the other propped on the chipped white paint of the porch railing, admiring the sinking dusk, still unwinding my thoughts as I picked through a classical cannon on my guitar. In the settling darkness, a distant porch light turned on—Daniel's. I paused my playing and wiped beads of sweat off my brow. I wondered what Daniel would think about everything I'd seen and heard, from the argument between Kipling and Ballings to Mark's presence outside the center, from Ballings and Trish together in his office to how Abby knew to associate me with the *Tribune*. I owed it to Abby's memory to tell Daniel what I knew. Maybe he'd tell me I was being an overly nosy reporter and jumping to conclusions again. But what if the information I knew was relevant to the case? Wasn't telling Daniel what I knew worth the risk of being laughed away? I made a decision.

In the amount of time it took me to close my window, trade my grungy T-shirt for a camisole and green semi-transparent top that set off my eyes, and pull on my sandals, I was out the door. But by that time, a splash of cherry red, a shiny Mini Cooper, was parked in front of Daniel's home. I slinked behind a tree and peeked down the street. I watched a pony tail of tangled, frizzy orange hair bob out of the vehicle. Kimmie. For a split second, I was thankful for humidity.

Kimmie clipped up the pathway and rang Daniel's doorbell. The door opened, and Kimmie stepped inside. I felt a tug inside me. I wanted to walk by Daniel's apartment and do some spying. Another part of me resisted. Let them have their privacy, it urged, or ring the doorbell and tell both Kimmie and Daniel everything I'd learned. But then, I thought, what would be the harm in first walking by, seeing if I could glimpse something? This was my neighborhood, too. I could go for a walk if I wanted.

Perhaps I could ascertain the extent of Kimmie's off-duty relationship with Daniel, though knowing my luck the bushes surrounding Daniel's yard would block my view. Reaching his property, I slowed and strolled into the alley. Picking a hopeful spot between two azaleas, I crouched down and pretended to adjust my sandals. Through the shrubbery, I could make out Daniel's den. I realized I was trembling as I felt a giddy surge of adrenaline course through my veins.

Kimmie and Daniel were standing inside. She put her hand on his shoulder and, laughing, threw her head back to reveal her white neck. I often envied Kimmie's milky, smooth skin, though it would have been too high-maintenance for me. I never needed to slather myself with sunscreen every time I thought about running to the beach. After about a minute of talking, Daniel left the room. Then Kimmie looked directly at me. I sucked in my breath and glanced around. Surely the bushes shrouded me. Kimmie yanked at a couple of strands of hair and examined her teeth. She was primping in her reflection off the glass. I sighed. Suddenly I felt a hand pulling me up by the scruff of my neck.

I stood and spun around, slipping against the gravel of the alley, and scraping my arm on the bushes as I fell.

CHAPTER 45

"Jonie!" Patrick pulled me up. Below his firmly gelled dark curls, one side of his mouth was crooked in an amused smile.

"I'm fine. I—I was just taking a walk," I stuttered, lifting my top back over my bare shoulder from where it had slipped. "I live a block away." I took a breath and decided to change the subject. "What are you doing here?"

"If you wanted to come to the party, why didn't you just say so?"

"Party?"

"Daniel likes to grill out every Friday for several pals on the force. We're all told we ought to bring dates, not that any of us have dates to bring, so I guess tonight is your lucky night."

"Hah," I said. "*My* lucky night? I—"

He grabbed my uninjured arm and led me around the house toward the front door. For a fleeting moment, I thought of running away, but Patrick' grip was unyielding. And I doubted he would take too kindly to any tae kwon do moves I tried to pull to break away.

While Daniel's face showed confusion when Patrick pushed me inside ahead of him, Kimmie's revealed anger. I hoped my face didn't show any emotion as I admired the way Daniel seemed solid and independent, almost commanding, among his colleagues, and even in casual attire—beige shorts made from cargo pants that were cut off just above the knees topped with a faded gray Army shirt. His mouth opened slightly, as if he wanted to ask something, before he quickly shut it. I wondered if we were going to spend the entire evening standing silently in the foyer when Patrick spoke.

"Now I know you all have met."

"She's a homicide suspect," Kimmie said.

Patrick rolled his eyes. "You know good as me she ain't."

Daniel shook his head slightly at Kimmie.

"I found her on the curb, and she looked hungry." Patrick draped his arm around my shoulder and squeezed.

"Welcome," Daniel said, frowning.

"By the way," Patrick said, "do you have a band-aid?"

"I'm fine," I said.

"Can't have you bloodying up my best friend's shack."

Daniel went upstairs to gather first-aid supplies.

"Really, what are you doing here?" Kimmie asked.

"You heard Patrick." I shrugged.

"You want a beer?" Patrick asked.

I nodded, and he wandered into the kitchen, leaving Kimmie and me alone.

"Why don't we go into the den?" I suggested.

"Why don't you go back to where you came from?"

"Actually, I'm just starting to enjoy myself," I said, sidling around her and bumping my shoulder against hers in a gesture that could be perceived as accidental. I selected a corner seat on the sofa with a clear view of the fireplace. I noted Daniel's mantle still held the ornate wooden box, the mysterious metal fragment presumably still hidden inside. I hoped one day Daniel would feel close enough to me to explain the box's content and, more, what happened to him overseas to cause him to be so afflicted by it.

Daniel returned with a handful of alcohol swabs and a band-aid, and Patrick passed me a beer. This evening could be extremely interesting, I thought.

"So," I said, after everyone settled in the den. "How's Abby's case coming? Are you close to arresting someone?"

"We're not playing reporter tonight," Kimmie said.

"I'm not. I'm asking as a friend."

"Let's not talk about open cases," Daniel intervened. "So, Jonie, Kimmie tells me you came here from Nashville."

"Near Nashville," I said.

"Do you miss it?"

I shook my head. "I like it here. I missed Wilmington, the downtown section, the beach, my family." I looked Kimmie in the eye.

She looked away.

"It's good to be home."

Kimmie made a grunting noise.

"As they say," I continued, "you can take me away from saltwater, but you can't take the ocean away from me. This place is in my blood."

"She fancies herself a surfer," Kimmie said.

"I did a little surfing myself," Daniel said, "back in the day."

"Back in the day?" I laughed. "What are you, 80?"

"It's been years and years."

"We ought to get together and go sometime. I didn't surf at all while I was away from here, but it came back to me easy enough, despite all the years." I was about to ask Daniel where he grew up when Patrick asked if I left Wilmington because of a job or college.

"No. I left because—" I looked at Kimmie examining the hardwood flooring as if the boards were chess pieces and she was about to try for a pivotal move. I figured now was not the time to rehash the past. "I left because I was at odds with my family."

"She left with her boyfriend to play in his band." Kimmie threw back her head, laughing. Only this time, instead of being flirtatious, the laugh came off as being embarrassingly catty, at least to me.

"I was stupid," I quietly admitted. "I thought our band could make it big in Nashville. I play guitar," I explained.

"So what happened once you arrived in Nashville?" Patrick asked.

"We played a couple of gigs and then the band fell apart. Later my boyfriend and I, our relationship—it was best to be rid of it all, him, the band. And since begging is such a fickle trade, I managed eventually to find a job at a small-town newspaper. But enough about me," I said, searching for a new subject. "Is sitting around interrogating innocent citizens what cops do for fun?"

"The tables are turned and Jonie can't take a couple of questions," Daniel teased.

"It'll all be worth it once you taste the meat," Patrick said. "You'll be over here every Friday night."

"I need to light the grill." Daniel stood.

I followed suit. "Can I help with anything?"

He eyed me. "Know how to sauté mushrooms?"

"Skillet, here I come!"

He smiled. "That's the attitude."

I followed him to the kitchen. He held out a colander of washed mushrooms. I grabbed it, but he didn't release his hold.

"Do you mind if I—" he shook his head. "Are you and Patrick…?"

Daniel stopped talking as Kimmie strode into the kitchen, followed by Patrick. Daniel let go of the colander and pointed to a glass cutting board. "Slice away," he said.

"What can I help with?" Kimmie asked.

"Want to chop some salad?"

Kimmie grabbed the lettuce and commandeered my cutting board and knife. I set the mushrooms beside her on the counter and popped one in my mouth. Daniel grabbed a lighter and a bowl of steak soaking in marinade and exited onto the porch with Patrick.

Kimmie chopped using vigorous swipes, the resounding bangs from the knife hitting the cutting board the only sound in the kitchen. I occasionally stole bits of lettuce or tomato from her piles and ate them. I could tell my actions aggravated her by the increasingly stiff jerkiness in her knife movements, so I kept stealing bits of salad while admiring Daniel outside turning knobs on the grill and talking with Patrick. Finally, Kimmie finished and set the knife down. I picked it off the counter and began slicing mushrooms. Kimmie shuffled behind me. I could feel her eyes watching my movements.

"Okay, Jonie, what are you really doing here?" she asked in an almost tired tone.

"Same thing as you."

"What do you want from Daniel, anyway?"

I smiled. "What do *you* want from him?" I set the knife down and turned to face her.

"You're not stealing Daniel away from me." She twisted a checkered green dishtowel in her hands.

"I don't see that he's yours to steal."

She reached out to my face and I sidestepped her hand. "You have something stuck to your cheek." She caught my face and scrubbed the moist dish towel across it, hard enough to leave a burning streak.

"What's your problem?" I pushed her hands away.

"I told you to stay away from Daniel, so my problem is you," she said, shoving my shoulders until I was backed into the counter. "You coming here, you trying to butt into my life." Her hands on my shoulders still pinned me against the counter. "You trying to make friends with me as if you could take back what you did."

"Don't you go pretending," I raised my arms and rammed my forearms against her wrists, busting out from her hold. I was amazed at the effort it took; Kimmie had toughened since I left town. "Don't forget you did things that were just as bad, just as humiliating. You were never spotless, though most everyone, Vicki, my father, Jason, might have thought you were Wilmington's sweet southern princess before I—"

Pow! Momentary blackness was shattered by blazing white stars. Kimmie had punched my eye, and my head had ricocheted against the cabinets behind me. I blinked the stars away just in time to see her lunging again at me. I caught her hair, the only thing I could grasp, and pulled hard while her momentum knocked again against the counter. Pots crashed on the floor. The cutting board, laden with vegetables, fell and shattered, scattering glass shards and greenery across the flooring. Kimmie let up, giving me time to sidestep away from the counter so we both had space to maneuver. She pounced on me, gripping my head in a lopsided lock. I tugged my knee up between us and kicked her away, then followed with a solid punch to her chin. But instead of doubling over and accepting defeat like I expected, she took the punch and came back at me. I blocked her fists. I aimed a front kick at her face, but before my foot made contact, thick arms pulled me back. Daniel was restraining me. Kimmie lunged at me but was pushed back to the sink counter by Patrick.

CHAPTER 46

"What are you doing?" Patrick yelled, his arms holding back Kimmie.

Both Kimmie and I were gasping for breath. I tried to push Daniel's arms off me, but he held me tight.

"She came at me," Kimmie panted. "I was defending—"

"You lie!" There I was, past 30; but feeling like an adolescent again—again wanting to expose Kimmie for what she was, to prove my case to people who should have understood Kimmie well enough to see through her hypocrisy, again caring too much about what others perceived.

My eye where Kimmie's punch landed already was swelling shut. We were glaring at each other, but we both had lost the momentum of the fight. Finally, Daniel's arms loosened. Patrick followed suit, and Kimmie sank to the floor, burrowing her head in her arms and emitting a hiccup-like cry. I recognized Kimmie's fake but believable cry. Patrick knelt beside her. I glanced at Daniel's concerned face as he rushed past me and also stooped down.

I stood alone, feeling distant, almost like I wasn't standing there at all and instead had dissolved into the faint buzzing coming from the kitchen light.

I found my voice. "I didn't instigate this fight." Instigate. Big word for a short-word situation, I thought. No one moved. No one acknowledged that I said anything. I felt the tension rising again, my muscles increasingly clenching. But instead of releasing myself, shouting like I felt like doing, calling Kimmie the names that were pouring into my mind, I took a deep breath. I looked at Daniel. "Sorry for the mess, Daniel." He glanced up at me for a moment. "I'd stick around to clean it up, but I have the feeling everyone would rather I leave." I turned around and walked from the house.

Halfway home, Patrick caught up with me. "I'll walk you the rest of the way," he said.

"It's okay. You can go back to consoling Kimmie."

"I think Daniel has that covered."

I cringed. Then I felt shocked that I cared so deeply about imagining Daniel's arms around Kimmie. Then I felt angry that Kimmie was manipulating again, making sure to milk her maladies from the fight she started.

"So a cat fight," Patrick said. "That's not something I get to see every day, even being on the police force."

I didn't laugh.

"Actually," he continued, "that's pretty serious, pretty violent. Are you going to tell me what that was all about? Was Kimmie not chopping the tomatoes fine enough?"

"I'm telling you, Kimmie is the one who started it."

Patrick didn't say anything.

"I suppose it was the physical part of a fight that should have happened years ago. Something Kimmie can't let go of."

"Must have been awful if she can't let go of it."

I nodded. "When we were in college, I hid a camera in our house, and it filmed Kimmie having sex when our parents weren't home. Then when my family was expecting to watch the action-adventure movie we rented, I switched films and showed my film, believing my father and stepmother would be appalled at Kimmie—they thought she was flawless—and hoping Jason, Kimmie's boyfriend at the time, but not the boy she was having sex with, would get a wake-up call. He was over that evening, too.

"See," I continued, rushing my words, "Jason and I had been dating for years when Kimmie stole him from me—not because she liked him but because she wanted to get to me.

At the time, it seemed like the end of the world—big drama college-days saga. Now it just seems silly. And my plan backfired—Kimmie's still my father's angel and perfect in everyone else's eyes."

"I don't know about that."

"Kimmie might almost have deserved it. We had been at war ever since we met. I never clicked with my stepmother, Kimmie's mom, though Kimmie became tight with my dad—closer to him than I felt, sometimes. And at school, Kimmie's friends and my friends, we just didn't mix. Who knows how it really started. She would do something to me; I would do something to her. One time, she knew I had a crush on this guy who used the locker below mine, so she stuffed my locker full of sanitary napkins. She must have spent a month's worth of allowance to buy that many. When I opened my locker, about a hundred of those things fell on that guy. Utterly ruined any chances I might have had with him."

Patrick chuckled, I eyed him, and he quickly turned his face stolid. Then I caught myself.

"No, it's okay; you can laugh. It is funny, looking back on it. Most of the things we did to each other are laughable now. When I ran my film, I was still hurt about her being able to steal my boyfriend away; but if he could have been stolen, why would I have wanted to be with him anyway?"

"You said it."

"I admit it myself. What I did with the x-rated tape was awful—one of the top items on my list of reasons I'm going to hell. I can't believe I expected everyone to suddenly switch sides and show their support for me. But I also can't believe Kimmie still won't let it go or that she's still pulling the same tricks on me that she did when we were younger."

We stopped at my apartment door.

"Like tonight, Kimmie struck me first. But she's got you thinking she was defending herself, and she's fake crying. You and Daniel buy her act. I know you don't believe me. You work with Kimmie, and you hardly know me, and police loyalty runs strong. I'm the outsider."

Patrick held up his hands.

"Sorry," I said.

He grinned. Patrick was becoming my friend. Not every guy could tolerate ranting so patiently.

"You want to come up for some food," I asked, "or do you think you'll go back to Daniel's?"

"I'd like to come up, but I should be heading back, seeing as how I work with both of them, and they might not look too kindly on me hanging around you tonight. Like you said, it's about loyalty. No offense."

I shrugged.

"If you're serious about making amends with Kimmie, put some distance between tonight's events," Patrick said. "Let the air clear out a little, let that bruise go away, let us tie up the case. Then approach Kimmie."

"At least you guys don't suspect me."

"Naw. Kimmie's just—you're not really on our radar screen. But it's not over until it's over," he said. "See you, Jonie."

I watched him turn and walk away.

CHAPTER 47

When I awoke to early blue-gray light Saturday morning, I lay still for a moment and listened to the steady hum of the ceiling fan, wishing I could wriggle out of the mother-daughter tea with Vicki and Kimmie. But because I didn't believe my father would applaud me using a fabricated excuse to duck out of the tea party he fought for me to attend, I was trapped. All I wanted to do was to get closer to finding Abby's killer and be vindicated at the *Tribune*. An afternoon tea wouldn't help that. I tried to numb my mind by following the progress of one of my ceiling fan blades as it circled, but the light was too dim or the fan was too fast.

Later, I stopped my truck at the gate to the bridge to Figure Eight Island and gave the guard my name and my parents' names. I was to meet Vicki and Kimmie at their house before traveling as a supposedly happy trio to the tea. I expected the guard to check my name off the guest list, nod lazily, and raise the gate. Instead, he spent an inordinate amount of time examining the visitor roster only to look up and ask if Dr. and Mrs. Waters were expecting me.

"Go ahead and give them a call, and tell them their other daughter is here." I passed my license out the window.

The sliding window of the guard building snapped shut, and I watched as the guard picked up his telephone. After a minute, he returned my license, and said, "Dr. Waters said

Mrs. Waters accidentally forgot to add your name to their list."

"Likely," I muttered.

"No matter; Dr. Waters told me to add you to the family list, so you'll be welcome to enter the island at your pleasure from here on out."

The gate raised, and I took my time driving across the bridge, taking deep breaths and making a concerted effort to divert my thoughts from Vicki and Kimmie. Why was I ever taken off the family list? I'd left town, not died. At least the low tide revealed the marsh mud, allowing its heavy stink to waft into my truck, drowning out the punch odor that somehow still lingered in the cab, even though I'd left the windows cracked since the alumni fundraiser. I had thrown away my purse and dress; the punch stains were past my abilities to remove. My cell phone had been totaled; I hadn't even bothered to retrieve it from the bed of my truck. I enjoyed hearing it rattle around when I drove over bumps or took a curve at more than 10 mph. The clattering reminded me of what to expect from family. Purchasing a replacement for the cell phone had taken a chunk out of my meager bank account, and while standing at the register, handing over my money, I couldn't help but itemize what groceries the cell phone money could have bought instead. I needed the salary of a fulltime reporter and wondered when, or even if, I'd be hired on as a regular staffer at the *Tribune*.

I locked my tires and skidded to a stop in front of Vicki's home. My father and Vicki waited on the front porch, where Vicki made a grandiose apology to me for the mix-up at the gate. Vicki's gold necklaces and bracelets glinted under the sun like costume jewelry beneath stage lights.

"Of course I forgive you," I said, acting my role.

I wanted to poke a finger down my throat and puke on her topiaries, but I followed Vicki to her car where Kimmie waited in the front passenger seat, her hair somehow pulled back tight into a thick braid from which orange ringlets were escaping and threatening a full scale riot. Maybe she'd explode before the tea was over. I tucked myself into the sedan, trying not to step on the hem of my sleeveless floral-patterned dress. We drove the two blocks to the brunch.

A fair number of cars already had parked beside the beachfront home, so Vicki parked several houses down. We almost would have walked as much had we not driven at all. Martha, with Mrs. Pridgen, parked behind us, and we all made our way to the house together, down the asphalt road that was so hot I could feel it through the thin soles of my flats. The thought of Mrs. Pridgen attending the mother-daughter tea without Abby struck me suddenly, but I supposed life had to continue; and I admired her for venturing out with Martha so soon after Abby's death.

The two-story house gleamed bright white with tall columns in front supporting a semicircular balcony. I imagined the house's color made it look imposing; but the structure also dwarfed the front yard's immaculate landscaping, small palm trees and numerous manicured bushes. Bony giraffe Vicki, Amazon Kimmie and I, somewhere in the middle but feeling on the outside, followed the Pridgens up the white tiled steps into the white marble foyer and then back into a living area that also displayed white walls and white marble floors. We all found a table together. I glanced around. While lacy white cloths draped each of the dozen or so circular tables, every table displayed a different pattern of tea pots and cups. Our set featured scenes of Holland, windmills and dancing Dutch girls. A maid wearing an all-white tuxedo, including even a white bow tie, served us immediately.

"How are you doing, Mrs. Pridgen?" Kimmie asked politely, not waiting for an answer. "Before we left our house, I noticed your irises in the side yard are looking beautiful."

"Thank you, dear," Mrs. Pridgen said. I noticed her eyes were unfocused, staring at the blank, white wall beyond Kimmie. "The only reason they look nice is because they need no maintenance. Everything else has fallen by the wayside, because of—" In a blink, tears spilled onto her cheeks. She bowed her head.

I scowled at Kimmie.

"You expect your peers to die in your lifetime, even your husband," Mrs. Pridgen said, "but not your daughter."

Vicki leaned over and patted her shoulder, her gold bracelets clinking with each pat.

Mrs. Pridgen began to sob. Women around us turned their heads to stare. "I came to this mother-daughter tea—" Mrs. Pridgen dabbed her nose with her linen napkin. "I thought I would be—" She hiccupped again loudly and stood up, her thighs jarring the table. "Excuse me," she blurted, hurrying off toward a hallway, which I assumed led to a powder room.

Martha stood to follow, but Vicki pushed her back down. "I'll go."

Martha looked at Kimmie and then at me. She then glared at the ladies at the surrounding tables until they looked away. She shook her curtains of thick brown hair behind her shoulders. Tears laced her eyes.

"Please tell me you've found something new on the case," she said to Kimmie, her voice low and soft. "I don't know how much longer we can take not knowing who, or why." She sipped her tea and put the cup down with a loud thump.

"We're working on it," Kimmie said, glancing at me. "I wish I could tell you more."

"What have you found out about Mark?" I asked. Abby's former fiancé remained devious in my eyes.

Kimmie hesitated. "We're investigating him, along with a number of other suspects." She lowered her nose and glared at me as if she was studying me over a pair of imaginary bifocals.

"Mark was stalking Abby," I said. I relayed how I had seen Mark the night of the alumni fundraiser. "He told me he was at the Dirty Bird the night Abby died; but when I went to the bar, the employee there said he hadn't seen him. Mark later told me he was at the marine center that night."

I was spilling my findings, offering my suspicions up for ridicule, but I didn't care. As much as I didn't want to give Kimmie a leg up, if she could use my puzzle pieces to help solve the crime and make an arrest, at least the killer would be brought to justice, Mrs. Pridgen and all of us would find peace, and my derailed life might return to its track.

Martha sat up straighter.

"Could Mark have killed her?" Martha asked Kimmie. She rubbed her hand across her cheek. "His temper always boiled over. I felt relieved when the engagement broke off."

"Sorry, but I can't discuss this case with you right now," Kimmie said. "Especially with you," she snapped at me.

"What about Professor Ballings?" I asked Kimmie. "Are you looking into him? He's not telling the police everything he knows. And I've seen him getting amorous with an undergraduate. He seems to get involved with most of the women he works with."

"We're investigating the case. I can't discuss it. Excuse me," she said, standing up. I watched her flounce away toward the bathroom.

"That bastard," Martha said. "Mark," she clarified.

"Has he bothered you since the funeral?"

Martha shook her head, and I told her about the report detailing Mark's stalking that I spotted at the police station.

"I hope they nail him," she said.

"I didn't like him from the beginning," I admitted, remembering the way Mark's anger seemed to expand from within him, stretching his skin, itching to burst out, and the freaky way he had appeared and disappeared like smoke at the fundraiser.

"Stay away from him," Martha said. "He makes me nervous. And Abby's research partner, Professor Ballings? Do you really think he could have something to do with her death?"

"Abby didn't mention anything worth noting or anything that seemed questionable about him?"

Martha shook her head.

"When I interviewed Ballings about his research with Abby, he couldn't give me precise details but kept trying to take credit for her work. He kept mentioning a backup disk with Abby's research on it." I steered away from discussing the possibility that Ballings' involvement with Abby could have been more than academic.

"But Ballings didn't know where Abby's backup disk was?"

I shook my head. "Ballings said pharmaceuticals in the waterway—pharmaceutical pollution—caused the fish kills. He didn't elaborate."

"You don't suppose the disk was destroyed or lost when the lab was vandalized, do you? But even if he doesn't find Abby's research, the work at least can be replicated."

We were silent a few moments.

"Look, Martha, do you know of a lockbox that Abby kept? Something she would need a key to open? Maybe something in her room? In Ballings' office, I found—" I noticed Kimmie reenter the room. "Just trust me. I think whoever vandalized Ballings' lab was looking for something, and I think maybe that something wasn't there in the lab; and if it wasn't there, it could be in her room at your house."

"Come over after the tea. We can look together." Martha took a sip of her tea as Kimmie sat down again.

A couple of hours later, Martha and I rifled through Abby's drawers and closet. We looked under her bed and in her nightstand. I quickly determined nothing in Abby's room locked with a key; a trunk in her closet buckled shut with no lock.

"What exactly are you looking for?" Martha asked.

"I don't know. I thought it would be obvious, but it's not."

I walked to the poster-sized map of the Cape Fear River and surrounding coast hanging on Abby's wall, the only obvious possession that connected her to her research. Abby had marked and numbered dots along the river. She also had scrawled annotations on the map, such as "Yarbrgh farm" and "WHGC," which I immediately recognized as the White Heron Golf Course, its pristine eighteen holes surrounding an infamous community known for its multimillion dollar homes. Upkeep on that grass was sure to generate a significant amount of fertilizer runoff into the river. In the river itself were dots with labels beside them. The dot closest to Wilmington was labeled M64, with another dot labeled M42 further downstream. Beside M64 was the notation "WWTP + runoff."

Martha saw my frown.

"What's WWTP?" I asked.

"All Abby's annotations were associated with places that affected water quality, places like golf courses and farms," Martha said.

"It's the wastewater treatment plant," I said as I realized it. "That must be near where the plant discharges into the river."

I left the house feeling disappointed about the lack of progress. With the sun hanging low in the sky, I sat at one end of Vicki's kitchen table, scooping dripping forkfuls of her candied yams into my mouth. My father, Vicki, Kimmie, and I still were pretending to get along. No one had commented on my black eye or Kimmie's bruised chin all day. We'd been immature to resort to a physical fight, but tension had been smoldering for years. I wasn't sure the fight had defused it.

As usual, the family conversation bordered on being nonexistent, so I swam in my own thoughts, wondering how Vicki made her yams so divine, probably by loading them with ungodly amounts of butter and sugar. Nowhere else had I ever tasted yams so sweet and creamy and soft. I had packed my swimming suit in my truck; and I dreaded seeing my bloated stomach on the beach after this dinner, but I continued eating courageously, scraping the last of the yams onto my fork.

I thought about Mark's confession at the marine center and his suspicions of Ballings. What could Mark hope to gain by lying to me? If he was guilty, wouldn't he have stuck with his former tactic of avoidance? My gut feeling was that Mark was telling the truth. Would Ballings have killed Abby because of her pregnancy? Unless Ballings was conning me, too, he didn't seem to know quite enough about Abby's research for credit to be the motive. If Ballings killed Abby, why was his and Abby's lab ransacked? If Ballings was looking for something, he had the time to conduct an orderly search. I took a swig of iced tea and noticed Vicki and my father both frowning at me.

"Sorry. Did I miss something?"

"I asked how you're liking work at the *Tribune*," my father said.

"It's good." I swallowed a bit of ham. "My job is flexible. Some days are long; other days are short. It all evens out. It's nice not having to clock in and out. I can set my own schedule, for the most part, around the stories I'm assigned."

"That's nice, unlike Kimmie, bless her and her job," Vicki said, stroking Kimmie's arm. "Depending on her case load, she can be out at all times of the day and night. She stays so busy. Of course, her work is so vital, so consequential. I can hardly say that if it were any less important, she would choose that type of lifestyle. She's like me; she honors a hard day's work."

I crinkled my nose but decided to let the comment slide as Vicki stood up and pulled a pecan pie onto the table. She doled out slices for all of us. I took a bite. Sweet, crunchy filling, soft, flaky crust: perfection. Surely a pie so heavenly couldn't come from someone who was all bad. Of course, I knew Vicki wasn't all bad, I reminded myself. My father loved her, after all. He married her and stuck with her, no matter how opposite she was from my memories of my birth mother. I pushed away a sudden aching loneliness by savoring another bite of Vicki's pie. Even her presentation of the pie proved immaculate. The plate my piece rested on matched the pie platter, light blue china dishes edged in gold with waterfowl, wood ducks and swans, flying around the border.

"Kimmie gave me these plates," Vicki said. "A special Mother's Day present."

Kimmie smiled at her. I clenched my fists.

"Such a wonderful, sweet, thoughtful daughter," Vicki said.

Something felt like it snapped inside me, as if my heart was a dried out dogwood branch bent over to breaking by a sudden weight.

"Can't you for once try looking at Kimmie, at this family, with just one toe in reality?" I asked.

Vicki gave me a look like I had incorrectly answered an elementary Sunday school question. She knew exactly what I meant.

"Jonie," my father said, holding out his hand.

"What?"

He shook his head, looking out the window over the creek grasses past the Pridgen's dock and boat house, their aged fiberglass skiff bobbing merrily inside its shelter.

"Don't you agree with me?"

My father turned back to his plate and took another bite of pie.

I felt sweat on my face. "Don't you get tired of sitting around this table, alternately ignoring each other, playing games, and pretending to be a family?"

My father and Vicki continued eating. Kimmie smirked at me.

I couldn't endure another second at the table. I pushed up, and in the movement, my pie plate fell to the floor and shattered. I felt a twinge of guilt in my chest, but I kept going, walking out of the kitchen, running through the living room, and slamming the front door behind me. I gunned my truck, like any decent grown woman acting like a rebellious teenager would, and ripped out of their driveway, nicking the mailbox with my side mirror as I cut the corner onto the street too sharply. It was then that I suddenly realized what Abby's key opened. It now seemed so blatantly obvious, I wanted to smack my forehead.

CHAPTER 48

The key opened a post office box, and I was betting it opened Abby's campus post office box. Why didn't I think of it before? I sped to the university post office, grateful its doors were open around the clock every day. A student exited the building as I parked.

I paused in the vacant post office lobby, a main hallway that connected longer hallways in a fork-like layout. Each prong of the fork held two long walls and one short wall at its end, and all the hallways were covered with boxes from eye level to a foot above the floor—thousands of mailboxes—one for every student and faculty member, and then presumably more to allow for university expansion.

I needed a way to narrow my search for Abby's mailbox. I looked around the lobby. A pay telephone hung near the corner. Clamped to the booth by a flexible metal rope were a regular phone book and a university phone book. Perfect. I flipped to the P's and found her, Abby Pridgen, 3034. I scurried to the mailbox and raised my shaking arm to shoulder height, jiggling in the key and turning the lock. I pulled the mailbox door open.

A few pieces of mail rested inside. I sifted through them: a schedule of upcoming university athletic events, a flyer for a concert held last weekend, and an envelope with the marine center's return address. Why would the center send Abby's mail to an on-campus post office box when she worked at the center itself? I held the envelope up to the light. The thick paper stock embedded with blue and gray fibers was nowhere near transparent. I glanced around. The hallway remained vacant. I decided to open the envelope. I pulled out the letter, took a deep breath and unfolded it. It was just a newsletter. I felt like a fool.

I decided to put Abby's mail back in her box and trash the newsletter and envelope I opened. I wanted to kick myself for getting my hopes up. I should have expected this; the key went to a mailbox, after all.

But why would Abby hide her mailbox key in the window track? I peeked through Abby's open mailbox into the interior mailroom hallway beyond. With the dim off-hours lighting, the hallway looked gloomy with aging, gray walls and a standard broad-faced clock, the elongated red second hand patiently clicking away. As I pulled my head away, I noticed a bump in the shadows at the top of Abby's box, like the box above hers was dented in its center. I ran my fingers over the bump. Something hard was taped to the smooth metal. Abby had hidden something on the top of her box! I used my nails to pick at the corners of the tape. After half a minute, I worked enough tape loose to peel it off. My hand emerged with a patch of clear packing tape and a USB drive no longer than my thumb and barely thicker than a few sticks of chewing gum. The high-density computer disk I held in the palm of my hand seemed so miniscule, so innocent, I wondered what secrets it held to justify its concealment. This had to be Abby's backup disk that Ballings wanted.

After closing Abby's mailbox, I hurried to my car, dragged out my briefcase, and snatched my laptop from it. I drummed my fingers against my dashboard, wishing my computer booted faster. I pulled the plastic cap off the USB drive and slid the disk into my computer. On my screen, the disk's contents popped up. I didn't recognize any of the file extensions, all of which were .lrf files. What was an .lrf file? I switched the disk's view to see which file had been modified most recently. It was conclusions.lrf, and it had been modified the morning of Abby's death.

I double clicked the document to see if it would open. Of course, it didn't. Instead, my computer asked me what software I wanted to use to open the file. After trying a few different programs unsuccessfully, I gave up. I logged onto the internet, thankful someone nearby operated an unsecured wireless server, and ran a search for ".lrf, software." A few different software programs were called up, the most promising being Laboratory Research Filer. I clicked on the link to visit the software's website. For close to $1,000, I could purchase the software. Even if I possessed the money and didn't mind burning it, shipping would take up to a week, the website informed me. I rolled my eyes. I wanted the software now. I bet the computers in the marine center ran the program, if only I could gain access.

I had found what the key opened, and I had found what Abby had hidden—from Ballings, I presumed, or possibly the dean. Now I needed to visit a marine center computer to open the research. If I was discovered using a marine center computer and reported, I would be terminated from the *Tribune* and possibly prosecuted. But if I wasn't discovered, and if the files on Abby's disk revealed something about who killed her or why she was killed, the mystery of her death might be cracked.

Face sweating, pulse racing in exhilaration, I cranked my truck and hoped the night air would cool me down and blow an idea into my brain on how to get into a marine center computer, soon.

"Fess up, Jonie. What are you up to?"

I extracted my second beer from the six-pack I brought to share with Phaser. We were sitting on Phaser's porch, the lights off except for a distant lamp in his den.

"Can't a sister bring her favorite brother a treat?"

"Your only brother, and this six-pack comes with strings attached, I bet."

I popped off the bottle top. "Didn't I bring you donuts just the other day, no strings attached?"

"But you didn't have that feisty glint in your eye and that toothy smile on your face. I saw it when I opened the door, Jonie."

Phaser still could read me; I supposed some things never changed. I decided to come clean. "You wouldn't happen to have software around here that can open .lrf files, or know someone who does, would you?" I asked.

"Never heard of an .lrf file."

"Then I need you to come with me and spot me so I can go into the marine center and open a file on a computer. Please."

Phaser set down his half-finished beer, a rare gesture, so I stepped up my plea a notch.

"It may help me move closer to figuring out who killed Abby."

"Aren't you in enough trouble as it is?"

"Kimmie exaggerates."

Phaser shook his head.

"If I'm already in such big trouble, what's a little more? With your help, I won't be caught. Besides, the center's a public place, sort of. It's public taxpayers' money that supports university education, right?"

"That's a stretch. Why don't you just let Kimmie and the cops do their jobs or call one of your contacts at the center and have him fax a copy of the file to you? They do know about the file you're talking about, right?"

I shrugged. I couldn't come completely clean, couldn't tell Phaser that I stole a key from Abby's office and used it to take a hidden disk from her mailbox. The risk of him tattling on me to Kimmie wasn't worth it.

"Please help me, Phaser. Trust me."

"The answer's no," he said. "Tell Kimmie about the file, if she's not looking into it yet, and let the police do their jobs."

I looked Phaser in the eyes, their moonlit luster slightly altered so that they looked dully reflective, almost like a muted gleam off metal doors. I knew I couldn't change his mind.

"Do you want me to pay for my half of the six-pack?" he asked.

"No," I said, failing to extract the sulkiness from my voice. "You're still my favorite brother."

"That's the spirit," he said. He chugged what remained in his bottle and grabbed another.

We finished all the beer in a consensual silence that should have been soothing, but my head slightly throbbed. Since Phaser denied my request for assistance, and since I wasn't going to turn over the disk to the police, and since I couldn't risk entering the marine center on my own, and since Jason and I were awkward, only one other potential partner I could ask remained, Stu. But I hadn't wanted to tell Stu about the disk. If Stu knew about the disk, he wouldn't take long to tell Jason.

The disk was my find, and what information that disk held mattered more to me than to either of them. The disk's contents might give me new insight, maybe even proof, about who killed my friend, simultaneously leading to my vindication with Montgomery. If I did tell Stu or Jason about the disk, would they believe me when I told them how I came across it? Would they agree with my actions, taking the disk, or would they reiterate what Phaser said; that Abby's computer files were a matter for the police?

The next morning, as I quickly whipped the couple of press releases assigned to me into stories, my fingers trembled with anticipation for what I was plotting later in the day. I knew I did a rough job, but I hardly bothered to polish my work before e-mailing it on. I couldn't believe my Plan Two was working. With surprisingly little prodding, not even pressing me for details on why I needed to sneak into Ballings' office, Stu agreed to back me up. As I put it to him in a late telephone call last night, he owed me after spying on my visit to Montgomery's office. Heading out, I nodded at Stu.

At my apartment, I rushed as I threw on some jean shorts and a pink v-neck shirt. I topped my attire with a ball cap. Glancing at my reflection in the mirror, I believed I could pass for a college student, albeit an older graduate student. I made sure Abby's disk and my new cell phone were with me. I also tucked a couple of sturdy pins into my pocket. I hoped, if I needed to break into Ballings' office, the lock wouldn't be much more difficult than the one on Kimmie's bedroom door I mastered picking as a teen. A few minutes later, I saw Stu's car pull up outside.

On the way to the center, we reviewed my plan. We were going to walk into the center like any student would and head to Ballings' office. My cell phone would be set to vibrate, so if Ballings—though he would be in the middle of teaching a class by the time we arrived—or the dean, or anyone else unexpected, decided to make an appearance, Stu could buzz me.

Stu parked his car at the center, and we exchanged a brief glance.

"Okay," I said, my voice barely more than a whisper. "Let's go."

CHAPTER 49

I slung my backpack over my shoulder and walked with Stu through the front door. At the branch in the main hallway, I paused and retied my shoe while Stu continued down a short hallway flanked with closed doors on the way to Ballings' room. Stu knocked. Just in case Ballings was in, Stu could be seen, make a lame excuse, and not find himself fired from the *Tribune* if anyone heard about his visit. When no one answered, Stu tried the door. He shook his head; it was locked. He walked back to me.

I pulled out the pins and waited until a couple of straggling students found their classrooms, then walked to Ballings' door. I inserted the pins into the lock and tried to find the sweet spot. I was rusty, but after a minute, I was in. I closed the door behind me and re-locked it. I had Ballings' office to myself, and Stu remained on look-out duty.

The professor's computer was off, so I pushed its power button and waited for it to boot, tapping my fingers and jiggling my foot. Finally the computer was running. I popped in Abby's disk and checked my list ordering the files I wanted to print. I opened the first file. A page that was blank except for *Pseudopersistent Pollution and its Effects on Marine Life: Conclusions* came up. I hit the print button. The program asked if I wanted to print the open document only, or if I wanted to print the open document and all linked files. I clicked on the latter option and watched as the computer pulled up every file on the disk and sent them to the printer. Even before the files finished queuing, the printer began spitting out pages. I crossed my fingers, hoping for no jams.

My cell phone vibrated. The caller identification showed Stu's name. I swore under my breath. I grabbed all the pages that had printed so far, but pages were still coming out. I looked around for somewhere to hide. I heard a key slide into the door. I dashed to Ballings' desk, crawled under, tucking myself as far back as possible, and pulled his chair forward to screen me.

I heard the door open. The printer was still going. I heard flip flops approaching. Then I saw feet with painted red toenails. The visitor shuffled close to the desk. I heard her rifling through papers. Then she walked away, pausing at the printer and then continuing out, closing and locking the door behind her. I waited a moment to make sure she had gone before letting myself out from under the desk.

When the printer finished, I checked the print queue on the computer, ensuring that all the documents went through. I shut down the computer and grabbed the rest of the pages from the printer, tucking them all into my backpack, fingers trembling uncontrollably. I hurried out, not pausing to look at Stu, ducking my head so the brim of my ball cap shielded my face.

Wham! I slammed into an unyielding body and fell backward onto the floor. Looking up at the person I ran into, I expected a jocular soccer player or fraternity boy but, instead, found compact Kipling looming.

"Dean Kipling! I—uh—I'm sorry." I stood up and dusted myself off. I assured myself that Kipling didn't know about my publisher banning me from the center, but still my heart raced.

"What are you doing here?" She frowned at me, her dark eyes piercing mine.

I glanced around for Stu but couldn't see him. He'd apparently melted into the students that flooded the hallway in the break between classes. "I was here to see Ballings, but he was out."

"He should be getting out of class now. I can accompany you until we find him."

"Actually, I wanted to ask you a couple of questions, too," I said.

A sudden cold shine in her eyes swallowed any openness present before.

"Not questions for the paper," I said. "The questions are for me. Abby was my friend. I'm not sure if you knew."

"No."

"When was the last time you saw her?" I asked.

Kipling frowned. "I don't owe you answers."

"Wouldn't you want—"

"Nevertheless," she interrupted. "Possibly a week before her death, passing in the hallway."

"Not the night she died?"

Kipling stared at me with an unmoving, slightly staggered expression.

"Did you see her the night she died?"

"No. Of course not."

After a few seconds, I rephrased my question. "What did you see at the center the night she died? Who were you meeting at 10 in the evening?"

"How did you—" Kipling caught herself. "Fine," she said so quietly in the busy hallway that I had to concentrate to distinguish her voice from the din. "She called me."

"Abby called you?"

"Early that afternoon. She said it was urgent; she needed to speak with me, it couldn't wait another day, and she wanted to meet when Ballings was certain not to be around. So we set up an appointment for late that night. She was to come to my office. After she didn't show, I walked to Ballings' lab. The lights were on, but Abby wasn't there. I waited a few minutes and then left. I didn't see anything that indicated she was in trouble." She shrugged, sinking her head deep into her shoulders and flinging her fingers open in a gesture that reminded me of an ostrich fanning its wings while sitting down.

"A night appointment with a professor? Is that normal?"

"Abby said it was urgent."

"Why did she want to meet with you?"

"She didn't specify."

"Do you think she wanted to talk about her research?"

Kipling shrugged again.

"Or, do you think she wanted to alert you to the fact that she and Ballings were seeing each other and she was pregnant with his child?"

Kipling's head jerked. "I don't know where you're conjuring that accusation—"

"Just answer my question, please. Was the meeting to discuss her intimate relationship with Ballings?"

Kipling slowly shook her head, as if she was calculating how to handle me. "I don't stand for professors fooling around." Her hands were clenched. "Nothing was going on. If Ballings was interested in Abby, it would have been strictly because she was his research partner."

"When I asked Ballings about the research he was doing with Abby, he couldn't give me specifics on any findings."

Kipling's face flushed. "Do you really expect every staff member to be able to recite spontaneous, miscellaneous details about research that's conducted under their oversight?"

"I'm not talking off-the-wall details. Ballings didn't know the main research findings. Shouldn't he, as Abby's research partner?"

Kipling paused, blinking. I considered Kipling. I had not pegged her as a woman who would want to be coupled with a complete fool such as Ballings, a man who ran around with students less than half his age, a man who clearly was trying to take credit for Abby's work. Yet Kipling seemed to be covering for him, and this wasn't the first time! But then again, perhaps Ballings was the only man to have nibbled at her bait in a while. Kipling wasn't exactly attractive or young. Her biological clock was probably ticking so loud her brain couldn't stop reverberating; but if I were Ballings, looking to settle down, and assuming he would side with me, I wouldn't want to settle with someone as rigid as Kipling. Was Ballings interested in Dean Kipling or using her for preferential research-funding assistance? Or maybe to Kipling, Ballings was a gem she was taking the challenge to polish.

"Perhaps," I said, "instead of appropriately assisting in Abby's research, Ballings was playing with Trish, the girl he drove around the evening of the alumni fundraiser. You remember. I saw you following."

Kipling stepped toward me. "That's enough!" She looked agitated enough to slap me. "Perhaps Ballings may be a little loose, but I can control him."

I found myself backing away from her. "Ballings fathering Abby's child is a very distinct possibility, isn't it?"

A sinister flash streaked through her eyes like lightning. Her teeth gnashed. "Shut—" She cut herself off and turned away. She strode down the hallway, her heels clicking loudly with each step.

"I thought you were busted for sure," Stu said, turning out of the marine center parking lot.

I let out a breath, unzipped my backpack, and extracted what looked to be more than 100 pages crammed full of small sans-serif type.

"Did you get what you needed?" he asked.

"We'll see."

I wasn't interested in talking. I flipped through the pages in my hands. Meth.lrf looked to be a summary of how Abby collected the research. Suppdoc.lrf was about 75 pages full of complex charts, chemical abbreviations, codes, and numbers. VitDat.lrf looked to be an abbreviation or continuation of Suppdoc, but Conclusions.lrf looked to be the goldmine, if there was to be a goldmine in the paper stack, except it didn't read clearly. The text was overflowing with chemical abbreviations and formulas, and complex words like "spectrometry" and "chromatography" that held no more meaning to me than words in a foreign language. I would have to concentrate, to sit down and wade through the document painstakingly.

"Well?" Stu asked. "What is it you have there?"

"Remember, you promised yesterday you'd keep us coming here together a secret, even from Jason, and no questions asked."

"We almost were busted by that student and then by Kipling. I risked my tail for you, and you're going to hold out on me?"

"I printed some research." I didn't want to lie or give too much away.

"Why did you print it? Why not just save everything to a disk and be done with it?"

I groaned.

"What is it?"

"Nothing," I said, but I suddenly felt nauseated. Sweat blanketed my upper lip. The disk! I'd left it back at the center, still poking out of Ballings' computer.

CHAPTER 50

In my haste, I'd only snatched the printouts, leaving the disk behind! I checked my watch. Ballings' class was long over by now. But maybe he didn't return directly to his office. I flicked open my cell phone and dialed Ballings' office number.

"Professor Ballings' office," a girl's voice said. She giggled and then gasped. I heard a shushing noise in the background. "Hello?"

"Is the professor in?"

"One moment, please."

The phone sounded like it clattered on the desk, then rubbed against something soft.

"Hello?" Ballings asked. He sounded out of breath.

I hung up the phone.

"What was that?" Stu asked.

"The professor's back in his office," I said. I didn't think he'd discovered the disk yet. He seemed preoccupied, but it was only a matter of time. I could see the disk in my mind, plugged into the computer, visible just beyond the keyboard, begging to be noticed. I put my hands to my face.

"Are you okay?" Stu asked. "You look a little green."

"I'm fine," I lied.

"No puking in my car. That's a rule."

I rolled down my window and took in some gulps of fresh air. There was no going back and getting the disk now. My head began to clear. If I looked at the situation from one perspective, the backup disk belonged to Ballings in the first place. It was returned where it was supposed to be. And Ballings wouldn't know I was the one who found the disk and left it in his computer. Looking at the abandoned disk from another angle, if Abby had hidden the disk from the professor, hadn't wanted the professor to take credit for her work, I had destroyed any chance for her to get her name on the research. But at least her work was going to be published and shared.

I looked back to the papers in my hands, more to take my mind off losing the disk. I tried to begin to make sense of the conclusion document.

"Have you ever heard of NCF6? CH—that's carbon and hydrogen, right?"

Stu shrugged.

"This is impossible," I said, skimming across the abbreviations. "DO? SPD? EPIs?"

"It's all chemistry to me."

"That's it!" I opened my cell phone again, called Martha, and set a time to meet.

"No, no," Stu said in a mocking, high-pitched voice. "Don't bother to fill me in or tell me what this is all about."

"I will when I can, I promise." I felt guilty.

Stu dropped me off at my apartment and drove on. I waved at Phaser, who was weeding the lawn, hardly looking my way, and bounded up my stairs. Although I was anxious to hear what Martha would say, I also felt glad for the couple of hours I had before I saw her. I wasn't going to show Abby's work to Martha right away since then I would have to explain how I came to possess it. The time before our meeting would give me a chance to look at Abby's printed files and write down the abbreviations of chemicals or phrases I needed to ask Martha to interpret.

I ordered a decaf; the last thing I needed was more nervous energy. I sipped it slowly while I waited for Martha at Port Java House.

In the couple of hours before coming to the café where I was to meet Martha, I had begun to grasp, but not understand, what Abby had discovered in her research. From reading and rereading the conclusions document and comparing it with her research, the chemical EPI seemed to be causing the fish kills in the Cape Fear River. EPI was one of the seven pharmaceutical compounds Abby had been testing. While in her research she said EPI didn't cause fish to become sick, if she combined EPI in the amounts documented in the river with levels of pollution and toxins fish could normally withstand without any adverse side effects, the fish died. Also in my studying, I found some of the abbreviations I originally thought stood for chemical names actually appeared to be places from which Abby was drawing her river water samples. For example, the most concentrated location where she found EPI consistently was M64, seconded by M42. I remembered from Abby's map that M64 was near where the wastewater treatment plant discharged, and M42 was downstream. Seeing EPI appearing most consistently in its highest concentrations at the discharge point and downstream jived with pseudopersistent pollution.

I hoped Martha could advance my knowledge by telling me what EPI was.

I didn't have to wait long for Martha to show. She slid into the seat across from mine, not bothering to order anything. She still looked faded, but at least her eyes weren't as shadowed as before.

"How are you doing?" I asked.

"Good. Better." She checked her watch.

"A lot has happened since we last talked," I said. "I've been checking out some things—Abby's research, actually."

"I thought you said it was destroyed when the lab was vandalized."

"As it happens, Ballings found the backup disk," I said. By this point, he probably had. "I don't know that it will bring us any closer to finding out who killed her, but I thought it might help to know more about what Abby discovered in her research. In Abby's car, the police found a printout of a newspaper article I wrote with the number for the *Tribune* on it. I believe Abby had a breakthrough, and she thought it was newsworthy. She wanted to get the word out about it."

I pulled out my sheet of abbreviations taken from Abby's research. "Do you know what any of these abbreviations are?"

Martha's eyes darted across the page. "C is carbon. N is nitrogen," she said, pointing at the chemical abbreviations. "I've never heard of M64. Mg would be magnesium; Mn, manganese."

"M64 is a location on the river near the wastewater treatment plant, remember? What about this?" I asked, pointing at EPI. "What does that stand for?"

"EPI? P is phosphorous and I is iodine. E is—I don't know. There's no E element. There's Es for einsteinium, but that ending up in the river is impossible. What does the E stand for, I wonder?" Martha mused aloud.

"I was hoping you'd know."

Martha shook her head. "*Extra* phosphorous and iodine? Have you asked Ballings?"

"Long story, but no. Anyhow," I said, hoping to change the subject away from why I hadn't asked Ballings about the abbreviations, "the chemicals in EPI, at least phosphorous and iodine, are they found naturally in the environment?"

"Everything, all the elements, really, are found naturally in the environment, unless you're talking about manmade elements, but—"

"What about the phosphorous and the iodine?"

"I don't know about iodine, but phosphorous comes from, one of the places it can come from, is fertilizer."

"So phosphorous and iodine at least don't raise any red flags?"

Martha never answered the question. Daniel whipped a chair from our table, whirled it around, and sat in it, while Kimmie took the chair opposite him.

"What's going on?" I asked.

"Why don't you tell us?" Kimmie said.

"I was just having coffee with Martha. What brings you in here?"

"An interesting story we heard from the undercover we had following you today," Daniel said.

CHAPTER 51

"Martha, would you mind giving us some time to talk with Jonie?" Kimmie asked.

Martha stood up. "I have to be on my way, anyway," she said, pushing her chair back beneath the table. "I'll call you if I think of any ideas, Jonie."

"What's the story?" I asked. My mouth was dry and my voice came out in a croak as if a ball of steel wool clogged my throat. Why would an undercover cop be following me? Daniel said earlier only Kimmie suspected me, and that was because our past history prejudiced her against me.

Daniel waited for Martha to leave the café. "Kimmie's brother seemed to believe you were going to sneak into the marine center today. When Kimmie told me what Phaser told her, I thought she was joking or being overly paranoid. So I thought, why not have someone tail you? Why not prove her suspicions about you wrong?"

Something in Daniel's glare made me wince, feel ashamed. I looked away.

"Imagine my shock," Daniel said, "when her suspicions proved correct, and you waltzed into the Cooperative Center for Marine Biology."

I tried not to reveal outwardly the inner panic that was racing through my veins. I needed them to contain this. Montgomery could not know I sneaked into the center. "What's wrong with me going to the marine center?"

"Were you there by invitation, or were you trespassing?"

"I was going to see Professor Ballings," I said, trying to make my voice sound nonchalant but thinking it sounded more greasy than anything else.

"Why?"

"I wanted to talk to him," I stalled.

"About?"

"Just to see how he liked the article I wrote from our interview the other day."

"Is this routine, personally checking up with subjects to see how they like your stories?" Daniel's voice sounded condescending. He wasn't buying my excuse.

"No," I said, thinking fast. "But I thought Ballings might make a good contact, maybe lead me to some other stories. So you could call my visit a meeting to cultivate a working relationship."

"And did you do that?" he volleyed.

"Ballings wasn't in his office."

"It took you the better part of an hour to see if he was in?"

"I looked around."

"Don't you mean, 'We looked around?' You went with a partner."

I shrugged. "Sure. Let's not split atoms."

"The only problem is, Phaser seemed to believe there was a file you wanted to open discriminately, to put it nicely."

"No," I said, in reaction to what Phaser had done. How could he? Before anger engulfed me, I tried to remember what I told Phaser. I hadn't told him about the disk. "I thought Ballings could open one of Abby's research files. I didn't think anyone needed to know, other than Ballings, of course. But as I just mentioned, I didn't catch him."

My cell phone rang. Because my phone was resting on the table next to my coffee, everyone could see Ballings' name come up on caller identification.

"Go ahead and answer that," Daniel said.

I snatched up the cell phone and stood up, but Daniel grabbed my wrist and beckoned me to sit down. His touch felt hard and cold. The bond that had crackled like fire between us was now a crumbling ruin of a memory in this icy connection. He was a detective at this moment, and a suspicious one as well.

"No need to leave," he said.

The phone rang again. I slowly returned to my chair and flipped open the phone.

"Hello, Professor Ballings. This is Jonie."

"I have some very exciting news," he said, giddy. "I've just had a major breakthrough in my pseudopersistent pollution research project, and I wanted to get a jump on publicizing my findings."

I squinted my eyes. So he had found the disk in his computer. Did he wonder where the disk came from? "Tell me more."

"Not over the phone. It's too complicated, and besides, I wouldn't miss a chance to see you again." His voice dripped with artificial flattery.

I tried not to grimace. "When do you want to meet?"

"Tonight. If you're not free, make yourself free. This is good."

"Okay."

"Meet me at my apartment, 313 Ashwyck Manor, at 9. I'd make it earlier, but I'm a busy, busy man, and I have a late class. 313 Ashwyck Manor. Know where that is?"

Of course I knew where the most glitzy, over-advertised, overpriced apartment building in all of historic downtown Wilmington was located. But I didn't want to meet Ballings alone in his apartment, especially if he was Abby's killer.

"How about I meet you somewhere else downtown? We could have coffee."

"No, the apartment's the place. We can have hors devours and champagne to celebrate."

"That's not necessary."

"This is a celebration! A momentous occasion."

"Then why not have a press conference at the marine center?"

"You want the scoop, don't you?" He chuckled. "And hey—I'll admit it! I want the credit. Press conferences are long, and Dean Kipling is there, ringleader of the department. She talks on and on, and I get buried, and she gets all the quotes. I need the credit for the prestige to secure funds to continue my research. She'd take all of it and keep me squirreled away in my office, and you are the gal to do my success story."

"Thanks."

"So you'll meet me."

"See you tonight," I said, planning to call Stu and persuade him to come with me. I closed my phone slowly.

"Hot date?" Kimmie asked.

"Hardly."

"So why don't you fill us in on what's going on?"

"I don't think that's any of your business," I snapped. "Besides, you're going to have me followed, anyway."

Daniel and Kimmie exchanged glances.

"I'm leaving." I stood.

"Going to hide back in the Tennessee foothills, back where you came from?" Kimmie asked.

The anger inside me suddenly roared. "This is where I came from, and I'm here to stay," I said. "You want to know what's going on? I'm going out to do your job for you because you obviously can't! You're wasting your time following me around town. Go pester a real suspect!"

I walked out feeling liberated and furious, nervous and betrayed. So long, Daniel, I thought. It was fun while whatever it was we had lasted.

Heading toward my apartment, I looked over my shoulder and glanced in my rearview mirror, wondering if I was still being followed. I couldn't tell, so I passed by my apartment and did some figure eights using the one-way residential streets as a track. Sure enough, far back, a vehicle with tinted windows followed my meanderings.

CHAPTER 52

I was surprised to feel relief. Maybe having an undercover cop
tail me would be good, I thought. At least the police would
know to come looking for me if I never left Ballings'
apartment later tonight.

I parked on the street in front of my apartment. Walking
toward my door, I found myself cognizant of the way my
arms were swinging with my stride. As I passed Phaser's den
window, I heard music. I paused. In the nerve-jangly state I
was in, I knew I shouldn't confront him about tattling to
Kimmie, but at the same time, my tense leg muscles locked
up; they wouldn't walk me past his door to the entrance to my
stairwell. Instead of knocking, I kicked. The music stopped. I
saw a shadow cross the peephole. In the back of my mind, I
knew he probably only ratted on me to Kimmie out of a
sense of righteousness; but I couldn't suppress my infuriation.

"Phaser!"

Phaser barely cracked the door. "Before you start in on me,
let me explain."

I closed my eyes and gritted my teeth. It took all the focus I
possessed not to yell at him, despite the police watching from
the street in the unmarked car. Phaser allowed me to pass
through into his den. I didn't sit down.

"I loved Abby," he said.

"We all loved her."

"No. I loved her."

So he loved Abby, romantically. I already knew this. How did that change anything?

"She only wanted to be friends," he said, "ever since high school, and although it was clear she never looked at me in the same way I looked at her, we had a—a *thing*."

Great, I thought: a thing.

"She always was dating boys. You know how she was. Telling me about how she received three bouquets on Valentine's Day or how she had a lunch date with one boy and dinner and a movie with another all in the same day. She went out with Mark—alright, became engaged to him—and then she told me he was getting too clingy. She told me about an affair with Ballings, and how the dean made Ballings end it. I was just waiting for her to see me for who I was; someone who would never betray her. And she never got that chance."

That's pathetically cliché, I thought, wanting to knock on Phaser's head and see if anyone was home. Instead I fought to keep my voice at a civil volume and said, "That still doesn't justify you siccing Kimmie and her police buddies on me."

"I went to Kimmie because I want Abby's case solved, probably even more than you."

"You—"

"I don't care whether you solve it, or whether Kimmie solves it. You don't want to share your information with Kimmie—that's politics. That's bull."

I wanted to say Phaser was wrong, that I didn't care who solved the case either, that the reason I hadn't disclosed the disk and the research to Kimmie or Daniel was because I was afraid of their faulting me for taking the key that led to the disk in the first place, and that I was afraid my possession of the key would cost me my job. But then I realized my point was what Phaser was getting at. If my top priority, my pure and singular motive, was finding Abby's killer, shouldn't I have relinquished the disk to the police? I could have taken the key to the police. I could have shared all my information with Stu and with Jason. To hell with my job. To hell with being at odds with Kimmie and Daniel. Instead, was I playing it safe and even hoping to land the story of finding Abby's killer? I realized I still was competing with Kimmie while Abby's murderer continued to walk free. I was no detective. I should have just let the police do their job.

"All I told Kimmie is that you thought something that had to do with Abby's death was on a computer at the marine center," Phaser said. "I'm sorry if you're mad, but telling Kimmie was the right thing to do."

After a moment, I nodded and tried to wipe the scowl from my face. "You're right," I muttered.

Phaser reached for me, pulled me into a tight embrace, and stroked my hair. I couldn't help but hug him back. I then trundled myself upstairs to call Stu. I considered coming clean before extending the invitation to the late-night meeting with Ballings. I considered telling him about how I found the key, how it led to the disk taped to the top of Abby's mailbox, how Ballings found the disk I mistakenly left behind in his office and how the research really hadn't been inside his computer. But when Stu answered the phone, all that came out from me was a request for a good-faith favor to accompany me to Ballings' apartment.

"Why can't Jason go?"

"I can't…Jason is—"

"I have a date tonight," Stu whined.

"What if Ballings is Abby's killer? You wouldn't want me there alone with him, would you?"

Jason and I have conferred on this matter. Ballings is a lover, not a killer."

"If he's a lover, I need you there at the meeting to stop him from trying to love on me!"

"The way you've been acting lately, you could use a little loving, even if it is from some skanky old pervert."

"Stu!"

"What do you want me to do? I've made plans, and I'm not going to ditch this girl—who I must admit is a hottie, and who I've been trying to connect with for at least a week now—to meet with some pompous professor to talk about boring research when there's not even a photo in it for me."

My head ached. I rubbed my forehead with my fingers.

"Jonie? You still there?"

"Bring your date to the meeting," I pleaded. "Ballings said he'd have champagne."

"I don't know. The best I can do is give you a maybe."

I thanked him and plunked the phone into its receiver. I paced around the apartment, trying to keep busy by tidying up knick knacks that littered the counters, considering how I might redecorate various rooms, fuming about Stu's uncooperativeness, and wondering what Ballings would have for me at the meeting. Where would Ballings say this new research information came from? Did he somehow know I left the disk in his computer? He could be Abby's killer, I reminded myself. But he sounded too exuberant on the phone, too triumphant, to be planning me harm.

Then I remembered the way he'd looked after his argument with Kipling about the bullet incident. He'd looked deranged, out of control. I wondered if I should meet him at all. But I had to go! I had to find out what was behind Ballings, find out what Abby's research meant. If Ballings was a killer, and if he murdered Abby for credit for her research, Ballings wouldn't kill me. I'd be writing the article to give him that credit. If Ballings killed Abby because she dumped him, and she was carrying his child, he wouldn't kill me. We didn't even have a relationship. Despite my rationalizations, I still felt edgy when I left the apartment for the meeting.

I selected jeans and a polo shirt to wear to see Ballings— something conservative and almost boyish, to discourage any romantic advances, and flexible enough to allow movement in case I needed to defend myself.

As I climbed into my truck, I noticed the unmarked patrol car no longer was parked within sight. Probably, I thought, the police switched cars and shifts on me. I parked in front of Ballings' apartment 10 minutes early. I glanced around at other parked cars, looking for Stu's red Civic, but I didn't expect he'd show. Anyway, I didn't need a college degree to know how Stu would choose between work and women.

I decided to go it alone.

CHAPTER 53

Ashwyck Manor was a large building with a central lobby decorated in gold and red, much like a fancy hotel. Except instead of bustling with porters and guests, the lobby was deserted. The front desk was manned, at least, but the stringy-haired employee slumped behind it didn't bother looking up from his skateboarding magazine while I passed and waited for the elevator.

Ballings' floor was decorated in the same red and gold décor as the lobby. Fake plants potted in reflective gold vases spotted the hallway. I reached Ballings' door and knocked. I didn't hear movement inside, and no one answered. I checked my watch. I was early. I backed up and leaned against the opposing wall to wait. After a few minutes, I heard the elevator ping open.

I straightened up and turned, expecting to see Ballings, but Stu stepped out of the elevator, accompanied by his date. While I was stunned Stu decided to show, I was even more shocked at the appearance of the woman standing beside him. What I first noticed was her clothing—a tight, very short, black leather skirt, fishnet stockings, and a silky top that looked more like lingerie than eveningwear. She might have had a pretty face; I couldn't tell for all the makeup that hid it. Her eyeliner was caked on so thickly, I wondered if she was going for a pirate appearance.

Stu introduced her as Steffie, who, in turn, gave me the once over.

"The professor isn't in yet," I said.

"We left Taversham's to wait in a hallway for a professor?" Steffie asked, crossing her arms and cocking a hip with her legs as far apart as her skirt would allow.

I wanted to warn her that if she moved her hip another inch her panties would be showing, if she wore any.

"I thought you said there was going to be champagne," she said.

Stu glared at me

"Once the professor arrives, there will be champagne," I assured her, checking my watch. It was exactly 10. "Are you two having a good evening?" I asked, more to stall for time than out of curiosity.

"We were until we had to leave the bar for this joint," Steffie pouted.

"The champagne will make it worth it." I smiled and waited for Stu or Steffie to continue the conversation. As the seconds accumulated, the discomfort grew and all smiles faded.

"Is he even going to show at all?" Stu finally blurted.

"He sounded like it—110 percent—on the phone," I said. I checked my watch again. "He's only five minutes late now."

"I need a drink," Steffie said.

I raised my eyebrows at Stu. He shrugged and gave me a perplexed half smile.

"Give him five more minutes, then go if he doesn't show," I said.

The minutes passed in silence. I admitted defeat.

"Sorry for inconveniencing you," I said. I felt like I should offer Steffie money for her time. "I guess Ballings isn't showing up after all."

Steffie strutted toward the elevators, not waiting for Stu.

"You're coming, too, right?" he asked, backing away as he spoke.

"I'm going to wait a few more minutes."

After Stu and Steffie left, no other traffic appeared along the hallway. I checked my watch for the last time at 10:35 and rapped again, hard, on Ballings' door. Of course, he didn't answer. I tried the doorknob; it was locked. As I trudged to the elevator, I chalked another line in my tally for Ballings' no-show interviews. Where was he at this hour, anyway? A vision of Ballings from last weekend, him in his sports car, his arm draped across Trish, sped through my mind. Most likely, that was where he was right now, out with her, maybe figuring he could meet me some other time.

Ballings had seemed exhilarated on the phone earlier, overly eager to meet with me, but I supposed academic excitement paled in comparison to the budding, wild buzz of an illicit romance. Next time I saw Ballings, I'd kick him, I promised myself, knowing I wouldn't, that I was too keen to hear about Abby's research to set the professor straight on making appointments and keeping them.

I knew I was in for an uphill struggle when Jason and Stu arrived together to work, early, and stood blocking the cubicle exit.

I had been glancing through the morning's paper, admiring the newsworthy stories other reporters covered the day before. I set the paper down.

"Good morning, Jason, Stu."

"Yeah." Jason's voice sounded dry. "Stu said you scheduled a meeting with the professor last night." He paused as if waiting for me to confirm it. "Why wasn't I invited?"

"The professor didn't show up."

"Was the meeting supposed to be an interview that I should have been at?"

I opened my mouth to tell a white lie, but Jason cut me off.

"No—wait," he said. "You've gone off on your own and covered stories without me. Remember your first story here? Remember your story on Abby's funeral? You don't want me around for the big stories."

"Jason—"

"And I'm certain you're not telling us everything you know about Abby's death." Jason wasn't even looking at me.

I took a breath. Had Stu belied his promise and informed Jason about our excursion to the marine center?

"If you leave me on my own, I'm leaving you on your own," Jason said. "You're just stringing us along."

"No, I'm—"

"Don't give me that dumbfounded look," Jason said. "Why don't you tell me what's really going on? You pounce all over me about not revealing every detail about my friendship with Abby. Why don't *you* try being open for a change? We're supposed to be partners here, but you're keeping me in the dark about who knows what, thinking you're going to benefit from excluding me by cashing in on some big story. Stu told me about sneaking into the marine center and printing out research—"

"I don't—"

"…when really it's just hurting you because, thanks to you, we won't be assigned the big story today."

"What big story?"

He sneered at me.

"What big story?" I repeated.

Stu shook his head. "A car ended up in the Cape Fear last night near the memorial bridge. The driver died. Took three hours just to pull the vehicle from the river."

I envisioned the steep drop down the bluff to the river near the drawbridge, almost could hear the oblivious clanging and whirr of vehicle tires speeding on the metal bridge more than 50 feet above the river, drowning out the splash and burbling of the sinking car as the current sucked it down and away.

"But," Jason said, "because of all the mess you've tripped yourself in, you're on news release duty. And since this story is a two-reporter job with all the leads to follow—"

"Hey, hey, hey!" Stu interrupted in a suddenly cheerful voice.

I looked up to see who he was talking to now. Kimmie stood beside Jason's desk, in uniform. The pants bunched around her hips. She ignored Jason and smiled condescendingly at Stu before turning her eyes to me. Daniel lurked just behind her, and he was looking at me also. His eyes, even more formally indifferent than yesterday, looked mechanical as they analyzed me.

"What's up?" I asked Kimmie, deciding Daniel was too threatening to broach. "Have you come to check in on me again? Better watch out; if you keep this up, I'll start thinking you're trying to befriend me."

Kimmie shook her head. "As we came in here, I couldn't help but hear Jason complaining about your no-show interview with Ballings last night." Kimmie ran a finger across the top of the cubicle and examined the dust before flicking it off. "You want to know why he didn't make it?"

"Sure," I said. "Why?"

"He's dead."

CHAPTER 54

"Ballings is dead, and you're coming with us to the station," Kimmie said.

"Am I under arrest? You heard—Ballings didn't show. I didn't do anything."

"Guilty conscience?" Kimmie asked.

"We want to talk to you," Daniel said.

"I have a staff meeting in a minute. Can't this wait?"

"No, you're talking now," Kimmie said.

"And this cubicle is not where we're going to talk," Daniel said.

I grabbed my laptop briefcase and edged past Kimmie, leaving Jason and Stu at my desk.

Daniel and Kimmie flanked me as we walked to the elevator. While we waited for the doors to open, they stood so close to me they were pressing in on my arms. Finally, the elevator arrived. I couldn't believe my bad luck; Montgomery and Lee walked off together. Montgomery seemed to be in the middle of telling a story, his booming southern twang was reverberating in the elevator, so I tried to lower my head and back away slightly, as if I could hide. It was useless.

Montgomery cut off his story in mid-sentence. "What's going on?"

"Jonie?" Lee asked.

"I'm assisting these officers on a case," I said.

"More like she's a person of interest in a case," Kimmie clarified with a smirk in her voice.

Montgomery looked from Kimmie to me. "That's it, then. I gave you my warning, and I'm a man of my word. I told you anything—anything else—suspicious, and you're out."

"I didn't do anything, sir," I said. "I'm not in any trouble because—"

"I don't care what you did or did not do!" Montgomery said. "I told you I would not suffer any suggestions of misconduct in a probationary reporter."

"Take a second and look at the facts."

"It's not about the facts; it's about perception! The *Tribune* does not need shadowy reporters. That's what this new reporters' probation period is for—to weed. And you're out."

I caught the tight grin on Kimmie's face as she turned in the elevator. On the ride down, I looked at my hazy reflection in the silver doors. So that was it, I thought. I had lost my job. Hot tears stung my eyes. I blinked them out, letting them roll down my cheeks, hoping Daniel and Kimmie wouldn't notice and that the trails would dry before we reached the ground floor.

Daniel seated me in the back of the police car. A metal grate separated me from him and Kimmie. The doors in the back had no interior handles and no levers to unroll the windows.

"Maybe I should drive separate to the station," I said.

"It's no problem," Daniel said, putting the car in gear.

"What do I have to do with Ballings' death? What's so important about me that you have to come to my office, make a scene that costs me my job, and chaperone me to the police station?"

"We'll talk when we reach the station."

"I didn't do anything," I repeated.

Daniel drove into the police department's parking garage beneath the station and let me out. Kimmie grabbed my arm and led me to an elevator. She released me in a room on the same floor as their desks. The room was empty, with the exception of a large wooden table and some chairs, and a dented gray filing cabinet in the corner, and, of course, the mirrored interior window.

"Do you want anything?" Daniel asked. "Water? Coffee?"

"No," I said, not wanting to reveal my shaking hands. I crossed my arms tightly and then wondered if that was a sign of being uncooperative, so I uncrossed them and clasped my hands together.

"We'll be back in a minute," Daniel said.

Daniel and Kimmie walked out of sight, closing the door behind them. I looked around the room. With nothing to see besides dirty linoleum flooring and generic beige paint, I sat down. I crossed my legs and then uncrossed them. I fidgeted with my bracelet. Where were Daniel and Kimmie, and what did they want? Were they trying to make me wait, make me feel nervous? Why did they have to drag me into the station?

I tried to calm down and check my emotions, and I found I was more concerned about losing my job, about now having no one to explain Abby's research to me, and about my estrangement from Daniel than I was about Ballings' death. I wasn't sure how I should feel about my lack of sorrow at his demise.

I was fired. That didn't even seem real to me yet. I was fired. I tried to let the thought sink in, but Daniel and Kimmie reentered the room. Daniel sat down across from me. Kimmie leaned against the head of the table.

"Let me guess," I said, forcing a smile as I gazed into Daniel's stormy eyes. "You're playing the good cop, and Kimmie's playing the bad cop."

Daniel didn't smile back. "I assume you know about the car that ended up in the Cape Fear River last night," he said.

I nodded.

"The car was driven by Stephen Ballings," Daniel continued. "I also assume you know that, per your telephone conversation with the professor at the café, we know you had an appointment with Ballings last night."

"I did, but when I arrived at Ballings' place, he was gone. No one answered the door, and I waited for a half hour." Using Daniel's terminology, I continued. "I assume you know that, and that I entered and exited the building alone."

"How would we know that?"

"Weren't you having me followed?"

"We pulled the tail off you, figuring you completed your mischief for the day," Kimmie said.

Daniel looked at Kimmie and nodded. Kimmie walked to the filing cabinet, unlocked it, and slid a photograph across the table. I picked it up. The photograph was of a cell phone identical to the one I owned.

"Look familiar?" Kimmie asked.

"We found that cell phone in Ballings' vehicle," Daniel said.

I pulled my cell phone off my belt. "This is my cell phone," I said. "I bought it after Kimmie pushed me into the punch bowl at the dance."

Kimmie shook her head. "This is your cell phone." She pointed to the photograph on the table. "One of our lab techs found that it's programmed for your number. It has your information on it."

I was in shock. Was I was being set up, framed? I set the photograph down as gently as was possible for my jittering fingers. I felt sick, like the time Phaser shot a squirrel with his bb gun and instead of keeling over immediately, the squirrel fell from the tree, screaming even after he landed, his last breaths spent screeching in incomprehensible agony. I still remembered the screaming, would probably carry the sound with me forever, like a cold, black pebble in my chest.

"When you knocked me into the punch bowl at the dance, my cell phone was totaled," I said. "I threw it in the back of my truck, in the truck bed. I never removed it."

"Let me clue you in on something," Daniel said. "Right now, we're fingerprinting Ballings' apartment and his office. It would be best for you if you cooperated with us and let us know now what you've been up to."

"You'll find my fingerprints on the apartment door handle. I checked it to see if it was locked when Ballings didn't answer the door," I said. "And you'll find my fingerprints in his office. I went into it the other day when we were supposed to meet."

Daniel looked as if he was staring through me, seeing right through my false premise for being in Ballings' office.

"What does it matter anyway, if Ballings died in a car accident?" I asked.

"The accident was faked by the person who wanted him dead," Daniel said.

"What about Mark?" I asked. "I know you suspect him of killing Abby. He was stalking Abby. Maybe he murdered Ballings. You heard his threats at Abby's memorial."

"Mark has a solid alibi for last night," Kimmie said. "He was getting booked for shooting at Dean Kipling's office. We matched the bullet to a gun we found in his apartment."

"Kipling," I said. "Have you checked into Kipling? She had reason to—"

"Now you're really reaching."

"No. Kipling—I saw a page from her appointment book with a late evening meeting at the marine center on the night Abby died. Kipling admitted to me she was at the center that night. I'm fairly certain Kipling and Ballings were romantically involved, but Ballings cheated on Kipling with Abby, and I saw him with a student just the other night, and Kipling was following them in her own vehicle. Kipling looked—she looked murderous."

"Does your wild imagination never cease?" Kimmie asked. "Dean Kipling was at a marine biology symposium in Charlotte last night. She lectured yesterday evening. We reached her in her hotel room this morning. She's skipping the rest of the conference and driving the two hours to return to Wilmington as we speak."

"Okay," I said, trying to mentally push away my headache, stall it so I could think clearly. "Still, I haven't seen Ballings in quite a while. The only recent contact I've had with him was verbal, over the telephone, and you both were present for that last conversation."

Kimmie shook her head. "You murdered him." Her statement resounded like a gavel in a courtroom. She and Daniel let the accusation hang in the air.

"That's absurd," I said, breaking the silence. "Why would I kill Ballings when you knew I had an appointment with him anyway? If I was going to kill him, it certainly wouldn't be when you knew I was going to be with him. I thought I was being tailed, too."

"You sound like you knew exactly when he died," Kimmie said.

"I don't know when he died. I only know what you told me just now. I didn't do anything." I threw up my hands. "I didn't—" I was beginning to think I needed a lawyer. "So you think you have this all figured out?"

Kimmie grinned.

"How would I overpower Ballings or get his car into the river then?"

"We're analyzing his blood for foreign substances."

I shook my head.

"It's going to be harder to prove you were involved in Abby's death, but we're working on it," Kimmie added.

"Why would I kill either of them?"

"You tell me."

I shrugged.

"For a story," Kimmie said. "For notoriety. Big-time journalist Jonie. You've always been strange, violent—"

"Kimmie," Daniel intervened.

They were both studying me.

"Kimmie, I loved Abby. And you, you're my sister," I said.

"Step sister."

"What I'm trying to say is you do know me. We lived together for years. You know I'm not a murderer."

"I know the vindictive acts you committed back then, and I'm beginning to understand what you're capable of now."

"You can't truly suspect me. You know I wouldn't do something like this."

"I don't know you at all."

I looked at Daniel. It was as if his face had shut down.

"I didn't do it," I said, staring him in the eyes. I then looked at Kimmie. "I didn't do it," I repeated. She looked at the filing cabinet. "I didn't do it!" I said, more forcefully than I intended.

Then I asked for a lawyer.

CHAPTER 55

I sat in my truck in the *Tribune's* two-tiered river-view parking deck with my windows rolled down and my keys in the ignition. A distant line of clouds promised an afternoon thunderstorm, if the front could push through the stagnant, sweltering air that drew beads of sweat to my face. Daniel and Kimmie let me walk with the warning that they would be in touch and for me not to leave the county, as if I had anywhere to go. I didn't know where to drive. I didn't want to go to my apartment, filled with the foreign remnants of my aunt, a woman I never really knew. I didn't want to see Phaser. I didn't want coffee. I couldn't go back to the newspaper office. The river walk was too open, too hot, too busy. I wanted to be alone and somewhere familiar. I wanted to go to the ocean.

I cranked my truck and began driving to my father's and Vicki's place. Since my name was down on the Figure Eight island roster as being family, I didn't have to worry about the security guard stopping me. And my surfboard would be there, waiting. At least that was something, I thought. Not quite realizing why I was doing it, I dialed Jason's number. After his voice mail answered, my words flowed smoothly.

"Hi, Jason. This is Jonie. I want to apologize. You were right. I shouldn't have kept information about the story from you. And I'm sorry for having become mixed up in the story, but I was trying to find Abby's killer the only way I knew how.

I was doing what I felt I needed to do for my friend. I didn't fill you in, not because I wanted to exclude you from a story but because I wanted to find the killer on my own—not for glory—I suppose it was more like a mission to me. I guess by now you know I'm fired from the *Tribune*. Anyhow, I don't know what else to say, other than I'm sorry, again." I hung up.

I blinked tears out of my eyes and tried to focus on the road, but my mind was over-occupied, wondering how I could untangle myself from this mess. I felt helpless, like I was being squeezed by insurmountable forces no more under my control than the storm clouds exploding on the horizon. My only options were to face the storm or to run for cover. Years ago, I ran. I could run now. Skip Figure Eight Island and keep driving like before.

"No."

I said it out loud, my voice deep and forceful, like thunder. My fingernails dug into the steering wheel. I shouldn't have to run. I shouldn't have to fight to keep my name clean. But that was what I'd do—fight. I wasn't guilty. But knowing I wasn't guilty wasn't enough. Claiming my innocence wasn't enough. Daniel and Kimmie were going to find my prints in Ballings' office. They were all over Ballings' keyboard and printer, and then Daniel and Kimmie might come to arrest me. Innocent people had been convicted on less evidence. But I wasn't guilty, and before they acted on erroneous conclusions, I needed to figure out the real culprit behind the crimes. Maybe the ocean and surfing would allow me to sort my thoughts.

Who else was left to look into? Mark and Ballings, my main suspects, were accounted for. Could Kipling have murdered Abby and then Ballings? A two-or-three-hour drive was nothing. Kipling could have left the symposium, driven to Wilmington, murdered Ballings, and then driven back to her hotel room in Charlotte as if nothing had happened. What would her motives have been: interference in her and Ballings' romance, Abby's womb harboring Ballings' child, unrequited love, Ballings' incapability of monogamy, research credit, or some combination of those factors? Ballings had seemed worried Kipling would steal his glory if he shared his findings with her. Kipling would have been able to ransack Ballings' lab, could have accessed the center at any time. Was I missing something?

What about suicide? Could Ballings have committed suicide, feeling guilty for killing Abby and perhaps pressured by Kipling? No; that didn't fit. In his phone call to me, Ballings seemed too excited, too jovial, to commit suicide. How could he swing from being exuberant about releasing the research to killing himself? Why would he go to the trouble of inviting me over to his apartment if he was just going to break the date and kill himself? And suicide didn't explain how my cell phone ended up in his vehicle. Someone was framing me.

After parking at my family's house, I changed into my swimsuit, grateful I hadn't yet removed my bag with the suit and the change of clothes after the tea. I left my windows down and my cell phone crammed in my backpack with the clothes I'd worn to work on the passenger seat. I braided my hair to keep it from tangling in the ocean, retrieved my surfboard from below Vicki's deck, walked to the beach, and was ankle deep in cold saltwater with my surfboard in tow in fewer than five minutes. The shore was deserted, and though the clear blue water was too calm to surf, I paddled out deep and straddled my board. The ocean lay eerily still, almost like a lake, the water translucent enough I could see to my toes. The placid water surface parodied the rapidly approaching thunderstorm clouds and the turmoil of my life now, but I guessed at least a half hour separated me from the dark rain lines sweeping the deeper water. Even if the rain caught up with me, I couldn't become any wetter. I needed to be in the ocean.

I wanted to forget everything that had happened in the last couple of hours. I wanted to forget who I was for a while, forget why I needed to be here on my surfboard. But I couldn't. If I was arrested, not only would my life be over, but Abby's real killer would remain free. I couldn't live with that knowledge. It was worse than death. Who murdered Abby and Ballings? I needed an answer. I needed it now.

I closed my eyes and reclined on my board, temporarily forcing my mind clear, focusing on the gentle bobbing of my board. What would become of me? Sweat broke out against my forehead. Was I going to be thrown in jail? My life was a disaster, had been a disaster for a long time now. Even if I wasn't arrested, what was I going to do with no job, no degree, and only a handful of years of reporting experience? My worst fear would come to fruition. My life would be forever null, like this ocean today, stagnant, futile, transparent. I shook my head. I couldn't think like this. I couldn't become preoccupied wallowing. If I wanted to go somewhere, if I wanted to find Abby's and Ballings' killer, I needed to focus— focus on the evidence, the facts—rely on my reporter's intuition.

Again, I forced my mind to clear. Again I let in only the sensation of the tender rocking of the waves, imagined the energy in the water pulsing its way through my skin, up my veins, filling my mind.

Then I let the images come, let the memories swirl through my mind. Abby's perfect smile that I remembered from adolescence. Then her lifeless body, crabs picking at her skin. Kimmie's smirk in the elevator. Kipling's red heels clicking on linoleum. Daniel's sweating body on top of mine, wrestling to keep me still. Phaser's tearing eyes. The fountain outside the marine center. Montgomery's tanned, elephant skin. Abby's mailbox key hidden in the window track at the marine center. Mark's angular face. Ballings' sports car. Kipling waiting, alone, at Southern Skillet. Her fight with Ballings about the bullet, her threatening to withhold funding. Mrs. Pridgen swooning when she heard of Abby's unborn child. Jason freezing at the press conference when he learned of Abby's pregnancy. The photo of my waterlogged cell phone. And the mysterious sheets of notations spitting out from Ballings' printer. A rogue wave bobbed my surfboard. I looked up at the dark sky. Wicked black clouds loomed like demons.

Where was I? Papers spitting out from the printer, and my disappointment at not being able to understand the meaning of Abby's findings. EPI. The fish kills were because of EPI in the water at and below the wastewater treatment plant. Something clicked in my brain. I felt like I had been sucker punched in the gut.

"I know." My voice came out a hoarse whisper. I sat up on my surfboard. My stomach flip-flopped. A rumble of thunder sounded overhead. "I know who killed them both!"

CHAPTER 56

I paddled out of the water, pulled on the shift I'd left on the shore, and jogged to my family's house. Rain drops—fat drops, the kind that splatter when they land—began to fall. Everything made sense now: what EPI was, why Abby hid the key in the window track at the marine center, how my cell phone ended up in Ballings' car, why Abby's death seemed less intentional than drugging Ballings and drowning him in his car. By the time I reached my truck, I was sweating, and my shins burned. I threw my surfboard beside my truck and reached through the open passenger window for my backpack, where my cell phone and keys were stowed. The bag was missing. But then I knew exactly where to find it.

"I need my bag back, Martha."

As I'd walked to their house, I'd seen her waiting for me at the nook in the Pridgen's aged dock that disappeared behind their boat shed. A flash of lightning streaked across the sky like a claw tearing at the black clouds. Martha remained statuesque, the tide falling around us and revealing a shallow oyster bed. The oysters spat water as they clamped shut.

"Where's my backpack?"

Martha cocked her head, directing me to my backpack behind the boat shed, as if she expected me to walk behind it and out of sight of the other houses to get it. "Don't you think its time you quit playing investigative reporter? It's not your job to find out who killed Abby."

"Too late."

"I thought I might have to do this," Martha said, waving her hand at me, a hand I now noticed held something as liquidly silver as mercury that mirrored another streak of lightning overhead. I'd forgotten about the gun. I knew I could physically control Martha, but I'd forgotten about the gun. The gun was so dainty; it was hardly larger than her hand. Martha noticed me eyeing it.

"My grandmother's," she said.

"I remember now." Suddenly my knees were shaking, and I tried to stop them but couldn't. I was standing alone on a dock with a murderer, the person who killed Abby—the person who killed her own sister—and then later killed Ballings. I could try to run back to land, but the straight pier would make me an easy target. I thought of jumping off the dock, trying to hurdle the oyster bed, and swimming somewhere. But Martha had access to a boat. She could catch me.

"Don't even consider it," she said, as if reading my thoughts of escape. Using the gun, she motioned for me to walk behind the boat shed. I hesitated. She cocked the gun. I obliged. The rain began to fall faster, soaking through my clothes and running down my back. Martha was now blocking the only exit back to land, her body and mine hidden behind the boat shed.

"You murdered Ballings. And you killed Abby, your own sister!"

"My grandmother offered this gun to Abby first, but Abby said she couldn't stand to hold something so deadly," Martha said, ignoring my accusations. "It's ironic. Before Abby died, she didn't understand that she held a weapon of her own that, if released, would have killed far more people than this gun ever will. Sit down over there." She used the gun to point to the back corner of the dock beside my backpack.

Her eyes were unwavering black bullets, sharply focused, even through the dense rain that veiled us like a translucent curtain. Long ago, when I had seen Martha at this intensity, she was playing a Bach fugue on the piano, fingers moving with frightening speed and uncanny perfection, or devouring a book and oblivious to everything surrounding her— screaming children, the rising tide, but never had I been their focus. Her eyes possessed a power, like metal bars, locking me in, making it impossible for me to shift my gaze.

"You can't shoot me," I said. "Your mother will hear."

Martha shook her head.

I glanced at the dock. There was nothing, no spear or even fishing pole or net that I could use to defend myself.

"Abby's weapon was her research," I said, hoping Martha would elaborate on my suppositions, hoping I could stall her somehow while I desperately tried to work out a plan, any plan, to escape.

Martha nodded.

"Abby was hiding the backup disk from you," I continued. "If she had been hiding it from Ballings or even Dean Kipling, she could have hidden it here, at her home. Abby found a chemical from your research in the river. Your company's drug is killing the fish."

Martha didn't respond.

"But I don't understand." I remembered Martha telling me so confidently that glassware at Prestol was rinsed into waste bins that stored the most hazardous byproducts from the testing.

"Because of the newness of the way our drug works, we had to complete extensive testing on hundreds of animals," Martha said. "The animals excrete the chemicals, the waste gets flushed down the drain, and the chemicals pass through the sewer plant undetected—undetected, that is, until my little sister became overly concerned about a few dead fish."

"So EPI isn't something with phosphorous and iodine. I remember from the day I visited Prestol—efflux—"

"Efflux pump inhibitors; EPI. That's what makes IEC work so well. The liver cancer cells can't flush out the toxins before they work. Abby came to me that afternoon, told me she had isolated the chemical that was causing the fish kills. Told me it was from my drug—the drug I spent years developing, the drug that will stop liver cancer and save lives. Abby told me that when fish absorbed the drug in the river, they couldn't expel the toxins at levels they had endured without problems for decades. Abby expected me to care, to drop everything I had been working on."

"What happened?"

Martha shook her head, her brown hair now a clumpy, black wet mane. "She wouldn't hear reason. If Abby had released her research, the FDA, EPA, PETA, and who knows who else would have been all over us. Research would have been halted just months before we were to wrap up everything and move on to manufacturing and distribution. Fathers, mothers, grandparents, siblings—people would have continued to die of liver cancer. All because my little sister's science project held up a few final months of testing. So I visited Abby at the center that evening. I made a decision, the only responsible decision that could be made under the circumstances. She was the one who needed to back away."

"You're crazy." I raised my voice to make it audible over the rain, which now pounded down in sheets, thudded against the wooden pier and boathouse, transformed the water's formerly glassy surface into a million pockmarked tremors.

"You know what's crazy, Jonie? Putting fish before people, a cold-blooded fish's life above a human life. That's what Abby did. She cared more about fish than about people. People like our own father. He died of cancer, the same cancer I've spent my career creating a drug to eradicate. I'm saving human lives."

Another flash of lightning seared the sky as the storm surged around us.

"Ballings was a human being, Martha. Abby was a human being," I said. "She was your little sister. She was pregnant."

Above us, thunder roared linearly like a wave crashing overhead.

"If there was any way to save Abby," Martha said, "I would have. But I made the only choice I could make. I determined what mattered most. I'm saving tens of thousands, eventually hundreds of thousands of lives, with the release of my liver cancer treatment. But Abby made it clear that evening on the garden boardwalk that she would not be dissuaded from releasing her research. We fought. She fell. She died."

"Someone else will find out that your drug is causing the fish kills."

Lightning flashed again, immediately chased by a roll of thunder.

"Wrong. I ruined Abby's lab and wiped out the computers, successfully making the destruction of her data appear to be vandalism, appear to be a crime unrelated to her death. Last night, I took away Ballings' disk, and I destroyed it, too. IEC nearly is ready for federal approval, and after that, all but a fraction of our testing at Prestol is through. The fish kills were happening because of the number and concentration of the animals we were testing the drug on. Once people begin using IEC, it's not like the waste from hundreds of people on IEC will all be going to the Wilmington sewer plant at the exact same time." She glanced at her gun and looked back at me, calculating.

"You can't pull this off, Martha. There's no one left for you to blame my death on."

"Who says your body will be found? That was my mistake with Abby; not hiding her body, leaving it in the open to be discovered. No, I think the cops will be very willing to continue believing you're the guilty party and that you fled, never to be seen or heard from again." She aimed the gun at my chest.

A bolt of lightning flashed so brilliantly, landing not 50 yards away up the waterway, I jerked. Continuing the motion, I grabbed my backpack and flung it at Martha, charging at her as she stepped back. I tried to knock the gun from her hand, but she fired. I felt a burning sensation sear through my bicep as I collided with her. She clawed my face and swung me sideways, toward the edge of the dock. My feet slipped, and I fell headfirst toward the water, my arms reaching up to shield my face as I hit the oyster bed and marshy muck, a thousand cuts screaming into my arms, torso, and legs. I pushed up, trying to move vertically to minimize the excruciating pain, pulling myself free from the blood-speckled oyster shells gouging into my body. I turned my head toward the dock.

Martha pointed the gun at me. Another crash of lightning split the sky, momentarily confusing me, making me think Martha had fired the gun. But she held it steady, adjusting it slightly to center the barrel at my chest. Stuck in the marsh mud, I had no escape. I caught movement in the corner of my eye and looked to land. Mrs. Pridgen was running from the house toward us. Her mouth was open, as if she was screaming. Kimmie and Daniel were also there, in the side yard, their guns drawn, running toward the dock. Kimmie's mouth was moving. She was shouting something, but all I could hear was a piercing metallic ringing. The pain from the oyster cuts and bullet seemed to have dissolved. Aside from my pounding heart, I felt almost blissful, incredibly lightheaded, like I was drunk. I looked back to Martha, who was staring at me still, gun aimed squarely at my chest, her black eyes set. The edges of my vision were fading. My whole vision was fading. My world was going black. I was sweaty and cold. Above the ringing in my ears, I heard another shot. I flinched and then tried to force my eyes to reopen, but all I could see was darkness, and all I could feel was my skin stinging.

CHAPTER 57

I gasped and opened my eyes. Somehow, I was on my back, on the grass beside the water. Kimmie and Daniel kneeled beside me, looked down at me, both as soaked as if they had been swimming. Kimmie looked peaked, even for her pale skin. Her hands and pant legs were mucky. She must have dragged me out of the creek. One of Daniel's hands was clamped on my bicep where I'd been shot, his fingers bright red with my blood, which mingled with the rain that fell soft and steady now. I coughed, and pain surged through my body. My arms and legs, even my torso, ached. I tried to sit up to assess how badly my skin had been shredded by the oysters and to examine my arm, but Daniel gently pushed me back down.

"Relax," he said. "The paramedics will be here soon. We think you passed out because of loss of blood, but you're going to be okay."

I looked to the dock. A couple of officers huddled around the corner where I remembered Martha last standing. Another officer sat with Mrs. Pridgen on the back patio, watching her sob into her hands.

"I shot Martha," Kimmie said. "I killed her. She's dead."

I tried to sit up again.

"It was Martha," I said, my voice sounding far away, like it originated from outside my body. "She killed Abby and Ballings because of Abby's research."

"We know." It was Daniel's voice. "Now, lie back and relax."

A patrol car rolled onto the wet grass behind Mrs. Pridgen's house.

My head was spinning, and my vision was ebbing again, so I allowed Daniel to lay me down flat.

"How did you know?" I asked. "When—"

"Yesterday, after we saw you at the coffee shop, we obtained permission from Dean Kipling to access the marine center's central computer database, which holds digital records of documents printed within the last 24 hours on every printer within the building," Daniel said. "We downloaded all the files that were sent to Ballings' printer. After we spoke with you today, Dean Kipling arrived at our headquarters. She interpreted the data that was printed off Ballings' computer and said that the chemical Abby identified as the culprit behind the fish kills in the concentration she found could have come only from one place—Prestol."

Suddenly Patrick, in his police uniform, appeared at my side. "Is she alright? Jonie, are you alright?"

"I'm fine—a little scraped up. Daniel just was telling me how y'all finally figured out it wasn't me who killed Abby and Ballings."

Daniel nodded. "About at that same time, a campus security guard on duty last night called us back and told us that he recalled Ballings leaving the school with a woman who matched Martha's description."

"But by that time," Kimmie said, "I already had told Martha we suspected you and that we suspected you met with Ballings since you saw Martha in the coffee shop. So then we needed to find and arrest Martha, and find you, too. We sent a couple of cars to Prestol, where we thought Martha would be, and Daniel and I went to your apartment. When you weren't there, I called the Figure Eight Island bridge tender, who said you were on the island. So we came looking for you here. When we saw Martha's car, too, I thought some confrontation might be happening. Then we heard the shot."

Kimmie touched my brow, a type of gesture I hadn't experienced before from her. Aside from the occasional obligatory hug for appearance's sake and the more frequent aggressive contacts, we had never touched each other in sisterly affection.

"You saved my life," I said, tears gathering at the corners of my eyes. "Thank you."

Kimmie shook her head. The sound of distant sirens rang across the marsh. The ambulance finally was crossing the bridge.

"Are you sure we can't have a do-over?" I asked. "Can't we try for a fresh start, try to be sisters?"

An officer walked up and tapped Kimmie's shoulder. She nodded. Then she frowned back at me.

"I can't deal with this now," she said. "I need to go and give my statement." Kimmie looked even paler.

"Try not to act stressed, Kimmie," Daniel said. "Investigating the shooting is standard procedure. You had to shoot Martha. Remember, it's a miracle you shot her before she killed Jonie."

Kimmie nodded and swallowed.

"Chin up," Daniel said.

Kimmie stood and walked away.

Patrick took her place, rain dripping from his hair, and grasped my other hand, the hand Daniel wasn't holding.

"Hey," Patrick said. A goofy grin spread across his face.

"Hey," I answered. "Could you do me a favor?"

"Anything."

"Call Jason at the paper. Tell him I have one hell of a story for him." I tried to laugh.

Daniel laughed, too, drawing my gaze to him.

"You're going to let a couple of cuts and a little bullet hole stop you from writing the story yourself?" he asked.

His eyes were twinkling again at me, and I felt a surge of something I knew wasn't adrenaline from my recent encounter with Martha. I grinned. The gesture sent pinpricks of pain through my scalp.

"Jason deserves the story," I said, "and seeing how I'm not employed with the *Tribune* anymore, giving him this story is the least I can do."

Daniel nodded.

"Kipling was a little unsure why Ballings hadn't released the research until the day he set up the meeting with you," he said.

"Abby had completed the research and hadn't shared it with Ballings. He didn't know what the research showed. I found a key," I said. "I should have told you and Kimmie about it immediately, but I initially thought it wasn't of much importance, and then once I found what it opened—Abby's main campus mailbox with a disk containing her research—I figured I'd see what the research meant before I lost my job over it. So I printed out the files on the disk while Ballings taught a class. I accidentally left the disk in Ballings' office, and he obviously found it. If I had taken the disk straight to you, maybe he'd be alive today. Maybe Martha, too."

"You couldn't have known," Daniel said.

"No, I should have—"

"Don't. You did the best you could. You couldn't have known," he repeated. "And I'll be forever sorry I doubted you, Jonie."

I shook my head. Simply hearing Daniel say my name, soft and low, washed a peaceful ease throughout my body. I tried to keep my eyes open, despite the steadily falling rain blurring my sight. The ambulance sirens drew closer and louder. I thought I heard Daniel whispering a prayer as my world faded once again.

When I awoke, I found myself tucked into a hospital bed and finally dry. Outside, the sky was dark, and I felt pleasurably numb and content. I glanced at my arms and noticed dozens of cuts, a couple of which sported black stitches. The bicep where the bullet entered was covered in white gauze. My father was seated in a chair by my side. He looked older than I remembered, and for once he sat idle. When I stirred, he stood and helped me sit up. We stared into each other's eyes for a moment. I thought of all the things I wanted to tell him, but I didn't know where to begin. He opened his mouth, as if to say something, but instead took me into his arms in a strong embrace. In that moment, I began to feel the years of separation, angry words, past hurts, and grudges begin to heal. We held each other for at least a minute, releasing our arms only when a nurse came into the room.

The nurse asked me how I felt and whether I was hungry. She told me I had been given morphine to ease the pain. The plan, she said, was to keep me from feeling through the night so I could sleep and then the doctor would take me off the drug in the morning. I had no objections.

CHAPTER 58

I awoke to the rising sun peeking over the treetops outside my hospital window and casting an orange glow about the room. Phaser snored in the chair my father had occupied the night before, and several flower arrangements beckoned from my bedside table, their sweet fragrance as soothing as their company. I reached to read one of their cards when I noticed a rolled-up copy of the *Tribune* beside them and grabbed the paper instead. In bold lettering just below the banner sprawled the heading *Police shoot campus murderer*. Beneath that, a smaller heading read, *Wilmington chemist murders sister in attempt to bury fish-kill research*. Stu's photograph of Martha speaking in the marine center's garden accompanied the article. I noted Jason's byline and quickly skimmed the story.

Jason had done a good job reporting and added some details that I didn't know, including that the police thought Martha drugged Ballings with ether she stole from Prestol before staging his death. Everything, from Abby's research findings to Martha shooting me before Kimmie shot her, was covered in the story. My favorite section of the article was a quote from Daniel.

"Without the investigative work of *Tribune* reporter Jonie Waters," Daniel's quote read, "it is quite possible that the death of professor Abby Pridgen would have gone forever unsolved, and that the culprit behind the fish kills would never have been identified. The *Tribune* and the Wilmington public are fortunate to have such a fine investigative reporter such as Ms. Waters at their service."

As if that wasn't good enough, later in the morning, Stu and Jason knocked on my door. Lee followed them in. Jason presented me with a mocha, and Stu opened a bag of fresh bagels. Better still, Lee offered me my job back. But instead of remaining on probation, Montgomery had been cajoled into giving me a salaried position, thanks to more than a few incoming calls that began as soon as the papers hit doorsteps. *Tribune* readers wanted to thank me, Lee said.

I congratulated Jason on his article.

"Thanks for getting Patrick to call me on it," he said.

"You deserved it after all I dragged you through."

"What about all I dragged *you* through?" Jason asked, most likely remembering the alumni dance.

I shrugged and smiled. "I'd say we're even."

"What about me?" Stu asked. "Kudos for having the foresight to take the photo of the supposedly grieving sister in the garden? What about my work and my loss?"

"I don't think Steffie was that big a loss."

We laughed.

By the end of the day, I had a promise from the hospital that I would be released the following morning and an invitation from Daniel and Patrick to join them, Kimmie, and others for their weekly grill night.

I was beginning to feel like myself again—free, strong, even halfway respectable.

I actually felt like I was sitting on my surfboard, looking toward the ocean at the endless lines of waves approaching me. Maybe Kimmie and I could be friends; maybe not. Maybe the relationship between Daniel and me finally would evolve into something tangible, something lasting. Maybe I'd become a distinguished reporter; maybe my work merely would pay the bills. The possibilities lay before me. All I needed to do was take the waves as they came and find my path through them as they carried me to shore.

ABOUT THE AUTHOR

Tamara Ward, whose journalism has won awards from the North Carolina Press Association, holds an MFA in Creative Writing from the University of North Carolina at Wilmington.

Tamara always has enjoyed writing. In high school, she often cut class to deliver columns to local newspapers and was called into the principal's office for interviewing teachers about how sports programs received more funding than academics, which resulted in an article that mysteriously never was published after she submitted it.

While an undergraduate, Tamara received her first paid writing job as a sports reporter. Since then, she has held jobs incorporating writing and editing for the North Carolina Museum of Art, the University of North Carolina at Wilmington, the North Carolina Department of Parks and Recreation, and the town of Holly Springs.

Her writing has appeared in various magazines and newspapers, as well as in Windhover, the literary and visual arts journal of North Carolina State University, where she graduated in English with a minor in music. Today, her writing regularly appears in the *Holly Springs Sun* as she covers the town council beat. She is a member of Sisters in Crime and Cape Fear River Watch.

A resident of a small town near Raleigh, North Carolina, Tamara enjoys wrangling with her two young boys, writing as a freelance journalist, and working on her next Jonie Waters mystery novel. She can't believe the trouble Jonie is in this time!

ACKNOWLEDGMENTS

Storm Surge never would have been completed without the support, encouragement, and guidance of many people. To name a few:

Tom: I treasure your love, partnership, and patience. Thank you for watching the kids and letting me escape into my writing world, and for speaking encouraging words to me when I needed them most.

My family: Thank you, mom, for so much that there's not enough space to write it all down here, including believing in me always and unswervingly, as well as the deliciously humorous insertions you vainly attempted to squeeze into the book. Maybe next time, but probably not! Thank you, dad, for your guidance and friendship, and Scott, for your contagious optimism and lifelong laughter.

Shiloh and Janice, among others, at Peak City Publishing and All Booked Up: Thank you for believing in my work. Thank you, Kerry, for your edits and camaraderie—and for em dash detail work.

I'm also very grateful for my innumerable personal, academic, and professional friends and mentors who helped me along, some of whom still are at my side today.

And last, but most of all, thank you, my Heavenly Father, for, well, everything.

Made in the USA
Charleston, SC
09 April 2011